MAREN MOORE

FOREVER

New York Boston

This book is a work of fiction. Names, characters, places, and incidents are the product of the author's imagination or are used fictitiously. Any resemblance to actual events, locales, or persons, living or dead, is coincidental.

Copyright © 2025 by Maren Moore

Cover design and illustration by Elizabeth Turner Stokes
Cover copyright © 2025 by Hachette Book Group, Inc.

Hachette Book Group supports the right to free expression and the value of copyright. The purpose of copyright is to encourage writers and artists to produce the creative works that enrich our culture.

The scanning, uploading, and distribution of this book without permission is a theft of the author's intellectual property. If you would like permission to use material from the book (other than for review purposes), please contact permissions@hbgusa.com. Thank you for your support of the author's rights.

Forever
Hachette Book Group
1290 Avenue of the Americas, New York, NY 10104
read-forever.com
@readforeverpub

First Edition: August 2025

Forever is an imprint of Grand Central Publishing. The Forever name and logo are registered trademarks of Hachette Book Group, Inc.

The publisher is not responsible for websites (or their content) that are not owned by the publisher.

The Hachette Speakers Bureau provides a wide range of authors for speaking events. To find out more, go to hachettespeakersbureau.com or email HachetteSpeakers@hbgusa.com.

Forever books may be purchased in bulk for business, educational, or promotional use. For information, please contact your local bookseller or the Hachette Book Group Special Markets Department at special.markets@hbgusa.com.

Print book interior design by Taylor Navis

Library of Congress Control Number: 2025935086

ISBN: 9781538773765 (trade paperback), 9781538773772 (ebook)

Printed in the United States of America

LSC

Printing 1, 2025

For the girls who got lost on #rugbytok, just as I did, and never wanted to be found.

*Cillian's thighs are for **you**.*

AUTHOR'S NOTE

Trigger warning:
On-page parental loss/grief.

When I started to write *Red Card*, I knew it was going to be something special. I knew it was going to be a fun and sexy, fast-paced college rugby romance. But what took me by surprise was how emotional this story actually became the further I got.

Cillian's story is like my own in a lot of ways, and the grief he experiences from losing his mother is something I hope that I have handled with the utmost care and respect.

I'm someone who has had a parental loss, so it was incredibly important to me to make sure I showed those who have experienced the same loss that I see and understand them.

I see and understand your grief, hurt, anger, and sorrow. I hope when you read Cillian's story that you feel as if you are not alone and know you are loved.

All my love,
Maren

CHAPTER 1

Cillian

"Welcome to Prescott University, *asshole*." The bloke wearing a Prescott Rugby Football Club jumper snickers, checking my shoulder roughly as he walks past me. I recognize him from the team roster I memorized on the plane ride from London.

I wasn't expecting a warm welcome from my new teammates. I knew better. I'd learned early on in life to set the bar low and that way you'll never be disappointed. And judging from the interactions I'd had so far, these wankers clearly don't want me here almost as much as I don't want to be here. Pretty fucking unfortunate for us all since we're going to be playing together for the next two years whether any of us like it or not.

"Yeah? Thanks for that. There a problem you want to discuss, mate?" I say, turning to face him. "Wanna have a talk about it?"

The laughter from his friends standing beside him dies down before he whips around. "Yeah, *mate*, let's talk about it. Let's talk about how you're the fucking *charity* case that walked on to this team while everyone else earned a spot because no one else would take your fucked-up ass."

"Seems like you're *threatened* or something. Worried I'll take the spot your mummy bought for you?" I smirk tauntingly and step forward, now toe to toe with the arsehole who's running his mouth.

Even though I know this is exactly what this wanker wants—to rile me up and make me react, to get me off the team before I even have a chance to prove what I'm capable of—hot tendrils of anger lash through my body, my temper rising by the second. My hands fist at my sides as I try to tamp it down. Lock it away. Stay in control of the situation so I can stay in control of my *future*.

Before he can respond, the door to the athletic building flies open and a tall, burly man with salt-and-pepper hair busts through.

"Cairney...my office. *Now*. You're late," he spits out before turning and disappearing back inside the building.

Goddamn it. Of course, my new coach would see this shit.

Less than twenty-four hours in this shithole, and I'm already regretting stepping foot on campus.

"Toss off," I mutter, my shoulder hitting his roughly as I brush past him toward my new coach's office.

I can't afford to start off on the wrong foot with Brody St. James. I can't afford any missteps, which means I can't let this happen again.

Not when my old coach, Coach Thomas, pulled so many strings to make this happen. Not when my shot in America is riding on me being a model player and staying the fuck out of trouble. If I don't, I'll be on a one-way ticket back to London, and my last chance at playing rugby professionally is gone. I can kiss my dream of playing professional rugby goodbye. Forever.

No more chances.

Simple as that. It's the same thing I've been repeating to myself over and over since I stepped off the plane. I've run out of chances, and playing at Prescott is a last-ditch effort to hold on to my rugby career.

I can't fuck this up. I won't. If not for myself then for Aisling and her future. My sister's all I have left, and I can't let her down.

All of this is in my hands. My responsibility.

The doors of the athletic building are painted a deep, rich burgundy, and the heavy wood creaks when I swing it open to step inside. It doesn't take me long to find the coach's office at the end of the trophy-lined hallway, with a bronze plaque outside the door inscribed with the name BRODY ST. JAMES.

My knuckles rap against the heavy wooden door twice before the voice on the other side calls me in. When I step inside, my new coach is sitting behind a large mahogany desk with a tight scowl on this face. I'll admit, he's pretty fucking intimidating.

Or maybe that's simply because this is the man who holds the strings to my future in his hands. Either way, it's a feeling I'm not accustomed to experiencing. I'm the player who the sports reports have deemed intimidating because of my aggression on and off the pitch.

And now... the tables have turned.

"Coach." I walk to the front of his desk and extend my hand. He looks down at it for a moment, his eyes dragging over the dark ink on the top that trails up and disappears into the sleeve of my jumper, before shaking it. "I'm sorry about that out ther—"

He drops my hand, cutting me off. "Sit. I've got ten minutes before practice starts."

Without hesitating, I drop down into the worn leather armchair across from him.

Coach leans forward and rests his forearms on the desk. "I'm not going to lie and say I'm particularly happy to have you here. I'm not going to bullshit for the sake of feelings. It's not how I run my program. Stay long enough and you'll see that. You messed up in London, and you're here because I owed a favor. *You* are now that favor, Cairney."

I grit my teeth together so hard that a deep ache forms in the muscle of my jaw. The old Cillian, the one who fucked up and landed us here in the first place, would've told him to fuck off and walked out of his office without a backward glance. Maybe thrown out a few more choice words. But I can't be that guy anymore. Or at least I'm trying not to be.

The guy who acts before he thinks. Who lets his temper, and grief, control him.

I've just got to keep it together, put my head down, and focus until I graduate and get the hell out of here. Until I can get back to London and play rugby. Really start my life.

Coach doesn't give me the chance to respond before he continues. "First and foremost, understand that whatever the hell just happened out there with Banes, it's not happening again. I don't give second chances. Being *here* is your second chance. The only chance you get. I don't baby my players, I'm not hand-holding, and I run a tight program. I know you've had a problem with aggression off the pitch. Fighting."

My shoulder dips. "Here and there."

Not exactly the full truth, but he's got the file in front of him, and I know he's read it.

We both know exactly what put me here. And it wasn't just my aggression.

"If you want to stay on this team, you walk the straight and narrow. No fighting. No drugs. No illegal activities. No fucking your way through the cheerleading team. No creating tension with your teammates. You're not the only one with something at stake here. This program operates on private funding. Boosters who expect a championship win this year, which means that we can't afford a fuckup. Of any nature."

"Understood," I retort, my jaw hardening again as we stare off over the desk.

He nods. "Good. We're on the same page then. Look, I've reviewed your tapes, Cairney... You're a damn good player. Naturally talented in ways that some guys work their entire life to be and never achieve. Don't waste it."

It's not the first time I've heard this. From my coach back in London, from scouts, from my teammates, my sister. From the voice in my head telling me not to end up like my father, who's never been anything but an alcoholic fuckup with a temper that puts mine to shame.

Truthfully, it's been a long time since I've felt like myself. The guy I used to be before Mum died. I've spent the last two years fighting to make it back to that person, and I've got the scars to show it. On every inch of me, inside and out. I spiraled so far down that sometimes I feel like I'll never make it out alive.

What I want more than anything is to leave the mess I made in London behind and start over. To take the opportunity I've been given even if it means moving to a new country and playing for a team of blokes who don't want me here. I can deal with it if it means that I'll have a chance at playing professionally and making sure that Aisling is taken care of.

"I have no plans to," I respond in a clipped tone. "I'm here to play rugby. That's it. I'm not going to cause any trouble. I know that doesn't mean much right now, and I get it—I haven't exactly shown anyone that my word means much, but I want to change that. Starting here. Starting now."

"All right then." Lifting his wrist, Coach glances down at his watch before looking back at me. "I've got to head to practice, but we can talk a bit more later. There's one thing I want to say before I go. You're walking on halfway through a season, Cairney. There's inevitably going to be some challenges. These guys have been playing together for years. There's a dynamic in place, and I know that it's going to take some time for everyone to adjust. And not only that...these guys have a lot on the line, and they know it. Doesn't help that they're feeling the pressure of expectation. I just need your assurance that you're going to give fitting in and becoming a member of this team everything you've got." His voice is low and solemn as he says exactly what I've been thinking since I got the transfer confirmation.

I already have a fairly good grasp on what it is I'm walking into, especially after the confrontation that happened a few minutes ago, but if anything, it's only making me more determined. To show not only Coach that I'm going to follow through, but also the arseholes who think they'll get rid of me as easily as I came here.

I nod, raking a hand through my hair. "I understand. You're not going to have any issues out of me. I'll make an effort."

"Good. Let's head down to the pitch and you can observe for a bit and meet Matthews, our assistant coach." Standing, he rounds the desk toward his door, and I rise, following behind him. "You'll officially meet the team tomorrow, before practice."

The pitch is a short walk from Coach's office and when we arrive, the team has already started their training session. He doesn't attempt to bring me out there to introduce me to everyone, and honestly I'm thankful for it. I'd rather observe from the touchlines and see how they operate as a team from the outside.

Coach St. James introduces me to a short, lean guy with red hair that's so bright it looks unnatural, and I almost wonder if the bloke dyes it.

"Cairney, this is Assistant Coach Matthews. I need to get out there, but I'll leave you two to it and I'll see you tomorrow before practice." He brushes past us onto the pitch, leaving us alone.

Coach Matthews turns to me and offers his hand. "Good to have you, Cairney. I've seen you on the pitch, and I'm impressed. I wanna see you adapt and do the same thing here," he says as he drops my hand, then shoves his back into his pocket.

"I plan on it."

"Got a good team this year," he says, nodding toward the pitch as they run a phase of play. "Powerful. A solid defense, disciplined. And that makes it hard to break through the line. Some fast guys that focus on moving the ball and exploiting gaps in defense."

I nod along but keep my eyes trained on the pitch, watching as they go for a try. He's not wrong; they're bloody good. Their bond is evident in the way they work together and execute plays. These guys are powerful and skilled playmakers. That's the best you could ask for in a team, and it's not just about being talented. It's all about communication and how it plays out on the pitch.

"And I think you'll be the perfect addition to the team if you can keep your head on straight." He adds, "Conditioning at least once a week, two sessions on the pitch until spring games start. I expect you at all of them, putting in the work just like everyone else."

I shove my hands into the pockets of my trousers and nod. "I'll be there."

A long, hard whistle blows down the touchlines, and we both turn to see a girl stomping out onto the pitch over to one of the blokes, her long espresso braid swishing behind her. From our position, I can make out the delicate slope of her nose, the high cheekbones, plump pink lips, pale, creamy skin, and a blazing fire in her eyes.

She's *pissed*. And proper fit. But who the hell is she?

When she makes it to the pitch she stops in front of the tallest bloke on the team and shakes her head while sporting a fierce scowl. "Soccer tryouts are in two weeks. If you're not gonna commit to a tackle maybe you should try out."

"But I—" he sputters.

"But I? But I? Drive with your legs and make the damn tackle, *Williams*. Jesus, are we playing rugby or ballet out here?" She does a mock twirl, which would be rather comical if she didn't *actually* look a little scary taking on a guy who's at least a foot taller and outweighs her by at least a hundred pounds.

Holy shit.

Coach Matthews chuckles next to me. "And that...is Rory St. James."

My gaze bounces to him, and then back to the tiny spitfire on the pitch who's now giving someone else a verbal lashing. Most guys wouldn't take a girl like this seriously, but these guys are looking at her with a mixture of fear and awe in their gazes.

"*That's* Coach's... *daughter?*" I mutter, my eyes still widened in shock.

"Yep. She's our equipment manager, but that girl knows more about rugby than half these guys do. You'll meet her when you meet the rest of the team. Look, all I'd worry about, Cairney, is putting in your time and making rugby your top priority. We're not asking for perfection. We're asking you to show up, do your job, and stay out of trouble. Earn your spot on this team. Earn their trust."

I nod. "I know. And I know that I'm an asset. If you give me time, I'll prove it not to just you and Coach St. James, but to them."

Silence hangs between us for a beat, both of us still watching what's unfolding on the pitch.

"You wanna know the *real* secret to getting in with those guys?" He jerks his head toward the feisty brunette on the pitch. "It's *her.*"

CHAPTER 2

Rory

There is *no one* more petty and dramatic than a group of college guys.

Specifically, rugby players.

Trust me, I know, since I spend the majority of my time with them.

You'd think that it would be girls who like the tea, but there is nothing these guys love more than being dead center in the middle of anything and everything.

Generally, I ignore anything that has to do with drama, but this situation can't be ignored.

And by situation, I mean *Cillian Cairney*.

Prescott University's latest headline straight off the plane from London. Six foot four, 230 pounds of tattooed, British bad boy for everyone on campus to lose their minds over.

Which they absolutely are. Everyone's obsessed with our new transfer.

Half the campus is falling over their feet to catch a glimpse of the guy who's been dubbed "Kill" on the rugby pitch, and the other half are too busy trying to figure out why he's been exiled here to begin with.

It's not a secret that he got expelled and a permanent red card from his team in London, and since no one truly knows *why*... everyone's desperate to find out.

Of course, the only person who knows the real reason is my dad, and that's only because he's Prescott's head rugby coach.

Even being the coach's daughter didn't give me access to that piece of information. All I know is that Cillian's apparently run out of chances, and a friend of my dad's called in a favor, which is how he ended up here, walking on to the team midseason.

During what could be our most important season yet.

Yesterday, I spotted him on the touchlines with Coach Matthews observing practice, but aside from the couple of stolen glances I allowed myself, I did my best to pretend he wasn't there at all.

I have no intention of feeding into the frenzy.

Cillian Cairney is a distraction.

One that I *nor* the team can afford.

The guys are having a hard time focusing with his arrival, and if we want any shot at the championship this year, they've got to bust their asses for it.

And now, that includes *him*.

I fidget in my chair, glancing down at my phone for the tenth time since we walked into the film room for this team meeting, chewing my lip. Better my lip than my nails since I'm attempting to grow them out long enough to keep them painted.

"Well, I heard that he got caught with like half a pound of cocaine. The guy's basically a low-level drug dealer," Ezra mutters from across the conference table. He's leaned back in his chair, tossing a ball up in the air as he speaks, and I roll my eyes.

Of all the ridiculous, made-up gossip I've heard about Cillian, this one might just take the cake.

"Brother, shut up." Brooks, the team's captain, scoffs from beside Ezra, reaching over and swiping the ball from midair. He starts tossing it back and forth in his hands. "First of all, like Coach would let someone on the team who deals fucking *drugs*, Ezra. Be so for real. Second, half a pound of cocaine is definitely not low level on the drug dealer chain."

Ezra's brow pinches as his lips purse, like he's only now realizing just how ridiculous his accusation sounded when his best friend laid it out for him.

"Regardless of what he did to end up here, I personally think this is a bad idea, letting this guy who's clearly a liability walk on to the team. I don't know what Coach was thinking," Fitz chimes in. He shrugs and glances at me. "No offense, Ror."

Sebastian Fitzgerald, better known as "Fitz," is my best friend. We've been inseparable since we met at his first rugby practice our freshman year, and he knows me better than anyone. So he knows just how protective I am when it comes to my dad.

And this team.

Lifting a brow, I narrow my gaze, dragging it over each of them before landing back on Fitz. "How about we not spread rumors? None of us knows the *real* reason why he's here, and I trust my dad to make the best decision for the team. Plus... say what you want, but he's *good*. Really fucking good. I've seen the tapes. I don't know him, but I do know that if he plays as well as he did in London, then he'll be good for the team."

No one has anything to say after that, not that I expected them to, so I pick my phone up out of my lap and scroll through my socials while we wait.

There's nothing else to say about any of it. It's already done. I know they don't want him walking on to the team, they've been antsy since they found out, and they're right to be distrustful when it's clear he was expelled from his last school, but...I trust my dad more than anyone. I know there's a lot at stake for everyone involved, but they have to trust that my dad knows what he's doing and is making the right choice. He's always been a damn good coach and put this team above everything, and I don't think that's changing.

A few minutes later, the door opens and my dad, Coach Matthews, and Cillian walk through. It's the first time I've seen him up close, and I'm surprised how much more...intimidating he seems.

He's taller than I thought, his thick shoulders even broader than they appeared from the try lines. A burgundy T-shirt stretches across them. Tattoos cover both his arms, the dark ink spilling down his skin onto the tops of his hands, painting a portrait that tells a story of some kind. His sharp, chiseled jaw is set in a hard line as his dark, smoldering eyes scan the room of unhappy faces peering back at him.

"Afternoon," my dad says, addressing his players. He's always been a pillar of strength, and it's one of the many things I've always admired about him. I know this can't be easy for him, bringing in this guy and hoping like hell that it works out, but I do believe that he's the best coach I've ever known, and he would never steer his guys wrong. If this new guy is here, it's because my dad believes that he's worth it. "I'm going to keep this short and sweet. We've got a practice to get to and I know that you've all heard what's going on. Let's just call this an official introduction. This is Cillian Cairney. He's transferring in from London and will be joining the team."

The entire time my dad's speaking, Cillian's quiet, his stormy gaze slowly moving around the room as my dad talks about the transition and how vital it is that they work as a team. *Play* as a team.

Honestly, Cillian looks completely uninterested in being here, and when we lock eyes from across the room, the scowl on his lips seems to deepen, a look of something I can't read passing through his eyes.

I lift a brow, holding his stare until he finally looks away, placing his gaze back on my father.

All right then.

Dad tells the guys that Cillian will be jumping in immediately, participating in all team workouts and practices.

Even though they all nod, the air in the room is tense and so thick you could practically choke. Everyone's aware the guys aren't happy to have Cillian walking on to the team, and it's clear that he's not happy to be here either. Which seems like the perfect recipe for disaster.

Sighing, I sit back in the chair and cross my arms over my chest. I knew this wasn't going to be easy, but it seems even more impossible after seeing him face-to-face. Seeing the guys' reaction to him.

Dad finishes his speech, then asks Cillian to hang back before dismissing the rest of the guys to head to the pitch. They file out of the room in a sea of whispered murmurs and stares, not bothering to hide their disdain.

I'm on my way to follow them out when my dad grabs my forearm softly, stopping me. "Hey, Ror, could you stay back for a second?"

Turning back to face them, I plaster on a small smile, tucking a strand of hair that's fallen from my ponytail behind my ear. "Yeah, of course."

Cillian looks annoyed that he wasn't dismissed with the rest of the team, shuffling from one sneaker-clad foot to the other before shoving his hands deep in the pockets of his dark gray joggers.

"Cillian, this is my daughter, Rory. She's our equipment manager and my right-hand girl. I just wanted to introduce you two since you'll be seeing her around. Going to head out to the pitch, I'll see you shortly," Dad says, jerking his head toward me with a smile before disappearing along with Coach Matthews through the door, leaving us alone.

In *painfully* awkward silence.

"Hi," I say, offering him a small smile. "I'm Rory, *unofficial* assistant coach. *Official* equipment manager."

Cillian's brow raises, but he remains silent, so I stick my hand out and refuse to look away, not backing down. "Nice to meet you."

He glances down at my hand before slowly dragging his eyes back up to meet mine. For a second, I think he might actually leave my hand awkwardly hanging there, making this entire encounter that much more unbearable, but after the longest seconds in history, he slides my small hand in his, and shakes it.

It's over before I can even register the feel of his hand in mine because he drops it like he's been burned.

"Likewise." The hoarse, growly, English accented syllables slip from his mouth, his tone flat and void of any emotion at all.

"If you need anything just let me know. I can help with whatever. I help a lot of our guys with nutrition plans, going over tape, anything really..." I trail off, tucking my hands into the pockets of my athletic shorts when he gives me a look that says he doesn't give a shit.

"Noted. We done here? I need to be on the pitch," he says sharply.

I shrug. "Yeah, sure. Have a good practice. Good luck."

Without another glance, he walks out the door, letting it slam shut behind him.

Well...okay then.

Nice talking to you too.

* * *

I knew that the first practice as a team would be rough, but I may have underestimated just how rough it would *actually* be.

Still, I choose to remain hopeful even though a disaster is currently unfolding on the pitch. It's like watching a train wreck, in ultraslow motion, that you just can't stop staring at no matter how bad it is. The tension is palpable and there's zero cohesion. Zero teamwork. They're practically ignoring him entirely. It's clear that the guys aren't making an effort to pass the ball to Cillian, regardless of him being a major playmaker.

"There might as well be a line drawn in the grass between them," Dad murmurs from beside me, clutching his clipboard so tightly his knuckles have turned white, a dramatic contrast to the shade of crimson his face currently is. He's the kind of man who doesn't get angry or upset and yell. No, he's the quiet kind. A simmering pot that continues to bubble until it finally boils over, burning everyone within reach. To me that's even more intimidating than someone who's constantly losing their shit.

I nod in agreement, my eyes trained on the obvious root of the problem. "They don't trust him, Dad. And you know they'll never be able to work together if they can't trust each other."

He sighs loudly as he pulls his hand down his face before turning to look at me. "I know. I just... The kid's a damn good player and I know he has potential. I can see it in him."

I look back to the pitch and watch as Cillian manages to get the ball, despite how badly his teammates are attempting to keep him from doing so. It's not exactly subtle. The way they're passing the ball around and purposely making sure Cillian is on the outside of the play. Hence Dad stressing about the situation even more than before he saw them together on the pitch.

I grew up on the touchlines of my dad's pitch. I fell in love with rugby when I was just a little girl and have spent all my life immersed in the sport by his side. The perks of him being a single dad with a toddler. I've seen hundreds of games, twice as many practices, and countless incredible players.

But the kind of talent that Cillian Cairney possesses isn't something you see every day, and I know that's exactly why my dad brought him here.

I can see it in his movements, fluid and graceful in a way that could only be natural talent. He's powerful and quick as he runs down the pitch, acting on pure instinct.

That instinct is what has made some of the greatest rugby players of all time... *great*.

"What do you think? Do you think him being here is going to hurt the team?" Dad asks, breaking through my thoughts.

I keep my eyes trained on the guys, taking a second to mull over his question as if it's not the same one I've been asking myself since I found out Cillian was joining the team.

And honestly? I still don't know the answer.

He's clearly a skilled player, but he's unpredictable, and his temper is a liability, so I don't know what's going to happen from here.

"I think... that it's only the first day and that's a simple question with a really complicated answer," I say, reaching out to place my hand on his arm. "And I think that you're the best rugby coach I've ever met. Your intuition is always spot on. But one thing I do know for certain is that unless we can somehow get them to trust each other and communicate, then this is never going to work."

"Yeah, I know it's the first day, Rory, but I didn't expect *this* much tension. I've gotta figure out a way to get them working together. Fast." He grimaces.

For a second, I'm quiet as I shuffle around the idea that's popped into my head. It might be a complete waste of time, but then again, we have to try something, and there's no time to waste. "Okay, I think I *might* have an idea. Do you trust me?"

He chuckles softly. "You know there's no one I trust more than you, sweetheart."

This could be fun. Or a disaster. Or maybe a fun... disaster?

But there's only one way to find out.

CHAPTER 3

Cillian

"Thank you all for coming in so early today," Rory St. James says with a saccharine smile as she stands at the front of the conference room holding a clipboard in her arms.

Shit, it's too damn early to be here, especially sitting in front of the human equivalent of sunshine. Most of us are still half asleep and she's bright-eyed and peppy as if it's not still 6:30 in the morning.

I wouldn't be here at all if attendance had been optional. The less time I have to spend around any of these tossers outside of the one job I came here to do, the better.

Sighing, I run my fingers through my hair and sit back, waiting for her to spit out whatever it is she's dragged us here for.

I've been here only a week, so this dynamic she's got with the team is something I'm still trying to wrap my head around. I'm trying to figure out why Coach allows it. I don't understand it. Why she's so involved and why everyone seems to put her on some kind of pedestal. It seems like everywhere I look, she's there.

"I know you're probably all wondering why we asked you to come in on an off day," she starts, her piercing gaze slipping around the room, pausing briefly when it lands on me. "I think it's pretty obvious we've been having a bit of a...rough start and that's okay. It's a big transition for everyone, I get it, and we were prepared for that. But we clearly need to work on team bonding. That's the place to start. Therefore..." She trails off as she looks over at Coach, who gives her a brief nod. "We're having an all-day clinic today that's going to focus on trust-building and team-bonding exercises."

The entire room erupts in a series of pained groans.

I sigh, crossing my arms over my chest.

Just what I wanted. To spend my only off day with these arseholes who clearly don't want shit to do with me as much as I want to do with them. They've made that abundantly clear.

Going out of their way to push me out of pitch play, talking shit every time the coaching staff is out of earshot, or ignoring me altogether.

Which I prefer.

All I want to do is play rugby. To finish these two years out at this damn school and go back home. Play for the Premiership.

But the only way I'll end up with a contract is by playing for a team where a scout can see me.

I know that I'm good.

But if I'm not on a pitch then my chances of that are gone.

I don't want to bond. I don't want to work on team building. I want to get in and get *out*.

Unlike the rest of the team, I stay quiet, keeping my thoughts to myself because I'm in no position to complain about today's activities. Truthfully, I'd rather take a hit right to the balls than work on some bullshit exercises that aren't going to make anything better.

Forcing us together isn't going to solve this problem, but I'll let her figure that out on her own.

"Look, I get it. It's not something you want to do on your only off day. But let's be real, it's necessary and you all know it as much as we do," she says as she crosses her arms over her chest, trapping the clipboard against it. Her navy-blue V-neck dips slightly with the movement, exposing the pale creamy swell of her tits. Which I ignore because that's the last bloody thing I need to be noticing.

The very last.

"Rory, please for the love of God don't do this to us." One of the guys in the back of the room groans loudly. "I'm begging you."

Her dark brow arches, and that sticky sweet smile returns. She doesn't look the least bit sorry for the torture I know is coming our way. Apparently the one thing we can all agree on is that we don't want to be around each other.

"Sorry, but it's happening," she responds. "Get your gear and put your game faces on."

Coach St. James steps forward when a chorus of murmurs ring throughout the room, a serious expression on his face as he says, "I expect everyone to give it their best today. I know it's not a normal practice day, but I support everything that Rory said up here. I'm giving the reins to her on this because it was her idea and you all know how much I value my daughter's feedback, and I know that you do as well. This is necessary for our team development, and I know that you're committed to making this year the best, most successful year we've had. Go gear up, let's do this."

He dismisses everyone with that, and the guys begin to file out of the room, most of them still muttering and complaining under their breath.

Not that it'll do any good because obviously this pointless clinic is happening whether we like it or not.

And I'm quickly beginning to realize that Rory St. James has this entire team wrapped around her finger and I haven't the slightest idea *why*.

* * *

"Today's team-building exercise will be fairly simple. You're going to split into two groups, a mix of forwards and backs, then run through an obstacle course relay. The first team over the finish line wins," Rory says, standing next to her father and Coach Matthews. She's got a bright yellow lanyard around her neck with a shiny whistle attached, and I already know she's going to blow the damn thing until our ears bleed.

She's on a mission. I can see the defiance in her eyes, and the way she's squared her shoulders as if she's prepared for an impending battle.

One that there's no doubt she's going to lose.

"Every station requires collaboration, which means you're going to have to work *together* if you want to succeed. Much like you have to do on the pitch," Coach St. James says. "You will need to lean on your teammates and communicate with each other. While this is Rory's exercise, I did suggest that we...*up the ante*—make sure you guys are really invested in being the winning team. Losing team will run a Bronco. *Before* you leave the practice facility today."

Bloody fucking hell.

A Bronco is without a doubt the hardest drill you'll ever have to do on a pitch. A series of sprints that leaves you nearly puking from a combination of exertion and exhaustion. It's fucking brutal. This might be the only way to get the lot of us to work together because not a single one of us wants to run a Bronco, no matter how much we can't stand to be around one another.

"Brooks, you're captain, you get first pick for your team and… Ezra, you pick the other team. Once you've split up, we'll briefly run through what each station's objective is. After that you'll be on your own. The coaching team and I will be keeping time, and an eye to make sure everyone's participating and playing fair. Remember guys, the purpose of this is to build trust and to learn to work better together. That includes *every* person on this team."

Brooks laughs darkly under his breath as his gaze locks on to mine, the corners of his lips curling into a sinister smirk while he lifts a brow tauntingly.

And then it begins.

One by one they pick guys for their teams until there's no one left on the try line but me.

I'm not surprised, but that doesn't mean that it doesn't piss me right off. I catch Rory's eyes, and she sighs defeatedly before shaking her head and turning to Brooks, then Ezra. "Really?"

They both shrug, Brooks with that stupid fucking smirk that I want to wipe clean off his mouth.

"Cillian you're with Brooks. Let's go."

Only then does the self-satisfied, arrogant expression on his face slightly falter, and now *I'm* the one smirking.

Arsehole.

It's clear that he and his dickhead of a friend are going to do whatever they can to ice me out and that's perfectly fine by me, because if there's one thing about me, it's that I don't give up. I might be keeping my head down and walking the straight and narrow, but that sure as fuck doesn't mean that I have to lie down and let these guys walk all over me as if I don't deserve a chance to prove myself on this team just the way they have.

Slowly, I walk over to Brooks's side of the pitch and stand next to Fitz who glances over and gives me a small curt nod. At least he acknowledges me, unlike the majority of the team.

The indoor training pitch has been turned into a series of obstacles sectioned off with fluorescent yellow rope and bright orange cones.

"Station number one, wave passing. Make a formation and pass the ball down the line. This drill is going to focus on precise, accurate passing, so I need to see everyone working together. You can move on to the next drill after completing four successful passes from one end of the line to the other." Rory instructs with her hands on her hips and that damn whistle hanging around her neck. Thank God she ditched the damn clipboard. "Next up we've got shadow running, and then partnered sprints where you'll carry another player to the try line and back before the opposing team. C'mon, guys, let's do this."

The first drill goes exactly the way I expected it to—the guys begrudgingly passing the ball my way because they have no other choice in order for us to actually complete it and move to the next station. When it's over, we pause for a water break before moving on to the next drill, and I step off to the side. Grabbing my water, I squirt a stream into my mouth, watching as Brooks walks over to Rory and tosses his arm around her shoulder like it's something that he's always done. He says something near her ear and then pokes out his lip like he's pouting, and she elbows him in the side, pushing him off with an eye roll.

He's smirking, clearly comfortably going back and forth with her. A few other guys from Ezra's team join in, and I sit back, watching the exchange.

These guys are friendly with her and not just in a "coaching" kind of way like I originally thought. In a *friendship* kind of way.

A loud, shrill whistle floats through the air. "All right let's get back to it." Rory says, putting space between her and the guys. "We've got a lot of work to do today and no time to waste."

The rest of the guys from my team filter back over one by one, and Ezra's with them. My eyebrow curves up when he grins, but then he shoulder checks me hard as fuck, knocking my water bottle out of my hands and onto the ground, where it bursts open, soaking my feet through my rugby boots.

"Might want to watch where you're standing, Cairney. Wouldn't want our new *star* player to end up hurt. Would be pretty tragic." His head tilts, lips curling into a smirk as amusement flashes in his eyes. Except there's nothing funny about it. His voice is low, so that only I can hear him, and I know it's because he's trying to pull this bullshit so no one from the coaching staff or Rory know he's mouthing off.

I roll my tongue across the top row of my teeth, counting backward from five.

Five.
Four.
Three.
Two.
One.

I add an extra second just for good measure so I don't do something stupid like beat the shit out of him.

For fuck's sake.

But that is exactly the response he's looking for, and I'm not going to give it to him. Especially not with the entire team as an audience.

I don't say a word as I bend and retrieve my water bottle, not until I'm twisting the top back on. "Yeah, thanks for that, mate. Way to look out for your teammates."

His shit-eating, sinister smile dims for only a moment, and then he's nodding, brushing past like he didn't just fucking threaten me.

Team bonding right?

It's going to be a long two years at Prescott, and it's only just beginning.

CHAPTER 4

Rory

I've never needed this fruity drink in my life more than I do right now. That sounds a tad dramatic, but it's painfully true and honestly, after the week I've had, I *deserve* all the alcohol I just watched my best friend pour into this red plastic cup.

"Mmm, sugar," I moan noisily after swallowing down another long gulp. "Calories. Carbs. *Vodka*. Do you realize how happy I am right now, Fitz? I would kiss you right now if the thought of that didn't make me want to barf."

He laughs and shakes his head. "See, aren't you glad you came out with us tonight?"

I nod. Although Fitz doesn't know that the *real* reason I'm here tonight is because the guy from my pharmacology class that I've been secretly pining over since last semester asked me to come.

Which is kind of a big deal for me. Well, actually it's a huge deal.

But it's not like a date or anything...I mean he didn't *say* that it was a date, but I really kinda hope that it is?

The invitation was unclear though, and because I'm *me*, I spent the entire day obsessing over it because I am painfully, horribly, tragically awkward when it comes to the opposite sex. Unless it's the guys from the team, and that's only because at this point, they're like brothers to me. That makes it easy for me to talk to them without getting flustered or having to second-guess myself entirely.

I have absolutely zero desire to flirt or date any of my rugby guys. *Gross.*

It's just when it comes to a guy that I think is cute or I'm slightly interested in, I immediately get in my head, and word vomit, saying all the wrong things and making a complete fool out of myself. At least that's been the case the few times I've attempted to flirt.

"You know that if I didn't drag you here, you'd be at home right now, working on a cross-stitch and watching reruns of *True Blood* like you're eighty," Fitz adds, his azure eyes dancing with a mixture of amusement and arrogance because he knows that he's right.

Scoffing, I reach out and push his shoulder. "Okay? And you say that like it's a bad thing. There's nothing wrong with my old-lady hobbies. They're... *relaxing.* Calming. You should try it some time."

He's right though. I'm absolutely a homebody and would prefer to be on my couch rotting at all times. This is my first time venturing out to a party that wasn't thrown in the backyard of one of the guys from the team. Where I'm comfortable and completely at ease.

This... this is an entirely different ball game. Or match if we're making rugby references.

"Yeah, I bet. My mom asked me last week when you were going to stitch my name on a sweatshirt for me."

Wait.

That's a brilliant idea and I have no idea why I haven't thought of it before now.

My eyes widen, and Fitz groans, dragging a hand down his face. "I shouldn't have told you that, should I?"

"Nope. Tell Mama Fitz I said thank you very much. And if you don't wear the sweatshirt I make you, I am going to be so offended and will absolutely be revoking your best friend card," I say before taking another long sip of my drink until there's only a teeny, tiny bit left at the bottom of the cup.

Would I prefer to be home, wearing my comfy pajamas, working on my cross-stitch, and binge-watching TV while I eat a pint of my favorite ice cream? Yes.

But I made a promise to myself that I would get out and experience what's left of my college career. Make new friends. Go to parties. Sleep with hot guys and sow every wild oat imaginable. No regrets.

Well, that would require me being able to *speak* to them first, but still. One step at a time.

I just don't want to look back on my life ten, fifteen, twenty years down the road and say, "I wish I would have…" I want to experience everything that college life has to offer.

I'm halfway through junior year, and I've lived in my new apartment for over a month and still have done none of those things, which is the real reason why I came here tonight: to meet a guy who makes my palms clammy and my heart race. Not normal Rory behavior.

I've spent the majority of my life taking care of not only myself but my dad too. It's not that he asked, or expected that from me, it's just kind of what happens when you're raised by a single father who's growing up alongside you. When I started at Prescott University almost three years ago, I thought I'd move into a dorm or an apartment and get the full college experience, but when it came down to it, I couldn't leave him.

Who was going to cook him dinner? Make sure he didn't mix dark colors and light colors in the laundry or make sure Teddy, our geriatric dachshund, was fed and had his daily vitamin?

Who was going to remind *him* to take his vitamins and newly prescribed blood pressure medicine?

I'm well aware that he's a grown man who did an amazing job raising me, but it's always just been the two of us.

Taking care of each other.

Spending Saturday nights at home watching game highlights or playing board games.

I've always been a daddy's girl, and I always will be.

Only now... I'm learning to be on my own. Without using him as a crutch to hide the fact that I'm afraid to put myself out there and do all the things I promised myself I'd do. It's scary to put yourself out into the world in any capacity, especially when you're doing it for the first time, but I have to do it. No matter how scary it feels.

It's time for me to spread my metaphorical wings and fly, to experience all that college life has to offer, and to hopefully check some things off my list.

Starting tonight.

"Rory St. James, get your ass over here and be my pong partner," Wren, my other best friend, who plays the prop for the team, yells from the opposite side of the hockey house's living room. "I'm not fucking losing tonight to these douches, and no one runs a table like you, boo."

I sigh, down the last of my drink, then thrust the now-empty cup into Fitz's hands. "Must I *always* show them how it's done?"

"Go get 'em, tiger." He chuckles.

I leave Fitz standing in the kitchen and make my way over to Wren, who's in front of a white folding table lined with red cups. Two guys from the hockey team are on the opposite side, and they eye me arrogantly.

Like, just because I'm a girl, I can't hold my own in a stupid drinking game.

Men. I wonder when they'll finally stop underestimating women, because I think we've proven that we're the superior creatures.

Wren peers down at me, a wide smile splitting his face, revealing his missing front tooth, and I bite back a laugh.

He's an idiot who never wears a mouth guard, and last season he took a particularly hard tackle that knocked his tooth out. Most of the time, he's too lazy to wear the bridge the dentist gave him.

And somehow he still manages to get more girls than half the guys on the team. He's kind of a gentle giant. Hard and unyielding on the outside, but squishy on the inside. It's what I love most about him.

Honestly, Wren Michaels is living proof that men can be badass *and* still be kind, compassionate, and sensitive. That they don't have to be one or the other.

"Time to eat your words, assholes," he says to the hockey guys as he thrusts the small orange Ping-Pong ball into my hand.

Seems like we've got a bit of an advantage here seeing as how Wren handles balls on the daily and these guys chase a puck around with a stick, so I'm already liking the odds.

"Thanks for being my partner, Ror. I know I can always count on you," Wren says, tossing an arm over my shoulder and tugging me close.

Of all the guys on the team, I'm the closest with Wren and Fitz. Don't get me wrong, I love them—they're my brothers in every sense of the word—but I don't hang out with anyone as much as I do them. They just get me, and our friendship has always been easy. They're my big idiots who I run to when the world's falling apart, and I'm...one of the guys to them. Which I've always loved—having people who understand and accept you without question—but also I'm realizing that being one of the guys puts me in the same territory with...all the guys.

Even the ones *outside* the team.

It's a stigma that has somehow become my reputation around campus.

I'm the beer pong partner. The one to watch tape with. The wing woman. The girl who plays fantasy football. And most important, Coach St. James's daughter who is a rugby aficionado and not afraid to go toe to toe with anyone about it.

And I love it. I do.

But...I just wish that it didn't immediately put me in *just*-bros territory with practically every guy I meet.

Lately, it's something I've become more...aware of now that I'm trying to meet new guys. I'm realizing this is how they see me, and it doesn't help the fact that the moment I open my mouth, I embarrass myself and can't seem to form a rational thought. It's never been like that with the guys from the team, which made me realize that it's actually the *flirting* that's the problem. I really wish that I could talk to Fitz or Wren about it, but they're men, and I truly doubt that they'd understand where I'm coming from anyway.

Cons to having *only* guys as your best friends.

One of the very few...but still.

I'm just the little sister they would never be interested in helping with guy stuff, and honestly, I would rather run through campus butt naked than talk to them about my "guy" problems, or lack thereof.

Because I'm distracted and in my head, I miss my initial shot, which makes the hockey guys entirely too confident. They think they have it in the bag, and that makes them sloppy.

That was their first mistake.

Little do they know, I'm kind of a beer pong champion—that's why Wren refuses to play with anyone else.

"Told you assholes," Wren boasts proudly when I sink the next three shots in a row and blow out a ball that circles the inside rim of the solo cup, preventing them from scoring a point.

I laugh. "Wrenny, it's not nice to brag. You know it's never too late to make a comeback."

Of course they don't though, because we're undefeated, and I am *not* giving up my title that easily.

After the game finishes, Wren wanders off to find a girl he's been texting all night, and I'm on my own, walking around the house to find the kitchen for another drink. It's barely midnight, but the three drinks I had earlier have my head feeling light and my limbs heavy as I push my way through the crowd.

All I had to eat today was a protein bar and a pack of gummy worms, which I'm realizing is not ideal when drinking, but it explains why the alcohol has hit me so quickly.

Note to self: no more vodka cocktails on an empty stomach.

Even if they're sugary and packed full of delicious carbs.

In the kitchen, I finally get another drink, eagerly swallowing the alcohol from the plastic cup.

"Rory, hey!"

My gaze lifts, and I see Carson Wright standing in front of me wearing a wide smile that shows two perfect dimples in his cheeks.

Oh God.

He's *here*.

Somehow between the alcohol and playing beer pong with Wren, I had nearly forgotten about meeting him here. That had been the perfect distraction, and now that Carson's standing in front of me, my stomach dances with nerves.

Lifting my hand awkwardly, I offer him a small wave. "Hi." It comes out as a squeak, and I'm not sure if it's because of the alcohol or the fact that he's talking to me outside of our pharmacology class. Or that he actually came.

He's tall, lean, and ridiculously hot, wearing a soft burgundy sweater and a pair of acid-washed jeans and old Converses. The thick black glasses on his face make him resemble a young Henry Cavill, and I think maybe I should just not say anything at all in fear of embarrassing myself, which is something I am very *very* likely to do.

You can do this, Rory. You've got liquid courage. You came here for a reason.

That reason is standing literally right in front of you.

"I've been looking for you. I saw Liam in the backyard, and he said you came with Fitz," he says with a raspy chuckle, pushing his thick black-framed glasses up on his nose. "You having fun?"

"Mm-hmm, yes. Definitely. How about you?" I nod enthusiastically, waving my hands as I speak. Jesus, what am I even doing? What am I even supposed to be doing with my hands right now?

His shoulder lifts as his grin widens. "Better now."

Oh God. My stomach flips, doing somersaults inside me.

What does that even mean? *Better now*? Better because he's seen...me?

Is this...Could *this* be my moment?

I've thought he was cute for like the entire semester but never had the courage to say anything to him outside of our conversations in class about homework and study guides. Until today, when he asked me to come here and I said yes.

I laugh and it comes out slightly awkward and a little too loud. "Uh, yeah? Th-thanks for asking me to come tonight."

He nods, stepping in closer and my heart actually begins to hammer in my chest as if it's trying to break free. "Yeah, of course. So this is embarrassing and stupid, but I just need to come out and say it," he starts, and I nod along with each syllable.

"No, totally, you can tell me anything," I say, blinking rapidly. My fingers tighten around the plastic cup in my hand as I wait for him to speak, trying to calm the rapid thrum of my heart.

The expression on his face turns sheepish as he reaches up and rubs his hand along the nape of his neck. "Uh...Do you think you could be my wing woman tonight? You know Adrina from class? She's here tonight, and I'm really into her and could use some help talking to her. I'm kinda really nervous?"

"Oh," I say, bringing my cup to my lips to hide my disappointment. "Uh...that's why you asked me here tonight?"

His brow pulls together tightly. "Yeah? You're so easy to talk to, Rory, like one of my guys. I thought maybe you could help me get a date with her? She's your lab partner so I figure that you probably know each other well?"

The hot, bitter sting of tears prick behind my eyes, but somehow I plaster on a smile to mask the hurt.

Of course. Rory the wing woman. Rory...*just one of the guys.*

God, I'm such an idiot.

Completely a fool to come here tonight.

I mumble a quick excuse to Carson and make a beeline for the bathroom, wiping away the silly, ridiculous tears and trying to pull myself together before anyone sees me upset. After a few minutes of pretending that it doesn't bother me that I just completely embarrassed myself in front of Carson, I find Fitz in the backyard and tell him I'm going to head home.

There's no way I want to stay at this party after what happened, and honestly, even though I'm sure the alcohol had a lot to do with the tears, I don't want to be here anymore. Tonight did not go the way I hoped it would, and my entire mood has completely gone down the drain.

"Let's go back to your apartment, Ror," Fitz whispers against my ear, tightening his arm around my shoulders as if he senses that something is wrong.

I nod wordlessly, leaning into him. The entire walk back to my apartment, I'm quiet, replaying what happened in my head.

I was so stupid to think Carson would want anything from me. Stupid to think my version of flirting, word vomiting and awkward giggling, was anything he'd ever be interested in.

Tonight proved exactly what I've been afraid of.

That I'll only ever be *just* the wing woman, and never anything more.

CHAPTER 5

Rory

"All right, spill. What's going on? You've been scarily quiet since we left the party," Fitz says, looking over at me with his eyebrow raised, gently bumping his shoulder into mine to pull me from my thoughts. Of course he's reading me like an open book, because my best friend knows when something's off. "Talk to me, Ror."

We've been sitting on my couch eating chicken nuggets and watching *Parks and Recreation* for the last thirty minutes and I haven't said a word. Mostly because I'm in my feelings about the run in with Carson, and I'm just kind of trying to process all of it.

Plus, talking to Fitz about this is kind of just weird?

Weird in the way of talking about wanting to hook up with guys...with your brother. I trust Fitz with my life, and I can't think of a time when he hasn't been anything but supportive and steadfast when I needed him, but there's a part of me that is just kind of embarrassed to admit all this out loud, if I'm being honest with myself.

I don't think he'd understand even if I tried to explain it. Guys like him are used to girls falling at his feet. Perks of being a hot D1A athlete with a stupid amount of charm. Hot objectively speaking because he's *Fitz*.

But... still.

"Uh... well something kind of happened tonight?" I mutter quietly, tearing my gaze from the TV and turning to look at him.

"Okay, what happened?"

Scrunching my nose, I shrug. "It's silly, it's not even a big deal. It's stupid, really."

I'm just permanently friend-zoned beyond my comprehension.

"Hey, don't say that." He shakes his head, blue eyes flickering with concern. "If it's bothering you then it's important, Ror. *Period*. Which means it's important to me. And I'm your best friend; you can talk to me about anything. You know that." The sincerity in his voice makes me want to cry a little bit and ultimately is the reason why I break.

In a rush of words that I mumble so fast I'm not sure if he's even really heard any of them, I recount what happened with Carson, and how incredibly stupid and foolish the entire thing made me feel.

"First of all, fuck that guy. He's a dick bag, Rory. You want me to fight him?"

"What!? Oh my God, Fitz, *no*." His response is a low, raspy chuckle, and I continue, "It was just like embarrassing. I thought that this was finally the moment where a guy, I don't know... *sees* me. For the first time. Me. Not Rory St. James, Coach's daughter. Or their *bro*. Like really sees me, and that didn't happen. I was yet again someone's wingman, and it made me feel like a fool. I spent the past several months trying to show him that I was interested and clearly that was a fail."

Fitz's eyes soften. "You're not a fool. That guy's just an idiot and clearly wasn't good enough for you anyway."

"Yeah, but I think tonight was just more of an eye opener? If it wasn't him, it would've been someone else. I just really thought he was interested in me. I thought that my sad attempt at flirting for the past several months translated into...something." Sighing, I pull my knees up to my chest before I continue, "I think I'm actually hopeless, Fitz. I don't know *how* to flirt, or how to even have an actual conversation with someone I find attractive. It's like something in my brain is wired wrong and I turn into a total klutz, stumbling over my words and yapping about the most random things. Mostly sports because it's what I know best. This is exactly why I'd rather just hang out with you guys. It's easy being with you."

"Maybe that's your problem, Ror. You need to get out, meet new people outside of the team. Hang out with people *outside* of me and Wren."

I don't respond, instead shrugging, chewing the corner of my lip.

"Put yourself out there and it'll happen exactly the way it's supposed to. Plus, how are you going to get any better at the things you're not good at if you don't practice? Pretty sure you've said that to me a time or two."

"I swear, I need some lessons on how to not be the most awkward person alive."

He rubs his hands together, then does a dramatic show of cracking his neck as he says, "Put me in, Coach, I'm ready. The only thing I'm better at than rugby is women."

"Shut up," I say, although I'm laughing, which is a step up from the tears of earlier tonight.

"Say, girl, you're cute tonight. Wanna hook up?"

"Ew. Stop. *Immediately.* I'm going to throw up." I fake gag, and we both laugh.

See? Talking to your best guy friend about wanting to find a guy to hook up with turns weird quick, especially when you're as close as siblings.

The easygoing grin on Fitz's face falls slightly as he sobers. "Seriously though, you're perfect just the way you are, and I think that if you stop putting crazy pressure on yourself, you'll find someone you click with. It'll happen."

He makes it sound so easy, but it feels anything but easy. Still, I nod, giving him a small smile. "Thanks, Fitz. For just...listening. It feels better just to get that off my chest. And thanks for forcing me out tonight, it was fun. Before all of that anyway."

"Well, you've been busting our asses hardcore so I figured you could use a break as much as we could from your tyranny."

"Ha ha. Dick," I deadpan, rolling my eyes. He can give me shit all day long, but he knows that a team-building clinic was necessary, even though I'm not sure it paid off. Yet. "How are the guys handling this? I mean *really* handling it, Fitz."

For a second he's quiet, rolling his tongue across his teeth as he stares back at me. Then he blows out a breath. "Still a fucking mess, Ror. Most of the guys are still pissed off that he walked on the team like he owns the place and didn't have to earn shit while they've had to work their asses off to get the spot they have. They don't trust him for shit, and I really don't know if that's going to change any time soon. Trust is earned, and so far he hasn't done anything to earn it." Fitz pauses, shaking his head. "You saw how the drills went, zero cohesion on both sides. He's an asshole, and he doesn't talk to anybody unless he has to. The rest of the guys are cold and closed off. We're all just caught in this in-between, and I have no clue how it's going to end up. Doesn't help that all of us, including your dad, have so much pressure to make it to the championship this year."

My chest feels heavy as I listen to him speak, but I knew that this was likely what was going to happen. It's been my worry from the start.

A huge change like this midseason is enough to throw any team out of rhythm and off-balance, but adding a new guy in the mix that they don't *want*... Well, that could potentially be catastrophic.

They don't trust him because he has a problematic reputation. He got kicked off his previous team and came here as a last resort. And to them, he doesn't seem very sorry that it happened. They think he truly believes he's a better player than anyone.

I know if they had their choice, he wouldn't be here.

But I'm not going to let that happen.

I can't. These guys mean too much to me, this *team* means too much to me.

"It'll work itself out. He's only been here for a little while, and everyone's still adjusting. We just have to keep trying, that's all."

Especially if I have anything at all to do with it.

CHAPTER 6

Cillian

"Fuck you," Brooks Thorne spits as he steps forward, forcing me backward until I slam against the cold metal of the locker door. I let out a low chuckle, shaking my head in disbelief that this arsehole is truly *this* fucking dumb.

I've had about enough of his bloody bullshit, and he has no clue just how much I've been holding back. Biting my tongue and ignoring the amount of dumb shit that's been spewing from his mouth since the moment I got here.

All because I can't fuck this up and lose my spot here.

"There's no amount of bullshit team building that's going to make you a part of this team. How about you do yourself, and all of us, a favor and go back to whatever Podunk town you came from?" he says.

"I'm not going anywhere, Thorne, so how about *you* do yourself a favor and fuck off," I say, my voice low and deadly, my temper on the verge of boiling over. "Maybe if you spent half the time you do worrying about me, actually being a bloody captain and leading this team like you're supposed to, then we wouldn't have to be running till we puke."

This time he laughs, and the sound pisses me off even more. He can hate me all goddamn day, but it's his job to lead this team, and from where I'm standing, he's doing a piss-poor job of it and everybody's suffering.

I don't expect them to invite me to parties or include me in their plans, and I don't even want any of that shit. I'm not here to make friends, I'm here to play rugby.

That's it.

They seem to think I'm the problem, but the issue is them. They won't even give me a damn chance to prove that I'm not here to fuck things up.

One word from the captain, and this grudge they're holding would be gone, but instead he's fanning the flame. He's pouring petrol on it, and watching it burn brighter.

That's his first mistake.

His second is thinking I have a never-ending amount of patience.

"You're the fucking problem, asshole."

"Yeah, well it seems to me that *you're* the problem, mate. You're making it goddamn impossible for us to find a rhythm on the pitch because the lot of you are too busy crying about the fact that I walked on to the team. Yeah? That's the problem, right?"

"You wanna know what my problem is? I don't like your fucking attitude. I don't like that you think just because you're good that you're above everybody else, that you're God's gift to this team," Brooks spits out, each syllable laced with a venomous disdain.

When the fuck have I ever said that shit? When have I ever acted like that?

I shake my head, a ragged scoff trailing from my lips. "Yeah, that's all in your head. You're fucking delusional. All I'm here to do is play rugby. I don't think I'm better than anyone, and I never acted like I was. All I know is that I am so goddamn tired of this shit already, so how about we solve it right here, right now? Put an end to it." I step forward until we're pressed chest to chest, nose to nose, waiting for him to decide where this is going from here.

His brow furrows, his eyes darkening as the corner of his lip curls up in a sneer. "Oh? You threatening me, Cairney?"

"You feeling threatened? Cause you should be. Now, what the fuck are you going to do about it, *Captain*?" The word is thrown his way as an insult just the way I intended it to sound. He might be a lot of things, but he's a right shit captain. I could lead this team better than he could and half these wankers hate me.

All I know is that I'm done with this back-and-forth bullshit. He's either going to do something about it or move the fuck on.

And finally, he grows a pair of bloody balls and flattens his palms on my chest, pushing me back roughly until I'm colliding with the locker behind me again. His chest heaves as he sucks in a breath. "You think you're going to come in *my* fucking house, *my* goddamn school, and threaten me? Fuck no."

I stay silent, arching a brow as if to say *then what the fuck are you waiting for*, and he might be the worst captain on the goddamn planet, but he can read that expression.

"Okay, chill the fuck out," Wren says, trying to step between us. He places his thick, meaty hand on Brooks's chest, but Brooks swats it away, pushing his mate back.

"Nah, if this fucker wants to talk shit, then let's go. The only way to solve this shit is to get rid of him, and I can't think of a better way to put him on a one-way flight back."

That's rich, coming from him. He hasn't shut the fuck up since I got here. Only difference is that I'm calling him on it and forcing the move instead of sitting back and yapping.

"Sorry, Michaels. Your captain seems to be too much of a pussy to do anything other than run his mouth," I say with a cocky grin, and a lift of my shoulder.

Brooks shoves me again, the sound of my back hitting the locker echoing around the empty locker room. I don't have a chance to say anything else before his fist is flying, colliding with my cheek, sending my head jerking to the side.

For a second I'm completely still, the only movement that of my chest as I heave in a breath. I think back to what the team therapist I was ordered to see after Mum died said to me: That the only person with control of my actions is me. No one could ever force my hand if I never give them the power to. Somehow, I hold on to that shit like I'm clinging to it for dear life.

Right now all I want to do is beat the living fuck out of the motherfucker standing in front of me, but I don't touch him.

I won't hit him back because I made a promise to my sister. That I wouldn't fuck this up, and I'm not ever letting her down again.

Summoning willpower that I truly didn't even know I possessed, I slowly turn to look at him, pain blooming around the split skin near my eye. "You done?"

He smirks. "Oh? You're not going to hit me back? Who's the pussy now, Cairney?"

"The difference between you and me is that I'll have to fight like bloody hell to keep my position on this team, Thorne. My daddy can't pay for my spot because he sits on the board of directors."

His pale blue eyes darken, and I know I've hit a sore spot. Funny the shit you can find out on the internet. He might be talented, but it sure as fuck doesn't hurt that his daddy bought a whole bloody wing for Prescott.

Money speaks louder, regardless of how talented you are.

"Go fuck yourself." He surges forward, crowding me against the locker again, but this time Ezra steps in between us, roughly shoving Brooks backward until he stumbles into the other guys standing behind him.

Ezra stares down at him, his jaw set in a hard line, eyes almost black. "Enough, Brooks. What do you think is going to happen when Coach hears about this, huh? We're going to get our asses handed to us."

Brooks shakes his head as he peers around the locker room at the rest of the team, who're watching the exchange between us. "Coach's not going to find out about this because no one is going to say a goddamn word. That right? This shit stays between us. No one talks, no one says shit. Got it?"

A few of the guys nod, while the others murmur in agreement.

As shitty of a captain as I've seen him be, he has influence with these guys because they trust him. In their eyes, they've been a solid team, that is, until I arrived and fucked it right up.

Part of me doesn't blame him for hating me. But the other part wishes he'd grow the fuck up and act like a captain should. Which means you do whatever it takes for your team. You sacrifice and show up no matter what the cost is. A good captain recognizes a valuable player when he sees one.

Not be threatened by it. A real captain wants what's best for your team, even if someone threatens your ego.

I'd know because I used to be one until my entire life went to shit.

And now I'm stuck here in this fucking hell.

* * *

"Would you hold still for the love of Christ?" Aisling mutters, softly placing the plastic bag of frozen peas over my eye. "Bloody hell, you look like shit, Kill."

Her eyes, the color of pale jade, are wide with concern as she peeks beneath the bag and winces.

"Thanks, Ais, appreciate that," I retort as I sink back into the couch cushions and close my eyes. "You don't need to take care of me, I'm good."

My eye is not nearly as bad as it looks and nothing in the grand scheme of injuries I've gotten over the years. I play one of the most brutal sports in the world, so getting hurt is second nature, and Ais has been there for most of them. But I think she just wants to fuss over me for a change because I'm generally the one taking care of her.

She was diagnosed with type 1 diabetes last year, and it's been something she's struggled with since. It's a little better now that she's got an insulin pump, but she still has to watch it constantly. Checking her sugar level, making sure she's eating properly. It's part of the reason I'm so protective of her.

"Shut up. I'm just saying it looks painful."

I nod. The movement makes the pea bag slide down, so I reach up to put it back, but she slaps my hand away, beating me to it, holding it firmly against my bruised skin. "Plus, someone has to worry about you, you know. You can't be the only one that worries, Cillian."

"Yeah, well, it's my job as your big brother to worry about you," I murmur. And trust me, all I do is worry about her.

Now that... that Mum's gone, it's just us.

And I feel so goddamn much guilt for uprooting her entire life and dragging her across the world all because I couldn't get my shit together. Because I was too broken to care about anything other than numbing the pain that was eating me alive.

The pain that still remains. A dull, constant throb in the back of my chest, reminding me that it'll never fully go away. I'll live with it for eternity. The guilt. The grief. The heartache. All of it.

But I'll do what I've always done. Push it down, pretend it doesn't exist because it's the only way I can survive.

"I know, but that doesn't mean that I can't worry about you too," she says. I feel her adjust the bag of vegetables on my face, making sure it's fully covering my eye. My skin is tingling and numb because it's so cold, but still I let her keep it there.

If there's one soft spot I have in the world, it's Aisling.

She's the only good part of me that's left. The *best* part of me.

"I'm really proud of you, Kill. Not just because you didn't hit him back—and I know how hard that must have been—but because I know this whole thing hasn't been easy for you. Even though you make it all look so easy," she says softly.

Reaching up, I pull the bag away so I can look at her.

She pushes her thin, purple glasses up on her nose, peering at me through the thick lenses. My little sister has always been fragile in a way. Soft and delicate. Smart, emotional, empathetic in a way I would never be.

She's always needed me to protect her, and I would. No matter what.

"You don't need to be proud of me, Ais. Not getting into trouble and handling my shit is the least that I can do after everything I've put you through since..." I trail off, hating to even say it out loud. It's been almost two years and thinking about Mum still makes my chest ache. It's too raw, and the moment that I feel the pain, I run from it. I'm fucking terrified that I'll end up back where I was. I'm a coward, and that's nothing for her to be proud of.

She blows her dark bangs out of her eyes, shaking her head. "You deserve to have someone be proud of you, Cillian. You've come so far, even if you can't see it yourself."

My throat feels so tight I can't breathe, thick tendrils of emotion clogging the passageway.

"Thanks, Ais," I say softly. The corner of my mouth tugs up in a small smile and she gives me the same as she pulls her knees to her chest and rests her cheek on top. She's wearing a pair of Mum's old worn flannel pajamas pants with an oversized jumper that has a photo of fluffy gray kittens on it.

We got it for Mum for Christmas one year, mostly as a joke, but the stupid thing ended up being her favorite. She wore it all the time till it practically had holes in it.

After the accident, Aisling would wear her jumpers around the flat, her eyes red and puffy from crying, and my chest would physically ache. I was grieving in ways I'd never known were possible and still trying to keep it together for her.

Aisling said that the jumpers smelled like her, and she was scared that if she took them off, the scent would fade and then she'd forget. She was terrified she'd forget.

"What are you thinking about?" Her voice breaks through the memory, and I swallow, pushing down the thick lump that's settled at the base of my throat.

"Home. I bloody hate America." I laugh, placing the peas that have begun to defrost back on my eye, desperate to change the subject.

"It's not *that* bad. They have amazing food, and their toilets are much better than ours." She giggles. "I'm just glad that we have each other. It's only been a few weeks, Kill. Give it some time, and I know you'll find your place. A new routine."

Ais is halfway through her freshman year and is seemingly taking the move, and all the changes in our lives, in stride, unlike me. I feel like I'm living someone else's life right now.

Like I'm a stranger walking in someone else's shoes.

I miss home. I miss the flat we grew up in even though everything there reminded me of Mum and the fact that she was gone. Some days it hurt too much to feel her surrounding me everywhere, but not truly *there*. Her rain jacket still hung on the coatrack, her favorite pajamas still folded on top of the dryer like she was going to walk through the door the next morning after her shift.

Neither of us could bring ourselves to touch any of it, not until we had no other choice.

As if the moment that we packed it up, put the things away in boxes, and donated it, we'd be erasing what was left of her.

A fucking nightmare. One I'm still living.

I didn't know how much I would miss all of it until we were

gone, now living in this small apartment just outside campus. We had to sell the flat and the majority of the furniture when we moved to America. I couldn't afford a mortgage, and by the time everything had happened we were already three months behind on the note. We didn't have much equity, so most of the money from the sale went to the solicitor fees handling her estate. Thank God she had a meager life insurance policy or there would be no way I could afford to live anywhere. Especially not at Prescott. Aisling being on scholarship has helped with cost, but for the most part, we cook at home and use any extra money we have to pay for rent and utilities.

The place isn't much, but it's ours.

"You and your routines," I mutter.

"Don't make fun of my type A personality. I just like things…organized. I feel more at ease knowing that I have a plan and the proper tools to execute it."

Chuckling, I reach behind me for the blanket that's stretched across the back of the couch. "Okay, Ais, whatever you say. You know, I was thinking, if this whole rugby thing doesn't pan out, at least you'll be able to take care of us with that big brain of yours."

"Way to look at the positives. Don't worry, if rugby doesn't work out, I've got a backup plan."

My shoulders shake with a laugh as I pull the old, soft blanket from home over me, suddenly dead exhausted from all the shit that's managed to transpire today. "I know. You always do, Ais."

CHAPTER 7

Rory

After my talk with Fitz the other night on my couch, I knew I had to take his advice and try again. He's right. I can't give up when I fail on the first... or third try. I owe it to myself to keep trying. To keep putting myself out there and meet someone new. Flirt with a cute guy—even if it all goes south, because practice does make perfect, and clearly I'm in need of lots and lots of practice.

Starting with tonight's party at the Delta house.

I've never been to a frat party, and I have no clue if it's even going to be my scene, but everyone knows that Delta throws the best parties on campus and anyone who is anyone goes. Which makes this the perfect place to be tonight.

Inside is packed with people, the bass from the speakers thrumming and making it pulse steadily in the pit of my stomach, adding to my already shot nerves. The air around me smells like sweat and stale beer, the result of cramming so many people in such a small space. I scrunch my nose as I make my way through the crowd to look for a drink.

I desperately need some liquid courage if I'm going to do this.

I find exactly what I'm searching for on a long folding table in the back of the kitchen in a large drink dispenser. The bloodred liquid inside looks slightly questionable, but there aren't any other options so... we're going with it. I fill the plastic cup I grabbed from the stack all the way to the rim and bring it to my lips, taking a heady sip that burns every inch of my throat as it goes down.

Holy shit, that's stupid strong, and surprisingly... *good*?

Great, I'll take four.

I drink almost the entire cup in two quick swallows while walking back out into the crowded living room and then I spot none other than Cillian Cairney, sitting on a folding chair near the back door, his arms crossed over his chest. Surrounded by a group of girls who seem like they're going to pitch themselves at his feet at any moment, he's looking particularly bored. Although he does flash a grin at one of the blond girls sitting beside him. Wow. I'm pretty sure that's the first time I've *ever* seen him smile.

And it's a bit unexpected if I'm being honest. His smile is disarming; it somehow makes his callous demeanor... softer. More human if that makes any sense. The girl leans in, pressing her ginormous boobs against his arm, and his gaze drops down to her chest, lingering there.

Of course he's got the hottest girl in this party drooling in his lap. I've heard all about his playboy reputation back in London. One of the guys did a social media deep dive and found a bunch of pictures with him and various girls partying.

Rolling my eyes, I push through the crowd toward the backyard so I can get some fresh air when someone brushes against my shoulder painfully, causing me to yelp.

"Shit, sorry," the guy says, and I glance up, my fingers curling around the cup of alcohol in my hand. Okay, he's...hot.

Immediately, my throat feels tight, and my heart begins to flutter wildly in my chest, battering against my rib cage.

"It's okay," I say nervously. "No big deal. I've been hit harder by guys on the team." Followed by an awkward laugh that dies down in my throat when he stares back at me blankly. "I mean...uh, not that I like that they *hit* me, or like even hit on me. Because that would be weird if they did that."

Why is it that I don't think twice about talking to guys on the team, yet the second I say a single word to a guy who's, I don't know, in the *chess* club, I word vomit things like sports statistics as if my brain has short-circuited and forgotten anything other than the top ten rugby hookers of all time.

"Oh, you're Coach St. James's daughter, right? The...equipment manager?" Recognition coats the guy's face. He's wearing board shorts to a sorority party, and not at all someone I'd normally go for but...here we are.

Not that I think I have a type, but if I did, I'm not sure it would be him.

I nod, bringing my drink to my lips for a sip and somehow missing my mouth altogether, causing a splash of bright red liquid to splatter onto the front of the white baby tee I'm wearing beneath my cardigan. I lick the pad of my thumb and brush at the stain roughly with zero luck. Damnit.

"Shit, that sucks," I mutter, blowing out an exasperated breath.

His gaze drops to the stain on my shirt, and the space between his brow furrows together tightly.

"Uh, yes, I am," I say, trying to draw his attention away from my clumsiness. "Coach St. James's daughter. Rory. That my name. What's yours? Beach boy?"

The laugh that tumbles out of me is possibly the most embarrassing thing I've ever done, and results in a snort that has me hiccuping. I probably shouldn't have had so much of this damn drink.

He chuckles. "Ryan. How's the team looking this year? I can't wait to see us at the championship. Ezra is a fucking legend on the pitch."

"Ezra? The guy that I made cry on his first day of college rugby practice? Yeah, that's a legend. *Sure.*" I snort, then drain the last sip of this magical juice and squish the cup in my hand, resulting in a god-awful sound that makes us both cringe.

Jesus Christ, why did I just smoosh that cup like it was a *beer* can at a NASCAR race?

Ryan's eyes widen. "What? Really?"

I nod. "Mm-hmm. If you ask him he'll say he got grass in his eye, but let's be real, the guy's softer than a flower."

"Man, that's fucking hilarious. And honestly? I can kind of see it. I feel like you're a ballbuster, Rory."

Shit. Shit. Shit. This is absolutely heading into bro territory. I've got to save it before it's too late. This is the easiest conversation I've had with a guy. Ever.

"Um...actually, I'm pretty gentle with guys' balls. Like... figuratively speaking." I giggle, which *has* to be a side effect of the alcohol, because giggling? Really? "I would never bust your balls, Ryan, I mean unless you were...into that?" I waggle my eyebrows suggestively.

"Into...ballbusting?"

I shrug. "I mean, I don't judge what anyone is into. You know, speaking of balls...we should totally go to a match. Together? I could get us tickets? One of the many perks of being the ballbuster. I have sideline tickets for all the games."

Why am I talking about balls so much? God, this turned weird fast.

I need to stick a figurative foot in my mouth because I'm officially about to walk into traffic as an alternative.

"Rory, you're fucking hilarious," he muses, reaching out and punching me lightly on the shoulder. "No wonder all the guys like you. Yeah, if you're serious about the tickets I'd love to go. My girlfriend, Miranda, is a huge fan too. I gotta get this back to her." He lifts the cup of the same drink I just downed in ten minutes flat. "But let me know about the tickets? I'll see you around."

See you *never*.

That's what he means.

I give him a dramatic salute as he turns and walks away leaving me ready to sink into the floor at any given moment.

Perfect. That was absolutely perfect and not at all the most embarrassing conversation I've possibly ever had.

I walk toward the back door, stopping to grab another drink at the table nearby, and then slip outside. Frigid winter air hits my cheeks the moment I cross the threshold, and I shiver as a chill racks my spine. I pull the thick cardigan I'm wearing tightly closed around me, trying to block out the small flurries of snow cascading from the sky.

I didn't grab my coat before making a run for it out here, but I have zero desire to go back inside so I suck it up and walk down the pathway to the side of the house. There's an old white wooden gazebo that sits just outside the living room window, and I make my way over to it, slowly sipping my new drink.

So tonight was a disaster, which is the opposite of what I hoped for, but then again, this is becoming a regular occurrence, so I'm not sure why I anticipated anything different. Actually, the definition of insanity is doing the same thing over and over and expecting different results.

Which means not only am I the equivalent of a bro's *bro* and painfully awkward around guys who I'm even remotely interested in, I'm also... definably insane.

"Perfect, Rory. You meet a hot guy and do nothing but talk about *balls*," I mutter as I stomp up the gazebo steps.

"That was an incredibly large amount of ball talk in such a short period of time." A deep, raspy, familiar British accent seeps through the air, causing me to startle and lose my footing on the rickety wooden step. I start to tumble backward but at the last second, a strong, tattooed arm shoots out, wrapping around my waist and stopping me from falling onto my ass on the sidewalk. Somehow, this time, my drink manages to stay inside my cup. Mostly.

"Jesus Christ, what are you doing sitting out here in the dark! Fuck, you scared the hell out of me," I cry, scrambling away from Cillian and leaning backward against the wooden rail for support.

He stares at me, remaining silent.

"Ah, I keep forgetting you're the broody, quiet type," I snark as I plop down on the bench across from him. Now that I'm thinking about it, I'm pretty sure his thoughts about my conversation were the most words I've ever heard him string together in a single sentence. Lucky me.

The chill from the wood seeps through my thin cotton joggers, causing another shiver to travel through me. It's too damn cold.

"That was almost as painful as watching what happened in there," he muses, placing his ink-covered arms along the fence behind him, doing the manspread thing that guys look entirely too hot doing. There's a bottle of water sitting between his jean-clad thighs. So he's at a party...not drinking.

I'm realizing it's the first time I've ever seen him in anything besides sweats or rugby shorts. The denim hugs his muscled thighs like a second skin, molded perfectly around his sculpted quads.

Jesus, thighs are *so* hot.

Something you become hyperaware of when you're constantly around guys lifting other grown-ass men clean off their feet.

Cillian's thighs are massive. Powerful. And he's got this slutty little tattoo on his upper thigh that I couldn't help but notice one day at practice. Not that I was looking...his shorts are just short an—

Never mind.

"And what exactly is that?"

He chuckles roughly, raising a brow. "Frat boy."

"Sorry, can you repeat that? I'm a little in shock that you're capable of having an *actual* conversation. What do you know, miracles *do* happen," I retort with a smile of my own as I set my drink on the bench next to me and run my hands up and down my arms to warm myself up. "And for your information, that was...a disaster. No need to rub it in."

"The bloke was wearing a yellow polo and *board* shorts, so I don't quite think you're missing much. Alas, very questionable taste, I see."

I open my mouth, then slam it shut because what a dick. And also...kind of true. Those board shorts were atrocious.

Cillian smirks.

"Yes, well, you've probably seen what the guys around here think of me. I've got to take what I can get," I finally respond, annoyed that he even witnessed that entire exchange go down. What's he doing out here anyway? The last time I saw him he was inside with his fans draped all over him. "What happened? You got bored with your fan club and decided you needed some fresh air?"

Another silent shrug, but the slight curve of his lips remains.

"Don't worry, they'll all show up at your games to cheer you on. Everyone at Prescott can't wait to see our new bad boy in action."

"Mmm, that sounds a bit like jealousy. Are you jealous, St. James?"

I scoff and a small puff of air slips past my lips. "Of what? Your ability to collect women like you do rugby medals? Not particularly."

For a second he's quiet, thick silence hanging in the air between us, and I wish I knew why my pulse was beginning to pound.

"You know, since you're apparently God's gift to women and can do so much better, please go find one of those girls, right now, and prove how easy it is for you."

He lifts his water bottle to his lips and takes a pull before shrugging. "Fine. Pick one."

I lift a brow and cock my head.

"Point her out. I bet you I can come back with her number in"—he glances down at the watch on his wrist before pulling his gaze back to mine and smirking—"two minutes."

Two minutes?

Seems like an incredibly short amount of time, but then again, the damage I could do in two minutes is nothing short of impressive. Honestly, after seeing him inside with those girls earlier I have little doubt that he could probably get multiple girls' numbers in that time, but now I want to call him on his bluff.

Just to see if he folds.

"Okay. Perfect. Her," I say as I point into the living room window at a tall girl with long, curly auburn hair.

I picked the first person I saw, but he just smiles, one that reaches his eyes causing them to crinkle at the sides, and stands from the bench.

"You going to time it, or should I?"

I nod, pulling my phone out of the pocket of my joggers. "Yep. Go get 'em, big guy."

He rolls his eyes before taking off toward the front door unhurriedly, more like a leisurely stroll. Okay, so selectively mute, grumpy butthole also has an overly inflated ego. Totally surprising.

Not.

I watch through the window as he strides into the house and walks directly over to the girl. He leans in, murmuring something in her ear, and her eyes widen slightly before she nods and then dips her head to his ear, whispering something in return.

A second later, he pulls out his phone and she quickly types something in it before he turns and walks away without another word.

My God, he didn't even *smile* at her. He just... did that broody, smoldering thing he does with his eyes, and she basically threw it at him.

When I glance down at my phone there's still thirty seconds left on the timer, and I have to admit, I'm impressed... slightly.

A little.

"See?" he says when he walks back up the gazebo steps toward me. He turns his phone and shows me the screen with a number and the name Larissa. "Do I get bonus points since she offered to let me fuck her in the bathroom?"

"Smooth. Tell me, how did you manage that when you're such a dickhead?"

He shrugs, pocketing his phone and taking his seat again. His expression is bored as he gazes at me, his eyes dark and stormy in the dim light of the gazebo. "They don't have to like me for me to make them come, St. James."

I can feel my cheeks heat at the crudeness of his words, but I shake my head, rolling my eyes with a dry laugh. "Whatever. You win. You get a trophy. God, I just don't understand how it's so effortless for you."

He grunts a response but otherwise remains silent.

Perfect, we're back to grunting as communication. Just the way I like it.

I wish I could flirt, and be sexy, and confident to guys like this. Any guy really. I wish I could walk up to a guy that I thought was attractive and have a conversation without making a fool of myself...or worse, immediately being friend-zoned.

Tonight was the prime example. So much for taking Fitz's advice. Wait...

The idea that pops into my slightly tipsy brain is ludicrous at best. But also...could actually work? It's literally what I said to Fitz the other night, and I was just joking then. Sort of. But, I mean, what if? The best players have a coach. Maybe Cillian could...teach me. This is probably the alcohol talking but whatever.

He seriously just walked into that party and the girl nearly launched herself into his arms. He's clearly good at this, even though it pains me to admit it.

Who better than him?

"So what if you...you know taught *me* how to flirt? Like that?" When he huffs, shaking his head and running a hand through his dark hair, I continue, "No seriously. You saw for yourself how it went tonight. Every time I even attempt to talk to a guy I either bro out and am immediately friend-zoned, or I attempt to flirt and end up making myself look like an awkward, fumbling idiot. I'm just permanently one of the guys. Nobody ever sees me as *just* Rory. They see me as Coach St. James's daughter or the girl who knows more sports statistics than your average sports *player*. You could help me, and I could...help you. In return."

Yep, definitely the alcohol. I would never normally blurt out something so...vulnerable, so embarrassing. But after what happened inside and the fact that it was nearly a repeat of the other night, with the addition of the two extremely strong drinks I've had, my give a fuck is not present.

His brows shoot up. "Yeah? What could *you* possibly help me with, St. James?"

My throat bobs. "I could...I could help you out with the guys. Get them to stop being so stupid and trying to ice you out. Help you really be a part of the team."

"What, with more team bonding? Yeah, no thanks, I'm good."

"I'm serious!" I groan, then continue before he can decline again. "This sounds stupid, I get it, but I'm just...so damn tired of feeling like this. And you know that Fitz is my best friend. I could talk to him and the rest of the guys. You also know they trust me and listen to my opinion. I'll put in a good word. Get them to give you a chance. In exchange, you teach me how to get out of the friend zone and how to flirt. How to be sexy. How to talk to guys."

"Some things can't be taught," he mutters gruffly, leaning back against the bench, sculpted arms crossing over his broad chest.

"I'm a great student. Four-point-oh GPA. Come on, Cillian, what exactly do you have to lose?" I ask. This is possibly the most idiotic, insane thing I've ever done, but truthfully, what do *either* of us have to lose? If anything, we both have something to gain here, and I am a newfound woman of opportunity.

It's not like I could ask one of my girlfriends to teach me how to flirt. Because, oh right, I have *none*. Fitz and Wren are really my only friends and just having that conversation with Fitz the other night was enough to solidify that this is not something that he can help with, nor do I want him to. Obviously, I would never go to the guys on the team because I'd quite literally rather die than embarrass myself that way.

I would die a slow, extremely painful death before asking any one of them to help me find a guy to hook up with.

Cillian stares at me intently, an expression I can't quite read on his face before he eventually shakes his head. "Sorry but I'm not that guy." He rises from the bench and starts walking down the stairs.

"Wait, you're going to just...leave?"

Turning, he looks back over his shoulder. "Yep. Cheers, St. James. Might want to head in before you catch a cold."

I don't bother to stop the groan that tumbles past my lips as I lean backward against the gazebo fence and drop my head onto the chipped wood once he's gone.

Just when I thought the night couldn't get any more humiliating.

CHAPTER 8

Cillian

"Cairney. I need to see you in my office. *Now*," Coach St. James barks from the doorway of the weight room, his expression a mask of tight irritation.

Nodding, I place the fifty-pound weights back into the rack and grab my water bottle from the floor, squirting a hurried stream into my mouth. Then I reach for the hem of my shirt and drag it down my face, wiping the sweat clean.

My stomach feels like it's full of lead as I make my way out of the weight room toward Coach's office. There's a huge possibility he found out what happened in the locker room the other day with Brooks, and this could end up a bloody fucking mess.

Nearly everyone on the team was there and saw what went down, but that was days ago, and unless shit changed, I was under the impression no one said anything.

Coach pulled me aside before film review and asked me where I got the black eye from, and I lied. Told him I tripped. Face-first into the locker. That I'm clumsy like that sometimes.

We both knew I was full of shit, but if no one else was talking neither was I.

I'm not giving them another reason to ice me out by snitching.

Wouldn't change anything even if I did say something to Coach. Thorne's still going to be a motherfucker who thinks he runs this team and this school.

And when Coach addressed everyone at the conference table, no one spoke up. That only seemed to piss him off more, the fact that he knew something had happened, but none of his players were talking.

I walk through the athletic building and down the hallway toward his office, pausing when I get to the open door. When he sees me standing there, he lifts a hand, waving me in.

"Shut the door behind you."

Fuck.

I nod as I grasp the handle and pull the door shut before turning back to face him. I take a seat in the chair opposite him, my teeth clenched together, my knee bouncing with nervous energy.

He leans over his desk, placing his elbows on the tabletop as he stares at me, letting out a long, deep sigh.

"You know I don't beat around the bush. I'm honest with my players, Cairney. It's the only way I know how to be, how to run my team. I know this has been a big change for you, and I also know how talented you are. I just don't know if it's enough."

My knuckles turn white as my fingers tighten around the arms of the chair. What the fuck is going on?

"I knew that it would take time for everyone to find a rhythm, to figure out how to mesh together, but it's just not happening, Cairney. There's still too big of a disconnect between you and the guys, and quite frankly I don't know if I can fix it. I can preach it all day long, schedule team-building exercises, work on establishing trust and a bond, but if everyone's not giving it all they've got, then what do we do next?" he says, chewing the inside of his lip when he pauses. I can tell he's on edge about it judging by the tightness in his jaw and the tired look in his eyes. We've *all* been wound tight about it, and he's not telling me anything that I don't already know.

I came here not giving a shit about letting anyone in, or get too close, but I guess... Coach is right. It's not working on the pitch. I guess I have to work to build a relationship with them. To form some type of... *trust* with them. I've just been keeping to myself and showing up because that's what's been expected, but now I realize that's not enough.

I can't give the bare minimum and expect them to give me anything but that in return.

He sighs again, leaning back in his chair and crossing his arms over his chest. "I can't force them, Cillian. If we can't get you guys working together, communicating, being a team, then I have no choice but to remove you from the team."

"Coach..." I start, and trail off when he lifts a hand, his expression softening slightly.

"I know you've been through a lot, son. Trust me, I do. But you know that me taking you on to my team midseason was a liability. One that I was willing to take because you're one of the most talented players I've ever seen. I think you made some mistakes in London, and while I hope that you've left everything that was holding you back behind, I don't know the future. But what I do know is that while I want this to work, and I want you to be a part of my team, it's not fair to those guys either. They've been working their entire college career for a shot at the championship. At playing professionally. There's a lot at stake, and jeopardizing the program while some of these guys have a year left is something I can't let happen. Do you understand?"

After a beat, I nod, my white-knuckled grip on the armchair the only thing keeping me grounded. I want to tell him *fuck* fair, and that I don't give a shit about these knobs who haven't made a single bloody effort to make this shit work because they don't want to, but I don't. I stay quiet because it's not going to do any good. And I know that this is a give and take. I've gotta give as much as they do.

"I'm not saying that you're off the team. I'm saying that you need to put forth more of an effort to bond with these guys. Whatever it takes, I need you to do it. You used to lead your team in London, Cillian, and you were damn good at it from what I hear. You're a leader. Not a follower. Make the effort, and make this work, or you're going to force me to make a decision I really don't want to have to make. Hell, maybe Rory was right, and we need to do more team-building exercises, I don't know."

More fucking obstacle courses? *That's* what he thinks the answer to this is? We're better off being locked in a room to—

Wait.

My thoughts drift back to the other night at the party. The one my sister insisted she go to and because I wasn't about to let her go alone, I ended up there with her and...Rory.

What if Coach Matthews was actually right all along, and the only real way for me to get in with these guys is *her*?

When he said that on the first day at the pitch, I had no clue what he meant, but now...I'm wondering if maybe he was right.

I don't understand it, not by a long shot, but for whatever reason these guys trust her. They respect her. They go to her for advice. She's clearly important to them. I've seen it with my own eyes these last few weeks.

Bloody hell, Rory St. James *might* just be the answer.

* * *

For the next few days, I'm so swamped with homework and training that I'm barely keeping my head above water. All while still thinking about the conversation in Coach's office, and the fact that I might not have a spot on the team for much longer.

Just thinking about it makes my stomach turn. I didn't come this far to lose my shot at a professional career because I couldn't play nice with these guys. I'm not the same guy I used to be. I'm better than this shit.

I'm losing my fucking head, and that's got to be why I find myself crossing the indoor training pitch when I see Rory sitting on the lush green turf of the try lines, the tip of her pen caught between her plump lips as she stares down at the playbook that's sprawled open in her lap.

She's got her long dark hair pulled up in a high slicked-back ponytail and is wearing a tight pair of lavender leggings and a baggy T-shirt that swallows her small frame.

When I come to a stop in front of her, hauling my bag higher on my shoulder, she lifts her gaze from the book and peers up at me. Her cheeks are flushed red, like she's just gotten out of a shower.

And my mind immediately imagines hot pelts of water turning her creamy, pale skin a feverish shade of red.

Maybe she showers in the locker rooms like we do.

Shit, now I'm thinking about her naked in the locker room while she's nearly eye level with my dick.

Fuck off, Cillian. Christ.

"Can I talk to you?" I ask gruffly.

I glance around the pitch to see who's watching, but thank fuck, most of the guys have already left for the day, and there's only a few left working on drills on the far side.

Not that I need to hide talking to her, but it might look... suspicious when I don't really talk to anyone, much less the coach's daughter.

"Um, sure?" She glances behind her then back at me. "Sorry, I thought you might have been talking to someone else."

Her plump lips curve into a shit-eating smirk, and I roll my eyes. "It's important."

She pauses for a second, her dark brows arching as her gaze travels over my arms, trailing over the ink before coming back to meet my eyes. "Oooookay."

She shuts the book, then stands, holding it to her chest. "So... talk?"

I shuffle from one foot to the other. "Somewhere... *private*." I'm on edge today after the conversation with Coach, and I sure as fuck don't want to give him any reason to question my spot here any further.

"Okay. Come with me," she says as she turns on her heel and takes off in the direction of the administrative offices.

I follow behind her, and I try not to watch as her hips sway in the leggings she's wearing, but I'm also still a man. So I do, and then I immediately regret it because I didn't realize how she filled out the tight fabric.

What the fuck is wrong with me today?

Rory leads me down the empty hallway before opening one of the last doors we come to. I slip inside behind her and shut the door.

There's a desk and a few chairs inside along with a mostly empty bookshelf, so I assume it's used as an office or something. She walks over to the desk and hops onto the edge, staring at me with a curious expression.

"So..." She trails off, lifting a brow and swinging her feet back and forth. She's wearing a pair of bright yellow trainers that match her personality perfectly. "What's going on?"

Sighing, I drop my bag at my feet and bring my hands to the back of my neck, lacing them together as I hold her gaze. "Were you serious about what you said the other night?"

"About... what?" Her voice is low.

For fuck's sake.

She's a cheeky little brat.

A smile splits her face, curving those pillowy lips as she pretends to suddenly remember our conversation from the party. "Ohhhh. You mean when I asked you to teach me how to flirt?"

I nod, remaining silent. It's bad enough that I'm having this conversation in the first place. I thought she'd lost her mind when she asked me to... teach her the other night at the party. Yet, I hadn't really stopped thinking about it. Trust me, I tried.

"What if I was?" she asks as she pulls her lip between her teeth and rolls it.

"What if I...said yes?"

Her eyes widen slightly and her lips part. "Seriously?"

I exhale. "Yeah, if you keep up your side of the bargain. The only way I'm doing this is if you help me with the team. Your dad said I'm cut if I don't make an effort and somehow get these lads to let me in."

She sucks in a sharp breath. "Shit. I'm sorry, Cillian. I can help with the guys, for sure. I don't want you off the team, and they don't either. They just...don't realize that yet."

"So if I help you with this, you'll help me with the team?"

Rory nods. "Yes. For sure."

I'm fucked if I don't make this work, but there's a sinking feeling of worry in the pit of my stomach about getting involved with Rory, even in a strictly platonic way. Her dad would probably cut my fucking balls off if he knew I was even breathing the same air as her that didn't revolve around rugby.

"Before I agree to this, I need more details. Like how this is going to work because I don't want your dad to kill me if he finds out about this. I'm already in enough shit."

She scoffs. "Jesus, Cillian, you act like I'm asking you to have *sex* with me." Her eyes roll and for a beat she's quiet, her gaze dropping to the floor before lifting back to mine. "I don't know how this works. I mean, I don't even really know what I'm asking of you. I just know that I'm tired of being awkward and atrociously horrible at flirting with guys. I'm tired of being friend-zoned. I'm tired of being the wing woman. I want to be able to get any guy that I want."

Is that how she sees herself?

My brow furrows, and she continues, "I just want you to teach me how to get *the* guy. To talk to them, to flirt with them, to be sexy and feel wanted. To be more confident. To not second-guess and question myself over every little thing."

I mean... yeah, she was shit at flirting with that bloke from the other night, but Rory's hot. Objectively speaking. There's no way other guys aren't interested in her when she's this bloody hot?

This should be easy despite what's at stake. Right?

A beat passes as I weigh the pros and cons of this, giving myself a chance to come to my senses before I ultimately say, "I'll do it, if you help me keep my spot on the team. I can't lose it, St. James. Okay? I can't. It's not even an option."

I'll do anything to stay on the team... including teaching my coach's daughter how to flirt.

"I know. I promise I'll help, and I won't let that happen," she replies softly, her voice dropping low.

Clearly, I'm desperate or I wouldn't be agreeing to this thing in the first place, but I think about my promise to Aisling. And how many times I've let her down in the last two years.

"All right. I'll see you around," I tell her as I pick my duffel off the ground, then hoist it on my shoulder and turn for the door.

"Wait," she says, stopping me. Her feet hit the floor as she hops down from the desk. "We need some type of plan."

I bite back a groan. She sounds like my sister right now with the damn plans. "Okay, so we'll come up with one. Right now I have somewhere to be."

"Okay, then give me your phone. Your *telly*, whatever."

I roll my eyes and fish it out of the pocket of my joggers before handing it over to her. "'Telly'? You realize English lads don't say *telly*?"

She smirks as she swipes it open and taps the screen before thrusting it back at me. "There. Now you have my number, and I texted myself so I'll have yours. And Cillian? Obviously, don't tell anyone about this. My dad doesn't get involved in my personal life, but I'm not really interested in him knowing about my *issue* or my dating life at all."

Her nose scrunches in distaste. Which shouldn't be so bloody cute.

"Who am I going to tell? I don't talk to anyone, remember?"

She nods. "True. Who knew you being a grumpy dick would actually come in handy."

"See ya, St. James," I say, walking away, her giggle echoing along the walls of the empty office. I'm still thinking about this stupid arrangement even when I make it out of the building and toward the quad.

I hope I'm not making yet another mistake, and this one? It could be the biggest one of all.

CHAPTER 9

♡

Rory

Rory: Hi, it's Rory.

Cillian: Figured as much.

Rory: Why? It could have been someone else. If I remember correctly, you collect phone numbers like they're trading cards.

Cillian: Not much of a texter.

Rory: This is me shocked 😯

Rory: Also completely unsurprising since you're so averse to talking to people. Makes sense that you'd hate texting too

Rory: I think you just hate people in general but also fair

Rory: Anyway, when should our first lesson be? 😊 😊

Cillian: Don't make this weird.

Rory: You're no fun.

Cillian: Now?

Rory: Like... right now? Tonight?

Cillian: I'll pick you up in an hour. Send me the address.

Rory: Cillian, seriously? What about the plan... this is not a plan!

Cillian: Cheers

I drop my phone onto my stomach as I stare up at the stark white ceiling above me, my heart battering wildly in my chest.

Holy shit. Is this actually happening right now?

I can't believe one slightly drunken ramble turned into this... I can't believe he *actually* took me up on it.

It just kind of came pouring out of me after the run-in with board shorts guy, and I just couldn't help myself. I'd been holding all that in for so long that I word vomited to the first person who doesn't know me as Rory, one of the bros.

But that's where Cillian is different. He's not one of the guys I've spent my entire college career around, that I've basically grown up with. He's not someone I consider a brother. He doesn't know me at all, which makes him unbiased.

Sure, this agreement is *mutually* beneficial. We both have skin in the game.

Except there are two things I didn't consider in this entire proposition.

One... *Cillian's* going to teach me how to do all of it and I am actually attracted to him because, I mean let's be real, how could I not be? He looks like a model. A broody, grumpy, hate-the-world-and-everyone-in-it model, and now that makes me feel nervous.

He's going to see me make a complete ass out of myself, undoubtedly.

And two, I haven't figured out exactly how I'm going to hold up my end of the bargain. How I'm going to get the guys to let him in, to trust him. They trust *me*, but I've got to come up with a plan to convince them to trust Cillian. At least enough so they can sync on the pitch.

Sitting up from my bed, I toss my phone beside me onto the mattress.

First things first: Figuring out what to wear tonight.

Because I have zero fashion sense and absolutely no idea how to dress for any occasion, it takes entirely too long to decide on something, and I end up pulling everything I own out of my closet and throwing it into a pile in the middle of my bedroom floor.

And *still* I end up in my favorite old sweatshirt that has the faded words PRESCOTT RUGBY across the chest. The fabric is soft and worn, and it's my favorite piece of comfort clothing. I put on a pair of black wide-legged yoga pants and realize that deciding what to wear is exhausting, and I am completely over it. I stare into the mirror at my reflection, trying to figure out where I would even begin if I wanted to put on makeup, or do something with my hair aside from putting it into my signature pony or wearing it loose around my face.

I don't even own makeup except for a few tubes of mascara that are probably well past the expiration date. Makeup does expire, I think?

I'm honestly just…hopeless at most things that deal with being a girl. I never had much interest in makeup and fashion, and since I was raised by just my dad, it's not something that he ever really knew anything about either.

So, I just brush my hair and toss it up in a high ponytail, and that is that.

Exactly an hour later, Cillian sends me a text.

Cillian: I'm outside. Bring a jacket.

Cillian: And a beanie, if you have one.

My brow furrows as I read the message. Ooookay.

I head to the front door, grab my keys from the bar counter along with my jacket and a beanie, then walk outside.

I realize the moment that I see him parked in front of my apartment exactly why he told me to bring it.

Because *of course* the tattooed British bad boy drives a freaking *motorcycle*.

In New England.

In the *dead of winter*.

This is the most cliché thing I've ever seen and honestly, I'm not even the least bit surprised.

"You *would*," I say as I come to a stop in front of him, my lips curved into a smirk.

He's leaning casually against the seat of the sleek black bike, his arms crossed over his chest, that smoldering, broody expression a permanent fixture on his face. He looks every bit the bad boy that his reputation paints him to be. He's wearing a dark gray hoodie beneath a thick black jacket with worn, faded jeans that hug his thick, muscular thighs.

Of course I notice the thighs.

He gives me a flat look. "I would, what?"

"You would drive a motorcycle. Fits the whole bad boy vibe you've got going on. Actually, where's the leather jacket?" I grin as I tug the beanie onto my head, over the tips of my ears.

He extends a helmet my way. It's midnight black with a dark glass visor. "Put this on."

"Where's yours?" I respond, taking it from him. I've never been on a bike before, but I've always wanted to. Yes, I too have fallen victim to the thirst traps on social media of hot bikers and immediately added this to my bucket list. Very high up.

Cillian jerks his head in a nod toward the helmet in my hands. "You're holding it."

"What? I'm not taking yours. You need one too, Cill—" I'm cut off mid-sentence as he tugs it from my grip and steps forward, sliding it onto my head in one quick, effortless yet gentle motion.

"You're wearing the bloody helmet, Rory. Now get on the damn bike." His voice is smooth like velvet as he speaks, each syllable rolling off his tongue with precision.

Okay, that's stupidly...attractive. Why am I turned on by this right now?

This growly, alpha energy.

I can feel the heat of his body as it brushes along mine, causing my nipples to tighten.

Oh God, am I falling...*victim* to the bad boy vibe? Is that what's going on here? Like this isn't already weird enough, I'm realizing just how attracted I actually am to him.

Perfect. Let's complicate this a bit more why don't we?

I blink rapidly, my brain short-circuiting for a moment before I clear my throat, nodding. "Okay, fine. But *not* because you told me to. Only because I've always wanted to ride one of these."

"Of course," he murmurs, the smallest hint of a smirk tugging at his lips as he pulls the hood up on his head and gets on the bike. "Use me for balance and swing your leg over."

I follow his instructions, placing my palm along his shoulder as I hoist my leg over and straddle the seat.

He looks back at me, twisting then grabbing my hands and sliding them around his waist until they're clasped in the front. I can feel the hard muscles of his abs beneath my hands, and I swallow roughly. There must be at least a dozen of them.

"Hold on just like this, and don't let go. Lean with me when we turn." He squeezes his fingers around mine to drive his point home.

I nod, suddenly feeling nervous. He flips the visor down before turning back and starting the bike.

The engine roars to life, vibrating beneath us as he grips the handlebars.

"Tighter," he says loudly over the sound of the engine, bringing his hand to the top of mine and squeezing again.

I tighten my hold around his waist, my fingers fisting into the front of his hoodie and with one last nod, he pulls off the curb onto the street. My thighs squeeze around his waist as he accelerates and my heart thunders. At first, I'm too focused on holding on to Cillian, making sure that I don't end up on the pavement, to take in my surroundings. But when I feel his hand on top of mine, there's something oddly reassuring about it and makes it easier to relax.

I watch campus fly by, the lights glowing little specks as we speed down the highway, and even though I'm wearing a thick sweatshirt, jacket, and beanie, the wind seeps through the fabric, chilling me to the bone.

Still, it's the most exhilarating thing I've ever experienced. It feels like freedom, like I'm flying. Part of me wants to throw my arms out and close my eyes, pretending that I am even if it's just for the briefest moment.

But I stay firmly wrapped around Cillian. Before I know it, we're on the outskirts of town, where everything's a bit less crowded and quieter, pulling into the parking lot of a small bar. Cillian parks in the front, cutting off the engine and sliding off the bike effortlessly.

"Wow," I breathe once he pulls the helmet off. "That was actually the most terrifying and *incredible* moment of my life."

I'm not prepared for the deep chuckle that fills the air between us, and it makes my stomach flip. It's...nice.

He sets the helmet on the seat, and then offers me his hand, helping me off the bike. "First few times are always like that."

There's a slight curve of his full lips and it almost feels like he's speaking about something else, but I'm not entirely sure so I just nod. We head to the front of the bar, and as we walk through the entrance I feel Cillian's hand pressing against the small of my back, guiding me through the door.

It's the faintest, barest brush of this palm, but for some reason it makes my heart race and my pulse thrum.

Get it together, Rory.

My God.

I'm being ridiculous. Absolutely ridiculous.

Cillian slides into the booth across from me once we've grabbed our drinks and he shrugs out of his jacket, leaving him in his gray hoodie.

"So..." I say between sips of my Cherry Coke, "what's the plan? How should we do this? Where do you think we should start?"

"Never given anyone flirting lessons before so I don't exactly have one, St. James," he says as he watches me toy with the black straw in my drink, moving it around the cup. "I only caught some of what happened the other night, so I guess we start by me seeing you in action. Fully."

This is what I was dreading. Obviously, I knew that he was going to witness me embarrassing myself yet again—it's inevitable when he's the one teaching me how to *fix* it—but it doesn't make it any easier to prepare for.

"It's going to be painful. Extremely painful. I'm warning you.

Last time was only the tip of the iceberg, I fear," I say after another quick sip. "Now that I'm thinking about it, we should probably just skip this stage altogether and get right to the good stuff. You know, the *teaching* part."

His brow lifts as his pupil's flare. "You want my help?"

"Obviously, yes, I want your help, Romeo." I roll my eyes.

"Then I need to see you in action. I can't fix something when I don't even know what's supposedly broken. All I know is what you've told me, and that might not even be the issue."

Okay... well when he says it that way, that's fair.

I huff out a breath and nod, crossing my arms over my chest and leaning back in the seat. "Okay, but don't laugh at me. What do I need to do?"

"Go sit at the bar, order a drink." He gestures toward the long bar that sits in the middle of the room. It's fairly dead for a weekend, surprisingly, and there are a few empty seats. "Smile, be approachable. Let the lads come to you. And I'm going to sit here and observe." Cillian shrugs, as if any of those things are so simple and easy.

Maybe for him, but not for me. Never for me.

I'm the queen of fumbling.

What does *approachable* even mean?

"The chances of someone coming up to me are very slim, Cillian."

His brow furrows, and he shakes his head. "Why? You're a hot college girl. Someone's going to talk to you. Go on. Stop wasting time."

Wait, Cillian thinks... I'm *hot*? A guy like him, thinks I'm hot? Well, that was unexpected, but okay.

Using his words as encouragement, I nod and exhale a shaky breath, releasing my shoulders while I work on internally hyping myself up.

I got this. I can do it.

When this is over I'm going to be the most confident, smooth, badass bitch ever and it will all be worth it. Every embarrassing moment.

Once I'm seated at the end of the bar, and I've ordered a double shot of vodka and Red Bull, my nerves are going haywire, a flurry of energy dancing in my stomach. It's one thing to make a fool of myself flirting with a random guy at a random bar when I'm alone, but an entirely different thing to know that someone's going to be *watching* as I do.

It makes me even more anxious about the task Cillian's assigned me. Like there's more pressure on me knowing that I'm going to be judged on this.

I'm already thinking about the disastrous outcome, and nothing's even happened yet. Something that I tend to do when I get nervous.

The bartender slides my drink across the bar to me, and I smile, thanking him. And then, I wait.

And wait.

And...wait more.

Sneaking glances at Cillian every few minutes because I can practically feel the weight of his stare on me.

God, this is mortifying.

I told him that no one is just going to randomly come up and talk to me because that's just how th—

"Hey." A smooth, velvety deep voice comes from beside me,

and I'm so lost in thought that it startles me, causing me to nearly knock my drink over.

I turn toward the voice and see a tall guy with dark hair, a short mustache, and a lazy, boyish grin wearing a hockey jersey.

He's...cute.

Which sends my stomach in a flip and my heart battering against my rib cage.

Okay, this is it. I can do this. This is exactly what is supposed to be happening, I remind myself. Exactly why Cillian sent me over here.

My gaze darts to where he's sitting in the booth, catching his eyes. He nods as he lifts a brow.

I can do this. I can do this. I can do this.

I'm just going to keep gaslighting myself into believing it.

CHAPTER 10

♡

Rory

"Well, that was actually a complete, utter, disaster," I huff as I slide back into the busted leather seat of the booth, dropping my head into my hands. "A category five disaster. Catastrophic, if you weren't aware."

When I finally lift my head from my hands, I find Cillian gaping at me like I've grown two heads.

"What? Why are you looking at me like that?"

He just shakes his head as he reaches up and drags his hand down his face, sighing. "Tell me why you think that was a disaster."

My eyes widen. "Did you not just witness the same thing I did?"

"Yeah, I did. Now tell me why *you* think it was shit."

"Because I scared him off in record time," I mutter exasperatedly.

"And *why* do you think that was?" Cillian asks.

Because I'm broken? Because I can't seem to stop being awkward and fumbling like I've never spoken to a guy in my life.

Every single time is the same, except I think I might actually be getting worse.

"Um... because he's not a rugby fan?" I say feigning innocently.

Cillian sighs raggedly. "St. James, you didn't let the bloke get a bloody word in. Literally, not one. All you talked about was rugby. *The entire time.*"

"That's not true! He said he's... never seen a rugby game."

"Yeah, and then you proceeded to tell him the entire history of rugby starting in the 1800s. I thought the bloke was going to have to fake a medical emergency to get you to shut up."

"Okay, well, that might be true, but I took the opportunity to educate someone who was clearly missing the best sport to have ever existed from his life. If anything, he should be *thanking* me."

"He might've if you would've let him say a single word," Cillian deadpans.

"Well, it feels a biiiit unfair for you to say he didn't get a word in when clearly he said he's never seen rugby, and you know he also said that he's a hockey fan an—"

"St. James," he says, cutting me off mid-word. "You're doing nothing but proving my point. How do you expect to have anything in common with any of these blokes outside of sports if all you do is talk. About. Sports?"

Fine. He does have a point. Ugh.

I bury my face in my hands again with a long, drawn-out dramatic groan. "I'm doomed. There's no hope. I'm hopeless. I *told* you I was horrible at this, and you didn't listen to me, Cillian! I. Told. You. I can't flirt. I can't talk to guys without word vomiting, and if I somehow manage to form words then it's all about sports because if you haven't guessed it, my entire life *is* sports. Literally,

I live and breathe rugby the same as you. Why do you think I asked you to help me? Now you've seen it firsthand for yourself."

Suddenly, I feel his fingers wrap around my wrist, tugging my hand away from my face until I lift my gaze to meet his. His piercing eyes seem to burn right through me. "You're not hopeless. What I'm hearing you say to me is that you need to feel more comfortable. More confident in yourself. That just means you need more practice. When you're not great at something you keep at it until you are."

While he's speaking, the rough pad of his thumb sweeps across the inside of my wrist, and I'm hyperaware of it, the feel of his skin on mine but I don't think he even realizes he's doing it.

"Okay," I say quietly, nodding in agreement. "I'll keep trying."

Slowly, he glances down at where his fingers meet my wrist, and then he drops my hand, nodding too. "If you want a lad to flirt with you, then you have to give him the *chance* to."

I push down a swallow with another nod. I know that; I just can't seem to get it together long enough to make it happen.

"What do you do outside of rugby? I know there's more to you than just rugby, St. James. What's your favorite movie, music, things you do for fun?"

The question is simple, but it still takes me a minute to separate *me* from *rugby*. Who am I without rugby?

It's deeper than intended, and the question makes me think.

"Um, I mean I really like to do puzzles, and color in these grown-up coloring books that Fitz and Wren got me a couple of Christmases ago." I feel the blush heating my cheeks, and I drop my gaze, looking down at the straw paper on the table as I fold it into tiny little squares to avoid his stare. I'm not embarrassed by the fact that I like to color; I'm more embarrassed that my list of interests outside of rugby is tragically short. "I like to bake cookies."

He leans forward, resting his elbows on the table in front of him. "Keep going. What else?"

"I like horror movies and homework. I actually like homework and being somewhat of a nerd. Oh, and cleaning whenever I'm stressed. Vacuuming makes me feel better."

"Of course it does." His voice is low as he lets out a quiet laugh before his indifferent mask slips back in place just as quickly as it left. "I think when you stop convincing yourself that all you're made of is rugby, that's when you'll realize that there are plenty of things people want to know about you."

I hardly have a chance to process his oddly...sweet comment when my stomach gurgles obscenely loud.

"Sorry." I wince. "I haven't eaten since breakfast and those vodka Red Bulls didn't help."

Cillian signals the waitress over and asks for an order of mozzarella sticks, pretzel bites, potato skins, and onion rings that makes my mouth water just thinking about them.

"I'm surprised you're eating fried food. Most of the guys on the team stay away from stuff like that during the season."

"It's not for me."

My jaw falls open. He ordered four appetizers...*just* for me?

"You need to eat," he says simply—that tiny, nearly indecipherable curve of his lips returning for a fleeting moment.

I realize that the moments when he allows his mask to come down are rare, but they're powerful. It makes me wonder just how much more Cillian is beneath what he shows everyone else now that I'm experiencing it firsthand.

Something tells me there's more to his story than I ever thought.

I nod. "Okay. Cool. Um...what about you? What do you like to do outside of rugby?"

"Not much. Class. Workout. Sleep when I can." He answered the question, yet it doesn't feel like much of an answer at all.

Still, I press on. He's not the only one who gets to ask the hard questions and expect an answer.

"There's got to be more to you outside of rugby, Cillian." I repeat his words back to him, and he rolls his eyes as he rakes his fingers through his hair.

At first, I think he might not answer at all, the beats of silence hanging between us stretching impossibly far, then he finally murmurs, "I watch stupid reality shows with my sister."

Now this...is surprising.

"Cillian Cairney watches *trashy TV*?" I gasp in mock surprise, unable to keep the teasing smile off my face. If I didn't know any better I'd say that the tips of his cheeks turn slightly pink at his confession.

He shrugs. "My sister likes it. I do it because I know it makes her happy."

So there it is. The big bad wolf does have a heart underneath all his rough exterior.

CHAPTER 11

Cillian

When my phone chimes for what feels like the hundredth time, I groggily lift my head from the pillow, peering around the darkened room.

Shit, what time is it?

I feel around the mattress for my phone, finding it underneath my pillow. I crack one eye open and swipe across the screen. I groan when I see the time.

It's barely six a.m. and I've already got four text messages.

Seeing as how the only person I ever talk to is Aisling and now... *Rory*, I know it's her before I even open them.

> **Rory:** Okay so, I have an idea and I know you're probably going to hate it but... Oh well.

> **Rory:** No you're definitely going to

> hate it but you asked for my help. Remember that.

> **Rory:** 😇

Cillian: It's bloody 6 am, St. James. On Sunday. I was out with you half the night.

> **Rory:** Yes, I know that but my brilliant idea came to me in the middle of the night and I couldn't sleep after.

> **Rory:** I'm working on a plan.

Cillian: Enlighten me so I can go back to sleep.

> **Rory:** I'm planning a small get together at my apartment tonight. With you, and some guys from the team, but I may or may not be telling them that you're ... attending.

Cillian: That's your plan?

> **Rory:** Yep. It's going to be like ripping

a bandaid off. Anyway, be at the place for 6 and don't be late.

Rory: Cillian?

Rory: I know you did not just leave me on read!?!

* * *

The *brilliant* plan Rory woke me up at six a.m. for is not going to be at all what she's hoping for, but I show up anyway because I know that she's just trying to uphold her end of our arrangement.

And even though I'd rather run until I puke than spend the evening with Thorne and the rest of them, I know I have no choice.

It's either I play nice or I'm off the team. And that's not something I'm even entertaining.

When I knock on the door, I can hear low, jumbled voices on the other side, and a moment later it opens. Rory peers at me through a small crack and nods, rolling her lips together. "Hi. Okay, you ready for this? No fighting. And no *leaving*. Okay? We have to do this."

I nod, and she opens the door wider, allowing me to step inside. I do my best to brace for the absolute shit show that's about to ensue, willing myself to keep my temper under control and remember that this is the only option, and my spot on the team depends on it.

My promise to Aisling depends on it. My *future* depends on it.

A mantra that I keep repeating as Rory leads me through her entryway into her apartment.

It's spacious, clean, and minimally decorated, which I think somehow fits her exactly. She doesn't seem like the kind of girl who makes a fuss over much, especially when it comes to things like decorations.

But then again, I barely know her.

Last night at the bar took me by surprise in more ways than one. First is the fact that she's actually as bad at flirting as she says she is, and now I know why she's asking for me to teach her. Even though I think the minute she gets out of her head, it'll work out, I'm going to do what I promised and help however I can.

But second, if I'm honest, I could've spent my Saturday night in worse ways. She's actually quite funny, and chill when she's not stressing out about what she should say or do. She's every bit the spitfire that I thought her to be, but it's kind of fucking hot. She's hot.

Not that I'm going to tell her that I didn't hate spending time with her. She'll think it makes us friends or something, and that's not happening. This is purely a mutually beneficial arrangement, and when I'm done satisfying my end of it, I'm out.

Period.

I follow behind her farther into her apartment until she suddenly comes to an abrupt stop, causing me to run into the back of her.

I collide with soft, warm curves, and I grunt. "Bloody hell, St. James."

She whips to face me, still plastered to my front, and places a finger over my lips, silencing me. Her voice lowers to a barely audible whisper. "Shh. Okay, listen. You and I both know that this is going to be a total... *shit show*. But I need you to promise me that you're not going to let them goad you. And promise me that you're not going to, I don't know, fly off the handle. That's exactly what they want."

It's not that I'm worried about right now.

It's the fact that she's pressed against my front, one hand resting on my stomach and the other still on my lips, that has my brain doing something stupid.

Liking it.

Christ.

My pulse thunders and I swallow, nodding against the pad of her finger.

What the hell is going on with me lately?

Her deep, dark eyes resemble chocolate as she peers up at me, slowly dropping her finger from my lips. "You want me to help you get in with the guys, I need you to trust me. It's the only way we're going to pull this off."

If only she had any idea how hard that is for me.

I'm giving everything I have, and trust isn't one of those things.

Our eyes stay locked, her body so close that I can feel the heat radiating off her, and for the first time I find myself wanting to touch her. To see how soft she feels beneath my hands.

"Rory, where'd you go?" a voice calls from the other room, and her breath hitches as she stills. "Roooooory."

"I promise to be a *good boy*, all right? On my best behavior," I murmur, taking a slight step back and creating distance between us before I do something even more dumb than liking the feel of her body pressed against mine.

I'm not really sure what I'm promising, but I'm here and I'm not going to leave.

With one last lingering look up at me, she nods. "Okay, let's go."

She leads me into her living room, and I see the guys spread out on various pieces of furniture, watching TV, eating crisps, and sipping beers. They look comfortable in Rory's space, and for some reason it makes me feel out of place.

Envious even. That they have this familiarity and friendship with her, and I'm destined to always be the outsider.

"What the fuck is he doing here?" My gaze flits to Thorne, who's in a plush, cream-colored armchair with a bowl of fruit in his lap that nearly falls to the ground when he sits up abruptly, his face turning a bright shade of scarlet.

There's an echo of murmurs around the room and I scan their faces, finding a similar expression on all of them.

They don't want me here.

But that's nothing I wasn't prepared for.

Ezra Keller looks at me with narrowed eyes as he shakes his head, a menacing smirk curling his upper lip into a sneer. "Seems like someone brought the trash in."

Bloody arseholes.

"Shut up, Ezra," Rory says sharply, her lips tightened into a scowl. She places her hands on her hips and looks around the room at each of the guys before focusing her attention back on Ezra. "You're in *my* apartment and you're going to respect anyone who's in my home."

Ezra's Adam's apple bobs as he swallows, suddenly looking slightly nervous, and I bite back a laugh.

"Fuck this, I'm out of here," Brooks says, rising from the

armchair and thrusting the half-empty bowl of fruit into Wren's arms. The stacked prop just blinks, holding on to the bowl with both arms as he looks back and forth between Brooks, Rory, Ezra, and me.

Rory stomps over to Brooks and pokes his chest, pushing him back down into the chair. He flops onto the cushion with an *oof*.

"No, you're going to sit down and shut up, Brooks Thorne," she says. "Listen up and listen good because I'm only going to say this once. Enough is *enough*. I get it, you guys are all pissed off that Cillian's on the team. Your routines are interrupted, and the chemistry with the team is out of sync. I get it, and I understand. We all do. But this whole...icing him out and being an asshole thing has to stop. This isn't just about Cillian, it's about you. It's about the team, and what you're doing right now is hurting the entire team."

Ezra opens his mouth to interrupt her, but when Rory shoots him a look, holding up her hand, he promptly shuts his mouth and sits back on the couch, crossing his arms over his chest like a petulant toddler who's just been scolded by his mum.

Make no mistake, that's exactly what this is.

She walks to stand in front of the TV, facing all the guys. "It ends here. Tonight. Because after this, you're not just going to have a problem with Cillian, you're going to have a problem with me. No one is walking out that door. We're going to continue our game night as planned, and nobody is going to be an asshole. Nobody is going to say one word. Or..." She trails off, as if she's contemplating something. "Or I'm going to tell my dad about the time that you all snuck out last year before regionals and got drunk when you were on a strict curfew."

Gasps ring out in the room along with a few groans, and Rory lifts a brow, an evil little grin flitting to her pink lips.

"Holy shit!" Liam squeaks, his voice a whisper as he stares at Rory with fear in his eyes. He's just a little pup, a rookie sophomore on the team, and of everyone in the room, he looks the most terrified.

Wren reaches his massive hand into the bowl that he's still holding and pops some strawberries into his mouth. When he chuckles, the sticky red fruit is stuck to his teeth, showing off his signature toothless grin. "Rory, girl, that is cold as fuck."

"Yeah, well, desperate times, desperate measures. And you know what? Not only will I be ratting you dickheads out, I will never ever *ever* make another batch of snickerdoodle cookies ever again."

"That's it." Fitz jumps up from the couch in an outrage. "That is crazy talk, Rory. Come on. Not the snickerdoodle cookies. You know how much those mean to us! What the hell."

"Yeah, what he said! You wouldn't do that to us," Wren adds around a mouthful of strawberries.

Rory just shakes her head, her long dark ponytail swaying with the motion when she places her hands back on her hips. "Try me. Seriously guys, you know there is no one outside of my dad and Coach Matthews that cares about this team more than me. You are my guys, and we've been with each other for almost three years now. This is disappointing to me, and I don't want to be disappointed."

Damn. I was not expecting this pep talk, but I'm impressed.

She just played the shit out of this lot, and they haven't a clue.

"Now, does anyone have any objections or can we please resume game night?"

I follow her gaze around the room, pausing on the two who

seem to have the biggest issue with me. Ezra rolls his eyes and looks away, and Brooks just shakes his head but says nothing.

"Perfect." She smiles, the cheerful tone returning to her voice. "You're going to love the game I got for tonight."

* * *

"You got fucking *Twister* for a bunch of guys to play together, Ror. Why do you love torturing us so much?" Fitz groans with his face entirely too close to Wren's balls.

"Seems to be her favorite pastime," I mutter, earning a snicker out of both Fitz and Wren.

"Yeah, well, jokes on you, Ror, because I happen to *love* having Fitz's mouth by my balls. There's nowhere else I'd rather be tonight. So, what now, huh?" Wren says, although his face is turning a bright shade of crimson from hanging upside down for this long, the vein in his thick neck bulging.

We might have a lot of stamina as rugby players, but shit, this is not the place to test it.

Right now I'm too busy trying to hold my hands on red and bloody green and not face-plant into the back of Liam's head.

Fuck, St. James has lost her mind.

When she said game night, I had no idea it would involve acquainting ourselves with each other's balls so intimately. I'm starting to come to the realization that she's got a thing for balls, and not in the kind of way that will benefit me.

I look up, peering over Fitz to see Rory perched on a chair with the spinner in her lap, a shit-eating grin on her plush, rosy lips.

She's enjoying every second of this. Watching a bunch of grown-ass college rugby players playing Twister in her living room while she controls the strings. I swear she's not even spinning the damn thing; she's just telling us to place our limbs in the absolute worst positions imaginable.

"You're doing great guys! Loving the teamwork. This is what it's all about." Her soft giggle floats through the room and Fitz groans again.

"I swear to fucking God, Liam, if you fart right now I'm going to break both your legs and you'll never be able to play rugby again."

For fuck's sake.

Rory giggles again. "Okay, Ezra, now you put your foot on… blue."

Ezra mutters a string of curses under his breath and attempts to wedge his body between Liam and Brooks.

Only he knocks all three of them over in the process, causing them to end up in a heap on the plastic game mat and Rory to nearly lose her shit laughing.

The only ones left are Wren, Fitz, and me.

Until Wren lifts a hand and shoves Fitz to the ground. "Oops, Fitzy's out." He smirks.

"Ooooh, just Wrenny and Kill left!" Rory says, bouncing excitedly in her chair.

"Ror," Wren whines, followed by a deep groan. "I told you, you *gotta* stop calling me Wrenny. It's fucking with my masculinity."

It's fascinating, watching the dynamic between all of them. How comfortable they are together, how at ease they seem to be.

If you saw Wren Michaels standing on a rugby pitch, the first thing you'd think is that's one big motherfucking bloke. Big, wide, boxy shoulders and built so solidly that he could withstand tackles from two guys at once. He's massive to say the least.

But then you see him around Rory and the bloke's a fucking teddy bear, all soft and squishy to her as if he couldn't pick her up and toss her around like a feather.

It's mind-boggling to witness.

She's got all these guys completely wrapped around her pretty little finger, and she knows it.

Even Brooks and Ezra, and they're arseholes to everyone, so it surprises the shit out of me to see them respect and value what she thinks.

"Wren, oh shit. There's a *caterpillar*!" Rory cries, jumping up from the chair.

What is she going on about? A caterpillar? The long...fuzzy little bug?

The next few seconds seem to pass in slow motion. Wren practically levitates off the bloody ground as he lets out a high-pitched scream. It's so loud and piercing and un-fucking believable that I blink, trying to figure out if I passed out from all the blood rushing to my head or if that really just happened.

"Motherfucker! Fuck. Fuck. FUCK. Where is it? Where the hell is it, Rory!" He's all but sprinting as he dives for the couch, jumping onto the cushions and wielding her fluffy green throw pillow like it's a weapon. "Those are *Satan's eyebrows*! Get it away from me."

Half the guys are in tears on the floor watching Wren lose his fucking mind over this mysterious caterpillar that I suspect doesn't even actually exist.

"Oh my God," Rory wheezes, doubling over as she clutches her stomach. Fresh tears are streaming down her face. "Wr-r-ren. S-s-top. I'm going t-to pee."

I drop down and sprawl on the plastic mat, watching her laugh. "Please don't while I'm on the floor."

This only seems to make her laugh harder.

"Glad you could come and witness this embarrassing shit first-hand tonight, Cairney," Fitz says from the floor beside me.

Wren retorts angrily, "Fuck you, Fitz, don't make fun of my fear. You're scared of fucking *carrots*."

Fitz sits up abruptly, his expression sobering and his gaze narrowing. "You dick. You weren't supposed to tell anyone that. Did you see the girl on *1000 Ways to Die*? Bet she fucking regrets that carrot."

"Yeah, only because she shoved it up her pus—"

"Oh my God, I told you fuckers to never tell that story in front of me again. I'm fucking scarred for life," Brooks says, cutting off Wren.

Shit, I know exactly what he was about to say, and that's pretty fucking scary to think about.

Rory finally admits to Wren that she was lying, and there wasn't *actually* a caterpillar, which I've now picked up is one of his greatest fears in life. He's come down off the couch, but still is not entirely trusting anything on the floor.

After that, he doesn't trust her, so they all begin filtering out until it's just me and her remaining.

"Well, that went...better than I expected," Rory says near her front door as she turns to face me. "I'm remaining positive that my whole blackmailing with the snickerdoodle cookies is going to work."

I nod. "They did seem very put off by that."

She grins. "My snickerdoodle cookies are out of this world. Maybe I'll make you some one day so you can taste for yourself."

My phone vibrates in the pocket of my trousers, and I pull it out and see a text from Aisling asking me if I want any Chinese takeout. At…midnight.

She's always up in the middle of the night studying so this question is not uncommon.

I quickly shoot her a text and tell her I'll be home soon.

"I've gotta get back to my flat, but are you free Thursday? For your next…" I trail off, lifting a brow.

"Lesson? Yes. I've got a study hall until like six but then I'm free."

Okay, that works because I've got tape review and team workout on Thursday. "Can we meet here around six thirty?"

Rory nods as she opens her front door, and I step through, looking back at her.

"Okay. Later, St. James."

I start walking toward my bike when I hear her call my name.

"Hey, Kill?"

"Yeah?"

She bites her lip, pulling it between her teeth, and leans against the doorframe. "Thank you…for trusting me. I know that it isn't easy for you, but I promise it will be worth it. You'll see. No matter how great a player you are, you can't be great just on your own. Rugby is built on family, and if you give these guys a chance, I know eventually they'll welcome you into theirs."

CHAPTER 12

Rory

By the time my study hall ends and I walk out of the library, my stomach is growling and I think I might actually be starving to death. I've been on campus since eight this morning, and all I packed was a protein bar and a bag of peanut M&M's because I was in a rush and it was the first thing I grabbed as I was walking out the door.

Not exactly a well-balanced meal.

More of a hot-girl snack.

Checking the time on my phone, I realize I've got a few minutes left before I need to head home to meet Cillian, which means that I have plenty of time to stop at my favorite food truck and get some birria tacos to go. They're the best in the entire city, and just thinking about them makes my mouth literally water.

I order some for Cillian too because I don't want to show up with food and not have any for him, and if he's been in weight training all evening he's probably as starving as I am.

My apartment is right off campus, so it takes me only a few

minutes to walk home. When I get there, I find Cillian leaning against his bike in the parking spot directly in front of my place, scrolling on his phone. His brows are pinched together, and his expression seems... sad almost?

"Hi," I greet him brightly, lifting the plastic bag full of tacos. "I wasn't sure what the plan for tonight was and I'm so hungry I could actually eat a cow, soooo I brought dinner."

He pushes off the bike, tucking his phone into the pocket of his gray sweatpants and nods. "Thanks. Came straight here after a shower."

"Everything good?" I ask.

Something feels off with him, but I don't want to pry because he's only just started to really let me in at all. I don't want him to shut down by pushing too hard and overstepping any boundaries. But I also saw the way he was staring at his phone, like whatever was on it was the most hurtful thing he's ever seen, then just as quickly, the mask dropped back in place, leaving his face blank.

"Yeah, I'm good. Thanks."

I give him a small smile as we walk to my door. I have a feeling he's not good, but I guess if he wants to talk, he will. He takes the bag from me as I unlock the front door and then he follows me inside, shutting it behind him.

"Wanna eat on the couch?" I ask him as we move through my apartment.

When he nods and walks over to the couch, I can't help but notice the way his ass looks in those stupid sweatpants. I swear guys have to know what they're doing to women when they wear them.

It's absurd.

Thirty minutes later, the tacos are demolished, and I couldn't eat another single bite even if I wanted to.

"Bloody hell, that was the best thing I've ever eaten in my life," he says after smashing four out of the eight tacos I bought, and I giggle.

"I *told* you. Trust me, as a foodie, I am on top of when and where to eat around Prescott. This truck only comes like once a month and no matter what, I make sure I'm there because only having these tacos once a month is hardly enough."

A low groan rumbles from his chest as he clutches his stomach, then lifts his arms in a stretch over his head. The T-shirt he's wearing lifts, revealing the dark dusting of hair covering his tan abdomen and the trail that leads into his waistband. I didn't notice until now how the dark green T-shirt he's wearing clings to every hard muscle of his upper body, molding to him like it was made just for him.

I feel my cheeks heat, and I clear my throat, a cough suddenly forcing its way up my throat.

Jesus, what am I even doing checking him out like this.

There are a lot of things I've been...noticing about Cillian recently. Some against my will, but still entirely impossible to ignore.

Obviously I'm just...horny. And I need a little time with my showerhead. That's all.

"So, I was thinking about the other night."

Pushing my thoughts of doing indecent things to him away, I turn to face him, pulling my legs up in a crisscross. "Okay...and?"

His fingers splay along his jaw, then he drags them across his mouth for a beat. "You need to practice on me, St. James. I know you said it's weird, but there's no better way for me to talk you through it than to see it face-to-face."

The thought of embarrassing myself that way is the absolute last thing I want to do but before I can even protest, he keeps going. "We're going to pretend like we don't know each other. Never met at all and we'll have a conversation just like we would if I was trying to take you home."

"And what makes you think that you *could* take me home, Cairney?"

The lazy, cocky grin he gives me admittedly has my stomach flipping, the feeling of a hundred flutters erupting in my lower belly in sync with the erratic beating in my chest. If Cillian were a stranger at a bar, there is absolutely no doubt in my mind that I would want to go home with him.

I'm not admitting that out loud, but it's painfully true.

"Damn. Okay, if that's the way you're doing it, I get it. You know, you should smile more. Makes you look less like a serial killer."

He chuckles. "Smart-arse. Now come on, let's practice."

When he turns to face me, scooting in slightly, I shakily exhale. We're almost touching now, his powerful thigh pressed against mine as he angles toward me.

I can do this.

It's just Cillian. We're almost, sort of, kind of even friends now. I think so at least.

Friends can flirt. Easy peasy.

"Tell me how I should start," I say, my voice barely above a whisper. "What should I do first when I see a hot guy that I want?"

It feels so incredibly stupid to say that out loud because I should know, but as painful as it is to admit, I don't. I'm a college girl who only lost her virginity because of a very awkward, very terrible drunken hookup at my high school graduation party that I immediately regretted and have done my best to never think about again.

Who's now being taught by the bad boy outcast of her father's rugby team.

"Smile. Introduce yourself. Don't worry about what he's thinking, or what you'll say next. Let the conversation happen naturally. No pressure, no expectations. Just a conversation," he says pointedly.

As if it's the simplest thing in the world.

"Okay." I nod, exhaling again, then square my shoulders and lift my chin. I plaster on a smile and say, "Hi. I'm Rory."

Cillian grins. He lifts his hand and extends it for me to shake. When I slip my shaking palm in his, he holds it for a second, letting it linger longer than I would with any stranger without it feeling awkward. But with him... it feels exactly the way that it should. "Rory. I like that."

Jesus, four words in and I'm already blushing. I can't imagine actually being the recipient of *real* flirting with a guy like him. This is just pretend and I'm already feeling flustered.

"Get out of your head, Rory." He leans in slightly and I swear he's so close I can feel his breath fanning across my lips. "Can I be honest about something?"

I nod wordlessly.

"I've been thinking about walking over and talking to you all night, love." The way the word rolls off his tongue, deep and thickly accented, it's possibly the hottest thing I've ever heard.

He smells so good it should actually be a sin. Like fresh sandalwood and cedar. Clean. Delicious. The combination of how close he is, how good he smells, how his voice is a velvet seduction has me completely overwhelmed. In the best way.

"H-have you?" I stutter.

His grin widens into a crooked smile, and his hazel eyes seem to darken. "Yeah. A pretty girl like you shouldn't be alone at a bar. Do you go to university around here?"

"Yes. I'm a junior at Prescott. Um...what about you?" I ask as my head swims.

"I just transferred to Prescott from London, actually. I'm still trying to find my way around campus." His shoulder lifts in a shrug. "Maybe you could show me around sometime?"

When he leans in and tucks a stray piece of hair behind my ear, I hear my own breath hitch. The moment his fingers brush against the sensitive shell of my ear, a shiver dances electrically down my spine.

I know that we're only pretending, and that this is just practice for the real thing, but honestly, I'm having trouble remembering that fact right now.

God, he's *charming* when he wants to be.

Now I'm starting to really understand why all the girls on campus are losing it over him. If this is how he acts with them?

I'd be down just as bad.

Calm down, Rory. This is all for show, and you're playing the same part he is.

"Definitely," I whisper back, my lips tilting into what I hope is a sexy smile. "W-what did you have in mind?"

Where's this charm when it comes to the team? Granted, they're guys and he's not trying to sleep with them, but still. He's too busy being grumpy and broody to give even a sliver of this away.

You're not thinking about the team right now, Rory. The hottest guy I've ever met is touching me, and my brain isn't entirely working correctly right now.

But you know what is? My nipples, which are currently taut and pressing almost painfully against the cups of my bra.

I'm irrationally turned on by a game of make-believe right now. I should probably feel ashamed of that since I went into it knowing this was just for practice, but my body has a mind of its own.

"You're in your head again," Cillian says, his dark brow lifted. "Where'd you go?"

"Yes, sorry, but I was just thinking about how…" I trail off, unable to pull myself together. There's no way I'm telling him exactly how much this affected me. How much it turned me on, so I pivot. "Charming you are. I mean… I know we're just practicing, but I still got a little flustered," I tell him honestly. "And I was thinking that maybe if you used some of that charm with the team, they may open up to you a little more. You know, instead of the selective-mute thing?"

He sighs as he pulls back, straightening his spine against the couch. "Not talking about me right now, St. James. This is about you."

"I know. I know. Okay, sorry, carry on." I flatten my palm and then wave it down my face as if I'm in theater class and attempting to get back into character, which only makes Cillian roll his eyes and shake his head.

"Yeah, I could *totally* show you around," I say, waggling my eyebrows.

"Stop that."

Nerves be damned, I grin and lean forward, ready to give him a taste of his own stupidly charming medicine. Well, the Rory St. James version of it. I place my clammy hands on his knees, slowly trailing them higher, watching as his eyes go wide.

"I know you're new to campus, and I could show you all of the best places... Where to hang out, where to hook up, where to..." I trail off, leaning even closer as I peer up at him through my lashes and pull my lip between my teeth. "Get *tacos*." My voice is so low and sultry that I hardly recognize it.

Okay, that was by far the most sexual thing that's ever come out of my mouth, and it was *taco* related.

I'm impressed with myself. I didn't know I even had that in me.

"Christ," he groans dramatically. "That really bloody does it for me, Rory. So fucking hot."

I toss my head back, a giggle escaping at how ridiculous this entire exchange has become. Cillian's laughing along with me, and I realize when I hear him, a real genuine laugh for the first time ever, I love the sound. Deep and raspy, it fits him so perfectly.

"Anyone ever tell you you're a shit student, St. James?"

I shrug, sitting back against the arm of the couch. "Nope. Maybe you're just a *shit* teacher."

"Bullshit. I'm a phenomenal teacher." He sobers after a moment, glancing over at me pensively. "Seems like you have no problem flirting with me. What's the difference?"

"Because you're... *you*? I don't know, I think maybe my brain knows it's not real. That it's just a scenario and not the real thing. It feels entirely different when I'm talking to a random guy that I find attractive. I either word vomit or find myself friend-zoned. I just freeze and then make a complete fool out of myself."

Cillian listens intently as I talk, his big hands folded in his lap, and when I'm done he says, "Then we'll just keep practicing, keep working at it until you feel more comfortable. For your next lesson we'll up the stakes, meet at a bar and pretend we don't know each other. See how you do with a change of scenery. We can work on cues, and how you can pick up on knowing when a guy is interested."

I chew my lip. "Okay. Can I ask you something? Not about the lesson or my...issues."

He nods.

"What's your dream girl? Not like a supermodel or a famous actress, but when you see yourself with someone, who is she? What does she look like?"

For a beat he's quiet as he mulls over my question.

It's something I've thought a lot about recently. Who my own dream guy would be, and I haven't quite figured it out, but I'm slowly working on it.

I want to know what Cillian likes. Who he'd be interested in. What kind of traits he looks for in a girl. I just want to *know* Cillian.

"Kind, smart, authentically herself. She'd genuinely like rugby and be compatible in..." My cheeks immediately burn when he trails off and smirks, dipping a shoulder. "As far as looks, I love *all* types of women, and I don't have a physical type."

That's surprising. Most athletes like cleat chasers. Puck bunnies. The girls who would do whatever simply because they play sports. I've seen it enough. But it seems that's not Cillian's type at all.

"Interesting."

"Yeah, what's interesting about that?" he asks.

I shrug. "It just doesn't fit the whole quintessential cliché bad boy thing. They usually want bimbos who think sucking their dick *is* a sport and have nothing important to talk about. Ever."

Cillian chuckles. "I mean most guys want their girl to love sucking their cock, St. James."

"That's not wha—" I stop mid-sentence. Hearing the word *cock* in his stupidly hot English accent causes me to flush, my cheeks burning. "Ugh, you know what...never mind. I'm just saying I didn't expect you to have an answer like that, that's all. So deep."

"Well, to be fair you don't really know me. Maybe I'm a deep guy," he says.

Okay, that's true. I guess it wasn't fair to judge him. I'm already beginning to learn that he's not at all like I thought when he first got here.

"Yeah, you're right," I say, because he is. "Won't happen again, promise. I'll just save all my judgment for your food choices."

When he laughs, I bite my lip to hold back the one that threatens to escape.

Something tells me there's much more to Cillian Cairney than what meets the eye.

And I want to find out what.

CHAPTER 13

Cillian

I would almost call today's practice productive... *Almost.*

It's not as if my teammates have rolled out a welcome mat and are throwing a party down at the pub, but the air doesn't feel quite as thick with tension as it normally does. I don't know if that had anything to do with Rory, but it does seem like after the game night at her place things are a little less heavy with my teammates. They're working with me as a team instead of shutting me out every chance they get.

I've said I wasn't going to worry about making friends or anything other than rugby in America since my stay here is temporary. Complete tunnel vision. That was always the plan. Not let anyone get too close, not after all the shit I've been through. After my trust had been broken by the people I had back home. The ones who dropped me like it was nothing when I was going through the hardest, most brutal time of my life.

But lately... I feel like that might be starting to change. St. James... has a way of burrowing beneath your skin.

I guess if I had to call anyone a friend, it might be her.

"Come in!" her soft voice calls from inside. I turn the knob and push the front door open, stepping into her apartment. "In the living room!"

When I walk into her living room, the first thing I notice is the giant whiteboard on wheels that's positioned in front of the TV mounted on her wall.

"You're late."

My gaze whips to Rory, who is sitting cross-legged on the couch, her hair piled high on her head. She's wearing a thick, oversized navy-blue jumper and a pair of tiny white shorts that have my eyes dropping to her exposed creamy thighs. She's all of five two, but her legs seem to go on for days. Staring at them makes me feel like I'm staring at something indecent even though it's just fucking *legs*.

Sexy, off-limits-as-fuck legs, arsehole. I feel like a bloke from the Renaissance peeping at bloody ankles.

I'm honestly not sure when I started to notice she was hot, but every single time I think of Rory in a way that *isn't* my coach's daughter, I force myself to shut it the fuck down.

Admittedly, lately, it's more often than it should be, and that worries the fuck out of me.

Clearing my throat, I rub the back of my neck as I flop down beside her on the couch. "Yeah, sorry, my sister had me hang some photos on the wall at the flat. Said we needed to make it more 'homely' or some shit and I don't exactly trust her with a power tool."

"Why, because she's a woman?" Her brow lifts.

"Christ, no. Because she's got a track record for putting holes in anything that she touches, so I wasn't going to let her anywhere near a seven-hundred-watt drill and old Sheetrock."

Rory giggles, covering her mouth. "Okay, that's fair. Coincidentally, I also suffer from the same problem. I usually just call one of the guys over to do it for me."

"Hell, the last time she used a hammer, my mum..." I didn't even think before saying that to Rory, and when my voice falters, her brow furrows in confusion.

"Cillian?" she murmurs, her eyes narrowed with concern. "What's wrong?"

I swallow, trying to breathe, but my throat feels so fucking tight I might suffocate. "Uh...My mum...she was killed in an automobile accident. And it's...I—"

Rory's face softens, her expression a mixture of sadness, sympathy...pity.

I hate the pity most of all. When people find out about Mum, it's like the puzzle pieces align, and they finally realize why I'm as fucked-up as I am, and I fucking hate it. I hate that me being fucked-up is aligned with the best person I ever knew. I hate that it still hurts as badly as it did the moment it happened.

"Sorry, I...I can't talk about it," I say, my voice rough as I drag my palm roughly over my mouth and pull my gaze away from her. To anywhere but the pools of pity shining back at me in her eyes.

Suddenly, I feel her soft, warm fingers curl around my forearm. She squeezes gently, and the touch helps to bring me out of my head and makes it a little easier to breathe. "That's okay. You don't have to. What about your sister? What's she like?"

When my eyes meet hers, a small smile tugs at her lips. I guess she's trying to distract me from the panic attack I almost just had, but at any rate, I'm grateful because I needed the distraction more than she probably even realizes. Anything to make my chest feel less constricted and my throat to not feel as if it's closing and cutting off my ability to breathe.

"Aisling's a freshman, two years younger, and she's... fucking *brilliant*. The smartest person I've ever met. Loads smarter than I'll ever be, without a doubt." A quiet, wistful laugh rumbles from my chest, and I see Rory smiling. "She's sensitive. Kind. I think she has all the best parts of Mum."

"I can tell how much you love her," she says, her rich brown eyes like melted chocolate, soft and full of warmth. "I know you don't want to talk about it, and I understand, but if you ever *do* want to talk about it, Cillian, I'm here."

A brief moment of silence passes between us until I finally lift my chin. This is a conversation I was wholly unprepared for when I came here tonight, and I'm not sure if I ever will be with Rory. Or anyone else.

"Thank you. For..." I trail off, and Rory nods, giving me an understanding smile. Jerking my head toward the giant whiteboard taking up most of her living room, I change the subject to something... anything other than this. "What's up with the board?"

Rory's eyes light up, and she bounces up from the couch and grabs a black marker from the top of her TV stand. "Okay, welllll, yesterday when we were talking about how stupidly charming you are... it gave me a brilliant idea."

I eye her warily. After the whole bloody Twister "idea," I'm not feeling very confident in any of her brilliant *ideas* right now. I never want to get that close to another man's balls ever again outside of a rugby pitch.

Christ, I don't even want to do it on the pitch, but it comes with the territory.

"Don't give me that look, Cillian Cairney." She huffs, crossing her arms over her chest, lifting a brow, and giving *me* a look. "You're supposed to be *trusting* me, remember?"

"I'm here, aren't I?" I snort.

"True," she says with a sigh. She places the marker cap between her teeth and pulls it off before turning to face the board. She writes OPERATION FAKE IT TILL YOU MAKE IT across it in big, block letters, then turns back to me wearing a cheeky smile.

"Okay so... it's *your* turn for a lesson. I was thinking about the best ways to *really* get you in with the guys, and then it dawned on me. What better way to get them to trust you than to learn everything you can about them? You'll get the inside scoop, and I think that we can use this to our advantage. You can use what you learn to connect with them, to bond. So, we're going to devise a plan and start at the top. Pluck them off, one by one. Take them down like enemy spies."

I'm not at all following, and she must read the expression on my face because she rolls her eyes. Then she turns back to the board and starts writing.

This gives me a full view of her arse in those tiny white, virtually see-through nightie shorts. I realize that I should be looking anywhere but there, but also I can't help it.

It's a bloody *fantastic* arse.

Lush and perfectly round, the soft swell of her cheeks practically hanging out from the bottom of the shorts.

I'm so engrossed with the view that I don't even realize she's turned to face me, catching me blatantly staring at her arse. "Cillian Cairney!"

Fuck.

"Were you just...checking out my ass?" Her palm flies to her hip as she cocks her head, glaring at me.

"Of course not." I smirk.

I can see the pink tinting her cheeks even from my spot on the couch, and my smirk widens into a shit-eating grin.

"Good. Because we've got work to do. Okay, Pay attention. Focus, Kill. This is important," she says before whipping toward the board and pointing animatedly at the name she's written at the top. "We're starting with the easy one. Fitz. He's Switzerland. The white flag you'll need. And he's our *first* target. You've already seen him starting to melt, like a scoop of soft serve."

I want to interrupt and ask her if she's lost her mind, but she's got a look of sheer determination on her face, so I keep it to myself.

"This is probably cheating a little, but I'm already going to talk to Fitz and have him help with the other guys. Besides the point. The point is that even though Fitz isn't captain, the guys still hold him in high regard. He's the guy they go to for advice, or for help with something. He's steadfast and loyal. He's the kind of guy we need on your team. Figuratively speaking of course."

I nod. "Of course."

I watch Rory turn back to the board and write WREN next to FITZ, then draw an arrow from his name to Wren.

"Next up: Wren. The prop equivalent of a big, squishy, fluffy teddy bear. Intimidating at first glance, but then you find out that he brings his mamas flowers every Sunday and is deathly afraid of caterpillars and centipedes. He's a sensitive little button. But he is *fiercely* loyal to the team. To my dad. He might be just a little harder to win over, but if you can get Fitz then I guarantee that you can get Wren. They're two peas in a pod. Good thing you have a secret weapon. Me."

She wasn't kidding about this being an actual lesson. I feel like I've learned more about the team in the past fifteen minutes than I have in the entire month that I've been here.

I learn that Liam is a reader who loves poetry and science fiction books. A weird combination if you ask me, but apparently he could talk for days about his favorite books featuring aliens and winged creatures. I would've never guessed that in a million years had Rory not told me. Another thing I wouldn't have known is that as much of an arsehole Brooks is he volunteers at the animal shelter every other Sunday since bringing home a three-legged cat when he got pissed after a night at the bar.

Go fucking figure. I thought the bloke was a psychopath, but I guess that's just what I see on the surface.

I'm actually pretty fucking impressed.

I knew Rory was close with these guys, but she's taken the time to actually get to know them beyond just rugby. It makes more sense knowing her dynamic with the team than when I saw her interacting with them at the start. They're not just players to her, they're her *friends*.

"So, your first step is going to be to extend an olive branch to Wren. Go out of your way to start a conversation with him, even if it's about something stupid. He's your number one right now. Let's call it your... *homework*. Maybe try and talk to him about that trashy TV show you and your sister watch. I'm like ninety percent positive he watches it too. See... there is something outside of balls that you two have in common."

A chuckle rumbles in my chest. "No way you're giving me

homework when I'm the teacher, St. James. If I'm getting homework, then so are you."

"Yeah? And what's mine going to be?" Her brow arches as she stares at me with defiance flaring in her irises.

Hmm.

"Talk to one guy this week. At class or at the gym. Hell, even the food court if that's where you want. But one guy who's *not* on the team. And don't mention rugby. Actually, don't mention sports at all. Got it?"

I watch as a small, adorable wrinkle forms on the bridge of her nose. An exhale rushes past her lips. "Are you sure I'm ready for that? We've only had two les—"

"Won't know until you try," I say, cutting off the long-winded ramble I know she's about to go on. The only way Rory is going to get the confidence she needs to date, or flirt, or fuck, or whatever it is she's in search of is to get out of her head and allow herself to be in the moment.

Can't do that if she's so afraid to fuck it up that she doesn't give herself the opportunity to try.

Sometimes the only thing holding you back is yourself.

CHAPTER 14

Rory

The roar of Cillian's motorcycle in front of my apartment has a bubble of apprehension settling in the base of my throat, my stomach doing a series of incessant flips.

I may have had a *slightly* dramatic, teeny intrusive moment where I texted him in a flurry of mass panic.

Well, I guess it's too late to turn back now seeing as how he's... already here.

Seconds later there's a loud pounding at the front door. I rush over, nearly tripping over my feet to wrench the door open.

He's standing on the doorstep, slightly winded and eyes wide as he says, "What's wrong? Are you okay?" He scans my body as if he's searching for something wrong. "You said it was an emergency. *SOS?*"

I wince. "I mean technically it *is* an emergency?"

His concerned gaze connects with mine, suddenly turning steely. "What do you mean *technically?*"

I reach out, grasp the front of his T-shirt, and pull him inside.

The space between his brows is furrowed, and he looks confused and still a little worried. I feel bad for worrying him but also this is an emergency. I didn't know who else to call so I called him.

Which is kind of weird... the fact that *he's* the person I thought about when something happened, but I don't have time to unpack that right now.

He's the one giving me lessons, so he's the only one who can help with this.

I think?

Yes.

"So clearly I'm not hurt, or dying, and there's not an intruder or anything, but to me this still qualifies as an emergency," I say to Cillian once we're in the living room. "Can you just, um, sit there please?"

I point to the cream armchair, and he gives me a blank stare, completely unmoving. Not even an inch.

I exhale noisily. "I'm sorry. I realize I should not have said 'SOS,' or I should've at least warned you that nothing serious was wrong. I just... was having a freakout, and you're the first person I thought to call about this."

He runs his hand through his still-damp hair, and I realize he must have been in the shower or fresh out of it when I texted. "Christ, St. James. What the fuck's going on?"

My teeth rake over my bottom lip before I pull it between them, chewing nervously. I think my palms are *actually* sweating right now. I haven't been this nervous in a long time.

He's going to think this is so stupid, and now I think it might have been a ridiculous idea to begin with.

"One second," I breathe, turning to sprint to my bedroom

and gather the armful of packages I've been hoarding for the past week. When I return to the living room, Cillian's on the couch, his tattooed arms spread along the back, staring at *The Office*, which I had playing on the TV.

I walk to the center of the living room and drop the packages on the floor in front of him.

His dark brow arches as he takes in the pile, clearly confused. "What is this?"

"These are packages."

He rolls his eyes. "Obviously, Rory. Can you fill me in on what the hell is going on? Because you're not making a bit of sense right now."

Dropping to my knees on the carpet, I pick one up and wrestle to get through the thick plastic of the poly mailer. "So the other day I started thinking about the fact that I've never really tried to, you know, wear dresses and makeup and things like that. And it's not because I don't want to, it's just I don't really know where to start."

Finally, I pop a hole in the plastic and rip it open, then pull out the satin dress inside. It's...pink. Which is obviously not a color I wear often, but I think I kind of love this shade? I unfold the dress and hold it up for Cillian to see. "I followed this girl online who's a fashion influencer and well, then that sent me down a rabbit hole and per usual I hyperfixated and, long story short, I've decided to try out a new wardrobe. Kind of. This is one of them. What do you think? Is it ugly? This is stupid, isn't it? I knew it pro—"

"Rory." His voice is rough, raspy, and low as he cuts me off. "It's not ugly. Or stupid. Put it on."

My brow furrows. "Really?"

He nods.

I rise from the floor and head to my bedroom, quickly removing my clothes and slipping into the soft pink dress. Once it's on, I run to the mirror in the corner of my room, and when I see my reflection, my jaw drops.

Holy shit.

The soft material hugs the dip of my waist, the swell of my breasts, the curve of my thighs, all the places that I never seem to pay much attention to since I'm always in a baggy hoodie or my workout clothes.

But in this?

They're impossible to ignore, and as much as I thought I probably wouldn't like wearing a dress, let alone a pink one, I wanted to step out of my comfort zone and try something new.

And I'm actually glad I did.

I exhale shakily, running my palms down the front of the dress as I take one last glance at my reflection before I walk back to the living room to face Cillian.

His gaze lifts when I walk in the room, and his dark eyes widen briefly, his lips parting.

It's almost as if something...*flares* in the depths. I'm not entirely sure, and I can't read his expression, but I think he doesn't hate it.

In an attempt to dislodge the nervous lump in my throat, I clear it and spin in a circle with my hands out. "What do you think?"

"Bloody hell, St. James." His voice is a husky whisper.

"Is that a good 'bloody hell' or a bad one because I honestly can't tell the difference sometimes." I laugh, but the nervous sound dies on my tongue when his gaze lazily glides down my body.

As if he's drinking me in, every single inch, slowly, one at a time.

And suddenly I feel as if I'm standing completely naked in front of him even though I'm fully clothed.

There's a silent, torturously slow pause before he says, "A good one."

I'm not sure what kind of reaction I was anticipating, but *this* was not it, and it makes me feel...good.

I decide I like that *he's* making me feel that way. A lot.

"Okay...good," I respond.

His lips curve. "Great."

"So does that mean I should try on the others?" I ask as I lean down and scoop up a handful of the packages.

He makes another slow perusal before nodding and raking a hand through his dark hair. I watch his throat bob with a rough swallow.

For some strange reason, my heart is thrashing in my chest. Maybe it's the attention from Cillian, or maybe it's something... different.

Something new that I've never felt before.

"Okay. Uh, I'll be right back," I say, giving him a small smile as I sprint from the living room. That was...interesting. Maybe I'm just being weird, but it feels like my brain is moving at the speed of light, and by the time I get to my bedroom and shut the door, slamming my back against it, I'm almost breathless. My head falls back against the wood with a loud thump at the same time a rushed exhale bursts out of me.

It takes a few seconds for me to calm my racing pulse and shallow bursts of my breathing, but then I move to my bed and set the rest of the packages on top. My fingertips slip beneath the hem of the dress I'm wearing and tug it over my head, tossing it to the side.

The next mailer I open contains another dress, but this one is... extremely tiny and now that I'm seeing it up close, I have no idea why I even ordered it in the first place.

It looked so hot on the model, and I thought I could maybe pull it off. But now that I'm staring at the leather material, I'm having serious second thoughts.

I don't even know if I can fit my *thigh* in this thing.

There's absolutely no way I can wear this bra with the dress since it's strapless and probably going to fit like a second skin, so I reach behind me and unhook it, throwing it on top of the previously discarded dress on the floor.

Okay, now to get this thing on.

It takes me ten minutes to even work it up to my hips, but I somehow squeeze into the tight, unyielding material. Then I realize... if it's taking me this long to get it *on*, then how in the hell am I going to get it *off*? Something tells me that it'll be even harder to remove.

It's so tight I'm pretty sure you can see the outline of my belly button.

Sweat coats my hairline by the time I pull it up over my chest, the tight leather barely covering the tops of my nipples before it stops completely.

My God, Rory, what were you thinking?
This is built for bodies that are not shaped like yours.

I can't suck in a breath in this thing.

Taking a couple tiny steps at a time, I turn toward the door and realize there's no way I'm making it another step.

I slip my fingers beneath the hem and try to tug it down, but it doesn't budge.

A single inch.

Groaning, I pull harder. Nothing.

Another thing I clearly underestimated? The fact that leather makes you *sweat*. And even with the sweat forming underneath the dress, making my body damp and slick, it's not going anywhere.

Shit. Shit. Shit.

Maybe I need to go from the top? I slip my fingers beneath the fabric cups of the dress and try to pull them down but I can barely get my fingers in the impossibly tight space.

In the shuffle, I fall against my dresser, knocking over a picture frame and a trinket tray from the top, making the heavy wood hit the wall behind it.

Great, I'm going to end up having to go to the hospital or something because I got stuck in a leather dress like some type of dominatrix.

"Everything okay in there?" Cillian's smooth, deep voice sounds from the other side of the door, and I suck in a sharp breath.

As big of a breath as I can in this…contraption.

"Um…well, that depends on the definition of *okay*?" I call back.

A beat passes before he says, "Elaborate, St. James."

I sigh. "Just open the door, and don't say a freakin' word, Cillian."

A few seconds later, the hinges of my bedroom door creak as it opens and he strides through. When he sees me leaning against the dresser with my palms shoved in the front of the dress, seemingly holding my boobs, he just lifts a brow, blinking slowly as he takes in the scene in front of him.

The space between his brows crinkles as he slides his gaze down my body, pausing at the dress that's molded to me. "Now, *this* dress is bloody hot."

"Yeah?" I retort sharply. "Great. Imagine wearing the equivalent of a latex glove. I'm stuck."

"What do you mean *stuck*?"

I try to pull my hands free, and they don't move like they're in one of those finger puzzles I did as a kid. "I mean I'm quite literally *stuck*. I can't get it off. You're going to have to I don't know...cut it off, I think."

Cillian holds it together for longer than I probably would have. I've gotta give him credit for that.

Then he loses it, tossing his head back and laughing. It's one of my new favorite sounds, deep and raspy, echoing off the walls of my bedroom.

I try to be annoyed, I really do, but God, this is so absolutely fucking ridiculous and something that would *only* happen to me, that I can't help the laugh that bursts out of me.

Except the material of this stupid, godforsaken dress is so tight I can't even really laugh because I can hardly breathe.

"Please, for the love of God, get this off of me," I wheeze. "S-Scissors are in the drawer. Over there." I jerk my head toward my nightstand.

"Okay, I'm sorry, but that's fucking hilarious. And hot.

Definitely hot too," he chokes out between a laugh. "In the literal sense, not the figurative one since I'm sure you're sweating in that thing."

"I'm going to murder you if you do not help me out of this dress, Cillian Cairney, I swear to God."

His hands lift in surrender, even though he's still sporting a shit-eating grin. "Okay, okay."

I stay rooted in place as he strides over to my nightstand, bending to pull the drawer open. He rifles around inside it for a second before turning back to face me, his cheeks suddenly red.

Why would he be tur—

Oh my God.

"Please pretend that you did not see that and carry on with your task." My words tumble out in a rush. Of course, he found my vibrator. Of course. Because what else could make this entire embarrassing fiasco that much worse? A hot guy finding your battery-operated boyfriend.

Perfect.

Not that it's something I use regularly because, sadly, I'm not that great at it. It's overstimulating, and I'm more of a finger kind of girl, but that's beside the point.

That's *not* something I need to defend to him. There's nothing wrong with self-care.

"Nice. Very *girthy*, St. James." The lazy grin curving his lips only furthers my mortification and I'm positive that I'm going to die any moment now.

Truly, RIP, Rory.

She's gone now.

Groaning, I squeeze my eyes shut and try to pretend that he's not standing there holding my vibrator in his hand. "You're going to forget this ever happened, and you're not going to tell a soul, I swear to G—"

"I wouldn't. I'm just fucking with you." He laughs. "I wouldn't judge you anyway."

Finally, freaking finally, he drops it back into the drawer, pulls out the scissors, and shuts the drawer. He makes it back to where I'm standing in two short strides.

He holds up the scissors. "How are we doing this?"

My brow arches. "What, you've never *cut* a dress off a girl before?"

"Can't say I have, but here's to the first." He smirks lazily, giving me a wink that makes my stomach flip.

I truly don't understand how someone can be so effortlessly charming but also a broody, grumpy dick sometimes. How does he do both entirely too well?

"Well, I'm also naked under here so..." I trail off, lifting my gaze to his. His green-flecked irises seem to darken, and I swallow the lump of whatever sitting in my throat. "Couldn't exactly get this on with anything underneath it."

"Right."

"So, I guess we just cut it down the center? I don't think you'd be able to get the scissors beneath anywhere else, but there's a small enough gap between my boobs," I add, nodding toward my chest.

Cillian's gaze drops down, and I watch his jaw tense as he swallows.

"I'm sorry, this is so embarrassing, I honestly would like to move to another country and assume a new identity. Witness protection of sorts, but the protection is from myself."

With a raspy chuckle, he takes a step forward until I can feel the heat of him sliding over my exposed skin, and his fresh sandalwood scent invades every single one of my senses. It's the first we've ever been this close and it feels…intimate. In a way I've never felt.

The air around us feels thick and charged, as if there's a current surging through it.

"Hold still," he murmurs as he brings the blade between my cleavage and begins to cut the leather fabric. "I don't want to hurt you."

I'm practically holding my breath as he works, but it's more so because of his proximity and not the fact that he's got a sharp object so close to my skin.

My pulse races as I watch him, concentration etched onto every inch of his face. Those dark eyebrows pulled tightly together, creating a furrow between them, his pillowy bottom lip held hostage between his teeth. He's got a small freckle just above his upper lip that I've never noticed until now.

Carefully, he cuts through the fabric with calculated precision, and after a few slow seconds, I can finally pull my hands free and suck in a deep breath. My body relaxes slightly at the liberation of breathing freely again, and I groan. "Oh God. I will never take breathing for granted ever again."

"When I cut this a little more, you're going to be…" Those raspy syllables trail off, leaving the statement hanging densely in the air between us as he slowly lifts his gaze from my chest to my eyes.

I slip my hand beneath the fabric to my boobs and cup them in my palms. "Well, I have to get it off, so you'll just have to be a gentleman and avert your gaze."

"And whatever gave you the impression..." he says, the warm caress of his breath cascading over my skin and sending goose bumps erupting over my flesh. "That I'm a *gentleman*, Rory?"

My God.

That may be the sexiest thing I've ever heard in my life, and instantly, every single nerve ending on my body feels like it might be on fire.

Sometimes, it feels so...easy with Cillian that I forget how insanely hot and intense he is, but right now it's all I can seem to think about. I've never been so aware of how good he smells, or how sexy his tattoos look as they wrap around his strong, corded arms.

The fabric of the dress falls around my rib cage, split open in the middle, and for a second he doesn't move. His gaze is pinned to my heaving chest, on my hands that are doing a poor attempt at keeping my puckered nipples hidden.

Both of us are breathing heavily, but we don't say a word.

My eyes flutter shut as shallow pants burst past my lips. It's no longer the dress that's controlling my breathing, it's...Cillian.

"Why'd you order this?" he rasps.

I find myself lifting my shoulder in a shrug, trying to tamp down a nervous swallow. "Because...I wanted to feel hot. I thought maybe it would help me feel more confident. And I guess to see if guys would be more interested if I wore something like this because they clearly haven't been so far."

He's quiet for a moment, his eyes burning into mine as he rakes his teeth across his bottom lip.

I feel the warm brush of his knuckles down the smooth skin along the center of my chest as he slowly drags the scissors lower, cutting through the fabric and causing a shiver to waltz its way down my spine.

"You're perfect exactly the way you are, St. James, and if any arsehole makes you think that you have to change to be what he needs, *he's* the problem. Not you." With every syllable, the rough pads of his fingers linger on my heated skin, the same way his words feel branded into my heart.

CHAPTER 15

Cillian

Of all the places I thought I'd be tonight, in a run-down cowboy bar watching my teammates ride a bloody mechanical *bull*, pissed off their heads, doesn't even come close.

Yet another thing St. James coerced us all into, but unlike the game night at her apartment, I'm not dreading being here. Which I'm sure is as much of a surprise to everyone else as it was to me.

"Let's get another round of beers... What about you, Cairney, you in?" Hollis, the team's right wing, asks as he leans over the table, a goofy, drunk grin tipping his lips. "This rounds on me."

I shake my head, lifting my water bottle. "Nah, mate, don't drink, but thanks."

Out of the corner of my eye I can see St. James smiling on the barstool beside me, no doubt pleased with herself that he thought enough to ask me.

Most of the team is here tonight.

Wren, Fitz, Liam, and even Ezra and Brooks came.

The latter made me a bit uneasy about showing up, especially knowing there would be alcohol involved, but Rory promised she'd keep everything under control and reminded me that I'm supposed to be bonding with the team. It's another step in the right direction that they were all right with me coming out tonight. That they're including me in activities outside of what the coaching staff implements. I never thought I'd be at a place with the team where I'm just thankful for the invitation, but I am.

Building a relationship with these guys is the key to keeping my spot on the team, and it makes it a helluva lot easier when we're not at each other's throats at every turn.

Wren's the first one to respond. "Yeah, but none of that IPA bullshit. I swear that shit tastes like what I bet your jockstrap smells like."

"Fuck off," Hollis retorts. "They're better than that girly sex on the beach shit you drink."

"How about we just do shots?" St. James interrupts with her brow arched. "Everyone likes tequila."

When she slides off the barstool to follow Hollis and Wren to the bar, some of my teammates head toward the dance floor. Liam, Ezra, and Brooks walk over to a group of girls clad in short denim shorts and cowgirl boots in the back corner of the room. I stay behind, sipping my water as I take in the bar.

One thing's for absolutely bloody certain, I've never been to a bar like this back in London. I've been to countless pubs and clubs, but this is something different entirely. The entire room is rustic, with various types of wood scattered around the room. Dark panels of unfinished planks line the walls, mismatched tables with peeling paint are paired with rusty barstools, and on a large dance floor in the middle of the room people line dance to old country songs. I didn't even know what bloody line dancing *was* until St. James explained it to me.

This is not exactly my scene, especially the new version of myself I'm trying to maintain, but it's been entertaining seeing the guys interact outside of the pitch.

Maybe even slightly...fun.

Fitz appears on my left and flops down onto the empty barstool, bringing his beer to his lips and taking a long pull. "Now this is the kind of team bonding I can get behind."

"Yeah, same. I'm okay with never getting that close to your balls again," I retort with a laugh. "Any of your balls actually."

"Cheers to that."

He taps the beer bottle against my water and we both take a sip, sitting in comfortable silence before he says, "The team's coming around, you know? It feels like we're making progress. I even heard Brooks commenting on the try you made the other day. Said it was one of the most clean, quick tackles that he's seen in a long time. He probably won't admit it, but still."

Damn. Now that's a fucking surprise.

Sure, shit isn't as tense as it was when I first got here, but I've had no expectation that the two of us would end up being friends, or anything close to that. I'll take teammates who can work together though. That's more than enough for me.

"I'm trying, mate. And I'm not going to give up. Not going to let you all down," I respond, my voice low.

I feel the weight of his palm on my shoulder as he claps it. "I know, man. It shows. I see it. The guys see it. Coach sees it. We'll make it happen. As a team, we're stronger together."

Before I can even respond, the rest of the guys come barreling back toward the table, St. James on their heels.

Wren shrugs out of his Prescott hoodie, tossing it onto the barstool. "I'm going to ride that fucking bull." Fitz shakes his head, unable to get a word in before Wren adds, "Rory bet me a hundred bucks I couldn't last eight seconds, and I told her I want two dozen cookies if I last *thirty*."

These fucking cookies must have magical goddamn powers as much as I hear them talked about.

I turn my head and let my gaze roam over Rory. Her cheeks are tinted pink from the alcohol, her long, dark silky hair is down, the ends curling near her waist. She's wearing a plain white T-shirt and a pair of tight jeans that are molded to her curves, along with a pair of brown cowboy boots that she's tucked the bottom into. I allow myself only a few seconds of drinking her in. She's a luxury I can't afford. Especially after the other night in her apartment and that goddamn contraption of a dress that I had to cut off her.

Every inch of her smooth, supple curves is branded into my memory like a hot fucking iron.

I haven't stopped replaying that night in my head over and over. Even though I shouldn't be picturing her wearing what was left of those tattered scraps of leather, I've been unable to focus on anything else.

And now it's like since that's happened, I'm hyperaware of *everything* about her. Noticing all the things I never allowed myself to before that night. The freckle on her collarbone that I want to press my lips to, or the swell of her breast that needs to be traced with my tongue. Those plump, pink lips, a pale and rosy color I imagine would be the same shade as her pretty little nipples.

"Cillian?"

My fingers tighten around the plastic bottle in my hand until it crumples under the pressure when her velvet voice breaks through my thoughts, catching me off guard.

She's perched on top of the old rusty barstool on my other side, a tipsy tilt to her lips. "I'm having so much fun. Come dance with me, pleeeease." When my brow curves upward, and I stay rooted in my seat, she groans. "C'mon. You can't just...*sit* here all night by yourself."

Before I can tell her that I absolutely am not going to bloody dance, that I don't dance, she's curving her small hand around mine, her soft skin pressed along my rough, calloused palm as she slides off the barstool and tugs me along with her.

The bar is packed, the music loud and thrumming steadily from the speakers while she drags me through the bar, pushing her way past the crowd toward the dance floor. The line dancing music from earlier is gone, replaced with something slower, the base heavy as the raspy singer croons something about wanting his girl in the worst way.

Tell me about it, mate.

All the lights have been dimmed, leaving us painted in the glow of neon light.

"God, Cillian, I love this song. It's so good," she murmurs, her hips swaying to the sultry beat as her eyes flutter shut and her arms lift above her head. I watch her for longer than I should, but I can't take my eyes off her. No matter how much I know that I *should*.

I'm fucking enraptured seeing her this way. Carefree and uninhibited.

Her teeth capture that plush bottom lip, pulling it into her mouth, and somehow she ends up in front of me, her back molded to my front. Despite every bit of better judgment I possess, my hand finds the shallow dip of her waist, palm curving around it, holding her there, pulling her even tighter against me. With every subtle shift of her hips, her ass moves against me and I can feel my dick starting to harden in my pants. My fingers tighten on the soft flesh of her hips.

Rory St. James has me under some type of spell and she hasn't a fucking clue. I don't think I did either until recently.

My skin feels hot, my blood simmering into a slow, rolling boil in my veins at the feel of her against me. At the sweet smell of her bodywash. It makes me wonder if her skin would taste as sweet, and something tells me that it would be even better.

Thank fuck the song ends a beat later because it's the excuse I needed to step back, putting space between us before we both do something we can't come back from.

My gaze flits around the semidarkened room, making sure no one was watching us dancing. If someone on the team saw us like that... Shit, I don't know what would happen. There's got to be an unspoken rule about staying away from your coach's daughter, especially when you're in the position I'm in.

Rory whips to face me, her warm eyes glassy from the alcohol. "That was fun."

I don't entirely trust myself to speak, so I just nod, rolling my lips together as I force down a swallow.

Not that she's in the least bit fazed at my inability to speak;

she's used to my selective conversation, so we walk side by side back to the table in silence. As I'm taking my seat, I watch her slip back onto the barstool, eyes pinned to the inflatable area where the mechanical bull is set up.

Cupping her hands around her mouth she yells, "Let's go, Wrennnnnyyyy!"

She's so bloody cute I want to kiss the fuck out of her.

And that thought is just as terrifying as losing my spot on the team is.

"Oh! Guess what? I forgot to tell you!" Her voice lifts a pitch in excitement.

"What?"

Lifting her hand between us, she turns her palm my way, wiggling her fingers. "Look."

There's a bit of black smudged ink scrawled messily across her palm.

"Did you get into a row with a permanent marker?"

Her head shakes as a laugh tumbles free from her lips. "Nope. This is a number. I got a number from a *guy*, Cillian!"

The weight of her words hits me unexpectedly, stirring up something foreign inside me.

"Bloody hell, way to go, St. James." My response is short, so I tack on a small smile. "I knew that you could." I'm not surprised it's happened. This is exactly what we've been working toward.

Only I never gave much thought about what would happen outside the lessons. About what would happen once she no longer needed me. It means we won't hang out anymore, eat dinner together, spend time in her apartment. Shit, I'm realizing how much I'd hate that.

If anything in the last several weeks, Rory's become my only friend at Prescott. The only person I really spend time with outside of Aisling.

And I don't want that to end.

I don't want to no longer be needed by Rory because then that means I lose this.

Lose... her.

Holy fuck.

My head is a jumbled mess of shit, and the realization hits me with the same weight a tackle on the pitch would, nearly stealing my breath.

I think I *like* Rory St. James.

"Aren't you proud of me?" She bounces in her seat. "He even asked me if I wanted to hang out. Like... *together.*"

The base of my throat feels tight as I nod, carving out a smile. "Of course I'm proud of you. You're ready to date then."

"Um, no, I don't think so. Not yet. I mean after he asked that, I just kind of squeaked and ran away because I was freaking out. Maybe a trial run first."

"All right then, let's go on a fake date. Put everything you've learned to the test." I shrug, hiding the fact that I hate her being successful in getting another bloke's number. But this is what she's wanted all along. This is what she's worked for. I should be happier for her. "Then you'll know if you're ready. This is the final exam, St. James."

CHAPTER 16

♡

Rory

"Happy Valentine's Day, sweetheart," Dad says, handing me a red heart-shaped box of my favorite chocolate truffles and a fluffy, oversized teddy bear that's nearly as big as I am.

I smile, stroking my fingers over the soft fur of the teddy bear. "Thanks, Dad."

Our annual Valentine's dinner is tradition, and thankfully it means that the girl who's hopeless at relationships doesn't have to spend the day alone. But as much as I love our traditions, I truly want him to find someone to share his life with. He deserves it, more than anyone, especially after what my mom put him through.

Imagine being barely a kid yourself and becoming a single dad to a toddler because your wife decides that she isn't ready to be a mother.

Ever since then, it's just been the two of us, and I love being a daddy's girl. I love that we have such a close relationship, and he wants to spend time together.

"But you do know that you don't have to spend your Valentine's Day with me every year, right?" I say as I place the chocolate and teddy bear next to me on his kitchen island, then hop up onto the granite countertop, watching as he walks over to the stove and turns the burner on. "I'm totally fine alone, sitting on my couch watching TV and eating a gallon of ice cream. Enjoying my new apartment."

He whistles, eyes widening. "A gallon, Ror? Seems like a lot of sugar at once." When I roll my eyes and cross my arms over my chest, biting back a smirk, he shrugs. "You know there's no one else I'd rather spend time with than my favorite girl. Plus, it's tradition."

And what he really means is that he's too afraid to put himself back out there and start dating again even though I'm in college and no longer live at home.

"I love our Valentine's dinner. But..." I trail off.

"But what?"

"But...I think you need to put yourself back in the dating game. Meet someone. Get out of the house and have fun."

Maybe I'm projecting a little bit about my own life, you know since I've officially secured a phone number and these lessons from Cillian are actually making a difference.

It feels good. And I just want the same thing for him.

Dad shakes his head and tears his gaze away, avoiding the topic as usual and busying himself with mixing the pancake batter in a bowl. "And the last time we talked about this we said that my daughter wasn't going to play matchmaker and would stay out of my dating life, remember?"

I let out a long sigh. That's indeed what we said, but I'm nothing if not persistent. "Fine. But for the record, I think that you should. No risk, no reward, remember?" I repeat the saying he's told me since I was a kid, and he eyes me for a moment before going back to the mixing.

The only thing I want is for him to be happy. That's what matters to me, and I just think he's a little...lonely is all. Even if he doesn't want to date, meeting new people outside of Prescott would be good for him.

If I can do it, then I know he can.

"Anyways, tell me about your week. How are your classes going?" he asks, pouring a round circle of batter into the pan. Our Valentine's Day dinner tradition has always been pancakes and bacon. Then we watch our favorite movie together, and I usually fall asleep before it's halfway through. Sometimes we switch it up and watch *Fool's Gold* instead. You know, just to be spontaneous.

Only this day is slightly different because I'm distracted by thoughts of Cillian, and I know that's the last person I should be thinking of. But I haven't stopped thinking about him since the whole dress fiasco and the bar the other night.

Even though I've tried. An exorbitant amount of times.

I keep thinking about the way his fingers felt along my heated skin, or the way my heart seemed to beat out of my chest when I stood so close to him.

How his thick, dark lashes kissed his cheeks before he dragged his gaze up to mine, his pupils blown and darkened with what felt like lust.

How, in my slightly drunken haze, I moved against him. I thought I felt him hard and pressing against me as we danced, but I'd had a lot to drink.

These thoughts were all-consuming and...confusing.

Things feel different somehow, but I'm probably just reading too much into it because Cillian being *actually* interested in me would be crazy.

Right?

Which is exactly why I've been trying to think about anything other than the bad boy who's supposed to be teaching me to flirt with other guys, not making me wet with that delicious English accent.

"Rory?" Dad's voice causes me to jolt, and my fingers tighten around the edge of the counter.

"Sorry, what did you say?" I respond after clearing my throat.

He's got three steaming pancakes finished on the plate, and I somehow blanked during that entire time thinking about Cillian.

"I said what have you been up to? Feels like it's been a few days since we talked."

Oh.

My cheeks still feel warm as I nod. "Yeah, just school and studying, the normal. I heard that the guys may be warming up to Cillian some? How is that going?"

He shrugs, flipping another pancake and exhaling. "Might be turning a corner, but it's still a little early to tell. They seem to be working better on the pitch together, and I've seen a few conversations happening. Fitz and Wren seem to be offering some support."

I witnessed that firsthand at the bar, and I could've kissed them both for it.

I knew that they wouldn't be the ones to continue to ice Cillian out, especially after I asked Fitz to make an effort. I'm just hoping and praying that we keep moving in the right direction.

It's all part of my brilliant plan. A little bit of luck and a whole lot of strategy. Just like playing the game.

"Yeah, I do think there's a whole lot less hostility between them, at least from what I'm seeing on the pitch? I think that it'll all work out, Dad. I mean we knew that things would be tense for a while as the guys adjusted; it's just taking a little longer than we planned, that's all."

My phone vibrates in the back pocket of my cutoffs, and I pull it out, swiping my finger across the screen to open the text notification.

Cillian: Time for your final exam.

Shit.
Now?
I tap a quick response.

Rory: You realize what today is, right?

Cillian: Yep. What better way to celebrate than a date?

Rory: A fake one you mean.

Cillian: Of course.

Cillian: You down or no?

I chew my bottom lip, my gaze lingering on the screen.

"Everything okay?" Dad asks, and I look up to see him observing me with a spatula in hand, brow lifted.

I nod. "Yes. Actually...would it be okay if I maybe...took a rain check on dinner? There's uh...I have a friend who wants to hang out tonight. I know it's our tradition, and I don't wan—"

"Of course, it's okay, Ror. Go, enjoy your night. Your old man will be fine. You're only young and in college once." He smiles, the corners of his eyes crinkling. "Do I know this friend?"

Yes.

But for the first time in as long as I can remember, I lie to him. Because telling my dad about Cillian is only going to complicate an already complicated mess when it comes to the team. "Nope. Just...someone I know from class," I say as I hop down from the counter and quickly respond to Cillian's message.

Rory: I'm down.

Cillian: Meet me at Ivy & Ale in an hour.

CHAPTER 17

♡

Rory

I spot Cillian as soon as I walk into the bar and grill, sitting at a table in the far back wearing a black long-sleeved shirt with the sleeves pushed to his elbows and the intricate tattoos on his forearms on full display.

It's truly absurd how hot those tattoos make him.

Not that he wasn't already hot, but there's just something about the dark ink that seems to make him more intimidating, more intense. It makes something in my lower stomach clench.

He glances up from his phone when I pull the chair out across from him and sink into it.

The corner of his lip curves into a lazy grin when he greets me. "St. James."

"Cairney."

"Ready to do this?" He leans back against the chair and crosses his thick arms over his chest, those stupid tattoos rippling as he moves.

I shrug. "I think so, but I can't be sure until we try. I tend to fold under pressure, as you know."

A low raspy chuckle rumbles from his chest, and my grin widens.

I honestly thought it might feel a little...awkward? After the whole pretty-much-seeing-me-naked thing. But our rapport doesn't feel any different.

The biggest difference is now I'm extremely aware of how attracted I am to him, and that I'm much more nervous than usual because of that.

The waiter comes by and takes our drink order, and when Cillian orders chips and queso, I stare at him from across the table with my brow lifted.

He ordered my favorite appetizer for me without having to even ask.

"What?" he asks.

"Ordering my favorite food is dangerously *sweet* of you, Cillian Cairney. Better be careful, you wouldn't want to jeopardize the whole broody, dick-ish thing you have going on over there."

My tone is light and teasing, so he rolls his eyes. "Never really been one to worry about my reputation, St. James. Not going to start now. I think I'm probably safe."

Before I can answer, my ice-cold Cherry Coke is dropped off at the table along with what looks like the cheesiest queso I've ever seen in my life, and I swear to God my mouth waters.

I swipe a still-warm tortilla chip from the bowl, dipping it into the cheese and bringing it to my mouth. Flavor explodes on my tongue, and my eyes drop shut as I groan.

"Christ, Rory." Cillian grunts roughly causing my eyes to snap open.

"What?" I ask around a mouthful.

He shakes his head. "I don't know how you make eating a bloody chip sound so sexy."

My eyes almost pop out of my head, widening. I swallow the chip down as I begin to cough, reaching for my Cherry Coke and sucking down a gulp to wash away the food lodged in my throat.

My God.

I can feel my cheeks burning, so I imagine he sees my flush, which is why he's wearing that stupid, hot, shit-eating grin.

"Shut up," I mutter.

He only grins harder.

There's one thing I've realized about Cillian: he's ridiculously handsome even when he's being his normal broody, closed-off self, but when he smiles?

It's *devastating*. To the point of almost pain. I feel an ache settling in my rib cage.

"Okay, back to the fake date, please," I blurt out, trying to steer the conversation away from my embarrassment. "What's the plan?"

Cillian leans in, placing his elbows on the table. "So we've established that your main problem when it comes to talking to someone is that you're nervous, yeah?" When I nod, he continues, "And when you're nervous, you tend to..."

"Ramble," I supply with a wince.

Word vomit. Whatever you want to call it.

"So we're just going to talk, St. James. Let the night go where it goes. No pressure, no expectations, just us," he says simply, his shoulder lifting in a shrug, and I try to keep my gaze away from the fabric of the shirt molded to the thick, corded muscles of his arms.

Obsessing over Cillian's arm porn is not on tonight's agenda.

Preparing me for the very real date that I need to be ready for is.

Focus, Rory.

My brow pinches. "That's it?"

He nods. "Yeah, why not? We've figured out what you do when you're nervous, but now you know how to handle a conversation without needing sports as a clutch. You know to take a breath and figure out exactly what you want to say before you say it. Just follow my cues, go with what feels right. Just like you would if I took you on a date. A real one. Just like you will…" Words trailing off, he swallows roughly before finishing, "With the bloke from the other night. This is just us making sure you're ready. That's all."

Okay, when he puts it that way, it sounds easy. It's just Cillian.

"I'll help you along the way if you need it. Guide you in the right direction. C'mere and sit beside me." He flicks his wrist and beckons me to his side of the table.

I swallow, rising from my chair and pushing it around to his side of the table before sitting back down next to him.

Cillian laughs. "We're not in Sunday Mass, St. James. You don't need to sit that bloody far from me." He reaches beneath the seat and hauls it closer to him with one effortless pull, sliding me across the floor until we're pressed nearly shoulder to shoulder beside each other.

Suddenly, my pulse begins to race.

It's not nerves per se, but… I'm not exactly even sure what it is.

It's like my body is recalling our proximity the past few nights, remembering the feel of his skin brushing against mine. Recalling how good it felt to have his hands on my body, to have his warm breath caressing the shell of my ear as he stepped closer.

"Now, here's what's going to happen. We're going to pretend we're strangers and start from the very beginning. And," he starts, tossing his arm across the back of my chair casually, "no sports talk."

"Like... none?"

His head shakes. "Nope. Not a word. I'm going to ask you things, give you shit to talk about that have nothing to do with sports. Just like any other bloke would."

Right, and what... Mr. Talkative is going to be the one just asking questions, and sitting there with his silent, one-word answers? Yeah, no.

This is the perfect chance to try to get him to open up more, maybe stop keeping me at arm's length.

"Okay, fine, but then that means *I* get to ask *you* questions too. And no grunts or one-word answers as responses. Fair is fair," I say as my brow arches.

For a beat he's quiet, those piercing hazel eyes holding mine in a stare. I know that answering things about himself is just as much out of his comfort zone than a date is out of mine. If not more. I know he's not much for talking about himself or his past in London, which is a huge part of who he is. That much I've learned since he's come to Prescott.

We've been spending a lot of time together lately, and even so, it feels like I've barely scratched the surface of who he is. I want to know more than the little crumbs he's started to give me. I want to know Cillian in more ways than I'm supposed to. I want to know all the little things that make him who he is. The relationship between him and Aisling, if he misses London, or if he's just glad to be away from it all. More about his mom. I want to know what actually happened that made him come to Prescott. What his favorite food is, his favorite band, his biggest fear.

And also...what his lips feel like, or the face he makes when he comes.

But I can't exactly tell him that, so I'll keep that little piece to myself, locked away in my spank bank.

"Okay," he says. "Let's do it. You first."

I rake my lips over my teeth, contemplating a safe place to start.

My stomach starts to do that flipping thing when I'm nervous, and I know that all the questions I want to ask are probably things he's not ready to divulge, and I'm blanking, letting those nerves get the best of me the second he puts me on the spot.

I'm lost in my head when I feel Cillian's fingers grasp my chin, tipping it up. He's staring at me with an intensity that has a flurry of goose bumps erupting on my skin.

"Stop worrying, St. James. There's no pressure. We're just two strangers, getting to know each other," he murmurs. "So, get out of your head. Introduce yourself and ask me a question."

I nod and exhale shakily.

He's right. It's just him.

I can do this. He's the world's biggest mystery, and he's giving me full access right now. This should be the easiest conversation I've ever had.

No pressure. Just like he said.

"Hi, I'm Rory," I say with a smile, extending my hand toward him.

He gives me the same panty-melting smile that I already know he must use on all the girls and slides his warm, rough hand in mine, shaking it gently. I can feel the hard calluses on his palm from all the time he spends training and, honestly, it's so sexy.

I know I probably shouldn't be focusing on his sexiness right now, especially because it's the reason behind the majority of my nerves at this point. But it's impossible not to. His charm is magnetic, and he wields it like a weapon.

When he wants to.

He doesn't immediately drop my hand, letting the handshake linger longer than would normally be acceptable if we were actually strangers.

"Hi, Rory. It's nice to meet you. You look beautiful tonight. I love that sweater."

I swallow as I glance down at the soft, baby-blue cashmere sweater that I picked out for tonight. "Thank you. It's...nice to meet you too."

Cillian smirks, shooting me a playful wink as he drops my hand and sits back in the chair. "How's your night so far?"

Weird. Kind of...exciting?

I don't say any of the things I'm thinking, and instead say, "It's good. Really good. This place has the best food, so I love coming here. I'm a bit of a foodie."

He nods. I swear I can feel the lightest stroke of his finger along the back of my arm, but I'm probably imagining it.

"Yeah, definitely a good place." His voice lowers. "This is the part where you smile and show the lad that you're interested in continuing the conversation. You're in control, but it gives him the opportunity to ramp up the flirting, keep it going. It's the small signals that you need. Let's skip to the questions, you're doing great, St. James."

His instructions give me an odd sense of reassurance, and it helps me relax some.

"What's your major?" I blurt out the first question that comes to mind. Honestly, I can't believe it's something I don't already know about him. It's simple yet hasn't been something I've thought to ask before now.

"Business management."

My brow lifts in surprise. He doesn't at all seem like a business kind of guy.

I open my mouth to say something about his rugby career, then I remember that I've been strictly forbidden from mentioning sports, so I snap it shut.

"What about you?" he adds, leaning in slightly.

"Sports medicine. I've always loved learning about how the body works, especially when it comes to athl—" I stop short, and Cillian chuckles, humor dancing in his irises.

Damnit.

Sports. Yet again.

"You said you were a foodie. What's your favorite?" he asks before I can retreat into my head, and I almost sag with relief.

"That is... an impossible question. I love all food." Laughing, I reach for my Coke and place it back down after taking a sip. My fingers trace the rim of the cup while I try to think of what my favorite food actually is if I had to choose. "Probably chicken nuggets from McDonald's."

"Bloody hell. You Americans and McDonald's." Cillian blanches, the disgust evident on his face. His brow pinches and his nose crinkles like it's the most horrid thing he's ever encountered.

And I nearly lose it. I've never seen someone be so personally offended by a chicken nugget.

I bring my hand to my lips as a giggle slips free. "Hey, no judging. I'm a chicken nugget kinda girl."

He eyes me warily, still shaking his head, but his lips twitch in amusement. "Out of all the foods, you choose fake chicken. Sorry, love, but I'm judging you for that. What do you like to do for fun? A hobby?"

"I don't even want to tell you because you're just going to judge me again!" I laugh.

He leans closer as he says, "I promise I won't judge you. Tell me."

I don't believe him in the least, but whatever. "I like to... cross-stitch."

"Fascinating. You really struck me as more of a crochet type of girl," Cillian murmurs with the most serious expression I've ever seen him wear.

I almost believe he truly thought that until his lips split in a smile that meets his eyes, crinkling them slightly in the corners. For a guy who tackles other guys on a regular basis, he has a flawless smile. Perfect teeth. Blindingly bright and straight.

His laugh settles around me, the low timbre making my belly tighten with something like arousal.

God, am I turned on right now from his... laugh? It's easily becoming one of my favorite sounds.

"Stop laughing at me, Cillian! I told you that you'd judge me. You shouldn't talk shit until you've tried it," I say defensively. "It's relaxing and a way to turn my brain off when I need a breather."

"Not judging you, St. James. It's cute." His lip quirks.

"Mm-hmm," I hum, lifting my drink and taking a sip from the straw.

That's when it hits me. We've been going back and forth for a while now, and his teasing and playfulness have kept me completely out of my head. Every time I retreated, he simply pivoted, pulling me right back out before I could stress about it.

Yet again, I realize how effortless it is to talk to Cillian. To laugh with him and talk about things that normally would make me freeze up around someone else. He doesn't make me feel like I'm not meeting expectations, or like I have to be worried that I'm going to say something stupid. Because even if I did, he wouldn't run in the opposite direction. Fake date or not. And despite my...growing attraction for him, I am able to have a conversation without rambling or going off on an awkward tangent.

"Wanna go play pool for a bit?" Cillian nods toward the tables tucked in the back of the bar that are currently unused.

Hesitating, I admit, "Uh...actually, I don't know how? I've never played before."

"Add it to the list of things I'm teaching you, St. James. C'mon. I used to play a lot back in London at the pub by my flat." His sneaker-clad feet hit the floor as he slides out of the chair and offers me his hand, gently pulling me up from mine. "Actually, my...mum, she uh...was the one who taught me to play."

I can tell by each tight syllable it was hard for him to tell me that. Every time he's mentioned his mom to me, a pained look passes over his face, his jaw tightening, his throat pushing down a swallow.

Placing my hand on his arm, I say, "Teach me."

After a quick rundown of the rules and how to win, Cillian thrusts a pool cue in my direction, instructing me to break. I've got beginner's luck in my favor.

"Do you miss it? Home, I mean. London."

There's a beat of silence hanging in the air between us before he says, "Sometimes. I miss the familiarity, our old flat. Going to Borough Market on Saturdays with Mum and Ais. Going to watch London Irish with the boys and the occasional England match at Twickenham if we were lucky. Shit, and I miss Greggs. Sausage rolls." He clarifies when the space between my brow furrows in confusion. "Bloody hell, what I would do for Greggs right now."

It's the first real peek into his life he's given me, and I selfishly want to hoard this side of him all to myself.

"Sounds amazing. I want to visit London one day; it's on my very long bucket list." I give him a smile as I bend, placing the tip of the cue stick near the bottom of the rack. This is going to be terrible because I have quite literally never done it before, but whatever.

"You should. Europe is an amazing place, to live, to visit."

When I pull my arm back to shoot, the tip blows past the balls, missing them entirely, and I can hear the low chuckle from Cillian behind me.

"Like this," he murmurs, and then I feel the heat of his hard body behind me, his breath causing the hairs on the back of my neck to rise and send my heart into overdrive.

His palm covers mine on the pool cue, and then he's bending me slightly farther, lining the tip up with the rack. His fingers are strong and warm against my skin. My breath stutters as my pulse begins ricocheting inside me.

God, he's so close that I'm having a hard time focusing on anything but him.

"Rory?"

I twist to face him, and now we're so close that I can practically count the constellation of light freckles that are scattered along the bridge of his nose.

His dark, thick lashes fan out along his cheeks as his gaze drops to my lips and lingers there, as if he's thinking of... kissing me, or *something*.

"You have the most beautiful eyes," he breathes quietly as he lifts his gaze back to mine. "And I really fucking want to kiss you."

I swallow. "Y-you do?"

He nods. "Fuck yeah, I do."

Holy shit. I mean... is this even fake right now?

Because this doesn't feel like pretend. I am pretty sure that my panties are soaked, and I'm going to pass out any second in this stupid bar from how hard my heart is pounding in my chest.

The song changes around us, suddenly an octave louder, the heavy bass causing the glasses on the table behind us to clink together loudly.

And only then am I able to pull myself together long enough to form a real thought.

When I open my mouth to speak, a wide smile flits to his face and he steps back, arching a brow. "A plus, St. James."

I blink, trying to clear the lusty haze from my head.

I nearly groan.

"That's it?"

He nods again. "Yeah, and you aced it. See? You took everything you learned and look what happened."

"Yeah, uh...yeah," I say, tearing my gaze away as I set the pool cue against the table. I can't believe I just got so caught up in that performance.

I realize it was an act, a moment in character, but it truly felt like something different.

And also just how badly I wanted it to be real.

Just how much I wanted him to kiss me too.

CHAPTER 18

Cillian

I've made a lot of stupid decisions in the last few years. More than I can even count at this point. Probably has a lot to do with the amount of hits I've taken to the head since I was a kid.

But *this*?

It might just be the most stupid of them all.

Bloody hell, I know better. I fucking *know*, and still I can't stop.

I don't want to stop.

I want to give in, fucking finally, and have my fill of the girl who's been plaguing my dreams every night.

My gaze slides over Rory, drinking in her still-wet hair, which is hanging around her shoulders after her shower, to the baggy maroon sweatshirt she has on and down to those tiny fucking shorts I'm convinced she wears just to torture me, all the way to the expanse of creamy, silky skin of her bare thighs.

I'm fucked.

Why?

Because I want Rory St. James. Preferably on her knees while those plump pink lips circle my cock, my hands fisted in her hair as she takes me down her throat. Or spread out on this couch, dark hair haloed around her while I drag my tongue up her soaked cunt until she comes, coating my face. Or even on her knees while I take her from behind, fucking her so goddamn deep that I can see the imprint of my cock in her stomach.

And I know wanting her, wanting all those things, is going to complicate everything.

I'm beyond bloody aware of that.

Only it doesn't seem to change the fact that the second I'm around her, I want to touch her. Kiss her. Taste her. Do everything that I've been thinking about for the past week without coming up for air.

Just like I almost did two nights ago when I had to play my feelings off like it was a fucking test and not me being weak and almost giving in to this insane need.

Fake date or not... it was one of the best nights I've had in a long time. It was fun being with her, and it would've been the perfect end to a perfect night if I just could've bloody kissed her as badly as I wanted to.

It feels like Rory is the only person who sees me just as clearly as I see her. She doesn't judge my past or throw it on my face. She doesn't make me feel like I'll only ever be the reputation that I'm desperately trying to leave behind.

"Okay, sooo, what are we starting with?" She huffs as she flops down beside me onto the couch, crossing her legs and resting the bowl of popcorn in her lap. "Something juicy?"

I clear my throat like I wasn't just having a fucking daydream about having her beneath me and pull my phone out of the pocket of my sweatpants. I find Aisling's message with the list of romance movies.

Never in my life did I think I'd be watching one by choice, but Rory thought it would be good for her to watch and learn—see people falling in love. In lust. In action. What better than a romance?

Even if it's *just* a movie.

"I've got no clue what any of these are, so I guess we'll just go with the first one," I say as I lock my phone and set it down on the couch beside me.

"Perfect. Popcorn?" She extends the bowl toward me.

I shake my head. "I'm good. Thanks."

What I really want to say is I'm having a hard time focusing now that she's sitting so close and I can smell the sweet floral scent of her bodywash, and it makes my dick ache.

Clearly, there's a pattern here.

But I don't, and I keep my gaze glued to the tube, feigning interest in the bloody rom-com because the alternative isn't happening.

The story isn't bad, and the acting is decent enough that I somehow end up slightly interested in what's going to happen. When the couple on the screen collides in a frantic, desperate kind of kiss, I feel Rory shifting on the cushion beside me, a few breathy sighs tumbling from her lips as the scene progresses. The heat of her bare skin blazing through my joggers, making my body run hot.

"I've been thinking... What happens if I ever make it past the flirting? Uh... the other night, you pretending you wanted to kiss me, it made me think about the *after*," she murmurs, and I whip my head to the side to look at her.

Her lips are parted, the tip of her finger tracing her bottom lip as she tears her gaze from the TV and looks at me. My eyes drop to the pattern her finger traces on her plump lip, unable to stop myself before raising them to meet her gaze. "What do you mean?"

She shrugs. "I mean, I'm practicing to be better at flirting and getting out of the friend zone, but what happens when I *actually* make it past that? How am I going to, you know...be great at kissing, or any of the stuff that comes once I actually get a guy?"

Before I can even respond, she's turning, angling her body toward me and capturing her lip between her teeth. There's a nervous edge to her words. "I've only had one sloppy, drunken hookup in high school that was absolutely the biggest letdown of my life, and so I'm just saying...I don't have much to go on. If my previous experience was anything to judge by."

"You just kind of know what to do, St. James. There's not a manual or a class to take on how to kiss properly," I say with a slight hitch of my shoulder at the same time I reach up and rub my palm across my mouth. For fuck's sake, hearing her admit all this is doing nothing for my desire to touch her. "It's the kind of thing you have to be in the moment for, letting instinct take over."

A shuddering exhale slips past her lips, then she looks back at the TV, watching the couple on the screen make a go of it. The bloke has the female love interest pressed against the shower wall as he fucks her, tracing his tongue along her neck while she whimpers and writhes against the tile.

When I glance back at Rory, her cheeks are stained bright pink, and her lips are parted as she watches. She's completely flushed.

"I just...I want *that*," she murmurs, not taking her eyes off the screen. "All of it. I want to get my brains fucked out against a shower wall while a guy looks at me just like that. Like I'm the hottest thing he's ever freaking seen."

Fucking hell.

I wet my lips, then I force down a swallow, nearly bloody *sweating* at her statement. My hands tighten into fists at my sides with the overwhelming need to reach for her.

To give her exactly what she wants.

She turns to look at me, and those rich chocolate eyes are molten, burning hotter than I've ever seen them before. "I think maybe that's what I need to do. You know just...practice"—her gaze flicks to the TV for a beat, then back—"*that*."

"Then...practice with *me*." The words come flying out of my mouth before I can even bloody think about exactly what I'm offering.

I'm out of my goddamn mind, and I should get the fuck up and walk away right now, if I knew what was good for me.

But fucking hell, I want to kiss her.

Until her lips are swollen and bruised. Until she's squirming beneath me, pressing her thighs together and begging me to touch her.

I *need* to kiss her. I'm so bloody fucking tired of denying it.

I watch her throat bob, her gaze never moving from mine as she nods, her shoulder dipping. "Yeah, totally. I mean, that would be the easy thing to do, right? You're already teaching me, and it would prepare me for when the time comes."

I don't even want to fucking think about her kissing someone else. Fuck that.

My chin lifts anyway, saying nothing as I let my gaze drop to her parted lips, lingering there.

I've never seen prettier lips in my life.

"I can teach you whatever you want to learn, St. James."

When she licks her lips, the tip of her tongue darting out to wet them before sinking her teeth into her lower lip, it's like something snaps within me, and I'm closing the distance between us. She leans forward at the same time, making us collide.

My lips slam against hers and she whimpers, the sweetest fucking sound that's a mixture of surprise and need, and I decide I'll do whatever the fuck it takes to hear it again.

Over and over.

I don't give myself the chance to second-guess the decision, or to worry about what the consequences may be.

Fuck it. Fuck the consequences. Fuck anything besides this. Right now.

My hands slide into her still-damp hair, curving around her nape as I tug her closer, angling her mouth to deepen the kiss when she scrambles into my lap, thighs fitted around each side of my hips. Her lips part, and my tongue sweeps inside as her hands snake around my neck, tugging roughly at my hair. The needy little sounds she makes shoot straight to my cock, making me so bloody hard it aches.

Christ, when's the last time I was so turned on by a fucking *kiss*?

I can't recall a time when I was this keyed up over something so simple.

Yet with her... it doesn't feel simple.

It feels like we're teetering on the edge of something. Something bigger than either of us imagined.

Her hips roll over my erection, and I groan against her mouth, my teeth grazing her plump lip. I'm about to slip my hand beneath her shirt when my phone goes off in my pocket. The obnoxious ringtone makes my teeth grit.

"Fuck," I mutter, tearing my lips from Rory's. She hovers above me, staring down at me with blown pupils and swollen lips that send a surge of possessiveness coursing through me.

I did that.

For a moment we just stare at each other, a heated exchange of shared pants. We stay like that, savoring the seconds that seem to drag by.

She looks like she's had the fuck kissed out of her, and if it wasn't for my ringing phone, I would keep going until the rest of her was marked by my lips.

"It's my sister. I'm sorry," I say as I reach between us and fish my phone out of my pocket. I know who it is because no one else calls me. It's not like I've made a bunch of friends since arriving at Prescott.

"No, of course."

Rory's lip curves into a shy smile, and I nod, swiping my finger across the screen to answer the call.

"Ais, everything good?"

My eyes remain on Rory still perched in my lap, and when she sits back on my thighs, brushing across my still hard, aching cock, I suck in a hiss.

"Sorry," she mouths, wearing a grin that shows she's not the least bit sorry for torturing me while I'm on the phone with my bloody sister.

I narrow my eyes at her.

Brat.

"Yes. I was just wondering if you could possibly pick up some migraine medicine? My head's been pounding for hours, and I still have this physics essay to finish."

I pull the phone back to glance at the time and see that it's after midnight.

I wish she would stop staying up half the night to work on homework, but that's Aisling. She's terrified of falling behind or getting a bad mark in anything.

"Ais, it's late. Shelf it till tomorrow, yeah? I'll stop by the convenience store on my way home and grab something. Be there soon."

She lets out a relieved sigh. "Thanks, Kill. Love you."

"Love you too."

When I press end and drop my phone next to me, Rory's already sliding off my lap and back onto the space beside me on the couch.

"I guess you probably need to go?"

"Yeah, I need to get that medicine to her." Even if there's nothing I'd rather do than stay right here, I have responsibilities. Aisling needs me.

I stand from the couch and tuck my phone back into my pocket, watching as she stands and adjusts her slightly askew sweatshirt.

"I'll text you?"

She nods, giving me a small smile. "Yeah, of course. I hope she feels better soon."

I feel like an asshole for having to stop what just happened, intentional or not, but I think it was probably for the best.

I lost my head tonight, something I apparently tend to do when I'm around her.

It doesn't feel like a mistake, but this can't happen again.

No matter how much I want it to.

CHAPTER 19

Rory

It was just a kiss.

A heat-of-the-moment kiss.

Just another lesson.

Absentmindedly, I trace my fingers along my lips, recalling the way Cillian's tongue followed the same route, and desire begins to pool in my lower stomach.

It's been days since the movie night, and I'm *still* thinking about it. *Cillian's* all I can think about.

And I've discovered two things since that night.

Number one, and probably most important, is that kissing Cillian made me realize that I'm not sure if I even *want* to... date anyone or even meet anyone anymore.

Second is that I am, without a doubt, into him, and *not* just as friends.

Tonight will be the first time we've really seen each other outside of the pitch since that kiss happened, and honestly, I'm nervous.

But mostly I'm thinking about how badly I want to do it *again*.

And again.... And again.

My God, kissing Cillian was an out-of-body experience. The way he kissed, slow and explorative, is exactly the way I imagine he...fucks.

I know we probably shouldn't do it again. Because of the team, and my dad, and that it will undoubtedly complicate things, but I also think I don't really care.

Because I loved the way I felt when his hands glided down the curve of my waist and the sounds he made deep in the back of his throat when my teeth raked along his bottom lip.

I want more.

More than just the hottest kiss of my life.

I want *him*.

The familiar rumble of his bike as he pulls into my complex parking lot has me jumping up from the couch and sprinting to the entryway. I grab my jacket off the hook and slip my arms into it. It's a soft black leather and makes me feel like a total bad bitch. I saw an ad for it online and thought it would be perfect the next time I rode on the back of Cillian's bike.

When I swing my front door open, he's standing on the doorstep, fist lifted mid-knock, and the sight of him makes me nearly breathless. He looks stupidly hot in a navy long-sleeved henley and dark-wash jeans, the fabric molded to all the sharp planes of his muscled thighs. The dark strands of his hair are still damp from a shower, the ends curling at his nape.

Jesus.

Is he always this attractive, or is it just because now I know how talented his mouth is?

"Hi," I murmur, a shy smile flitting to my lips.

His dark hazel eyes drop to my outfit and his brow lifts as the corner of his lips tugs up in a slight smirk. "That new?"

"It is. What do you think?" I do a little spin, giving him a full view. I'm wearing a new pair of jeans that are so tight they're practically a second skin, with a deep burgundy sweater and a pair of short combat boots.

Not at all something I'm used to wearing, but I'm pushing myself to step out of my comfort zone. Try new things and see what I like.

And this outfit makes me feel *hot*.

"You look good," he says as I shut the front door and lock it before turning back to him. "Ready for your next lesson?"

Is he asking if I want to kiss him again, because the answer to that is yes.

"I thought since that dickhead that gave you his number the other day ghosted you, we'd go to the bar and keep practicing on putting yourself out there, even if it doesn't work out," he adds with a serious expression.

What?

So... he's just going to not acknowledge that... we kissed?

Oh my God.

Have I really spent the last few days obsessing over this stupid kiss when he's not even interested in it happening again?

My stomach plummets and a sharp pang of disappointment shoots down my spine.

Embarrassment washes over me in a torrential wave.

Of course I thought... I don't know what I thought. I thought after the last couple of weeks and finally that kiss, that he was interested in me.

But why would he when I'm *me*? It's the same torturous history repeating itself, and I was foolish to think Cillian would ever want me the way I want him.

The girl who's only ever had a handful of sloppy kisses who has absolutely no clue what she's doing.

Why would he want that when he could have any of his fan club with a single effortless smile? I've already seen that much.

"Uh…sure, yeah. Sounds great," I respond, pasting on a bright unaffected smile when I feel anything but. We make it to his bike, and I take the helmet from him, sliding it over my head without his help.

Fine. If that's the way he feels then okay. *Perfect.*

I tamp down the sinking feeling and the hurt. He's not even going to *acknowledge* what happened between us. He still wants me to go and find another guy.

If he wants me to go find someone else, then so be it.

* * *

My hurt has morphed into something much bigger as we walk into the packed bar on the outskirts of town and slide into an empty booth.

The air between Cillian and me is unbearably tense, and I hate that it's the result of a kiss I enjoyed more than I should have. A deep exhale rushes past my lips as I sit back in the booth.

I spent the entire ride here with the hurt and disappointment colliding together in my head and leaving me frustrated but determined to show Cillian just how capable I am.

I'm not at all interested in finding another guy. Not when

the one I want is sitting right across from me in this stupid, run-down bar.

But I'm going to do exactly as he wants: find someone else.

Even if it's just to show him that I can and that I'm not hurt by his rejection. Even if it makes my stomach and heart ache just the same. I'm going to put on a fake, saccharine smile and pretend that I'm not affected at all.

Cillian glances around the bar, his eyes raking over the patrons as he settles back into the booth and places his large, ink-stained hands on the top of the table.

Completely unaffected.

"What about him?" He jerks his head toward a guy leaning against the bar watching the hockey game on the big screen. He's around six feet tall, lanky, with black curly hair and really, really tan. The guy must live outside or in a tanning bed. Jeez.

He reminds me of one of the guys off *Jersey Shore*.

While this guy is cute, sure, there's no doubt that Cillian is the hottest guy here. Which makes me more annoyed with him.

Part of me wants to throttle him as much as I still want to kiss him.

And now I'm even more annoyed.

"Yeah... I mean, are you sure about him?"

His dark brow arches. "What's wrong with him?"

I narrow my gaze at him. "Nothing's *wrong* with him. I'm just making sure that he's the right one."

Besides the fact that he's the color of an orange from the amount of fake tan he's wearing.

Whatever.

"The only way to find out is if you"—he gestures to the guy

once more, pointing a long, thick finger in his direction—"go talk to that lad."

Sighing, I shrug, then cross my arms over my chest. "Fine."

"Let's see it then."

With one last dramatic, drawn-out sigh, I slide out of the booth and walk over to the guy by the bar.

He doesn't seem to notice as I walk up, his gaze zeroed in on the hockey game as he sips a dark amber beer from a glass.

"Uh, hi!" I say a little too loudly, causing him to jump. He looks over at me, dragging his eyes down my body in a slow, pervy way that's not at all gentlemanly. Completely unattractive behavior.

Great, add that to the list of things I'm already checking off about him.

"Hi," he finally says when he's done eyeballing me. "What's up?"

I smile before pulling my lip between my teeth. "Not much, just you know, enjoying a night out." I laugh, but it sounds a bit manic, so I clear my throat and spit out the first thing I can think of. "Are you a big hockey fan?"

He nods, smirking. "Yeah, what gave it away?" When he gestures down at the hockey jersey he's wearing, I laugh again and shrug.

"Mmm, yeah, that was it. I'm not much of a hockey fan, but I really love Jean Béliveau. He was such an incredible player. Did you know he won the most Stanley Cups in history? Like, wow, what a fucking flex, you know? Not many other players can say that an—" Abruptly, I shut up when I realize that I'm once again rambling about sports and the guy standing next to me is looking at me as if I've grown two heads. "Sorry, I uh...really love sports."

"Yeah, I can see that. That's pretty rare. Most women don't

understand sports even if I give them a play by play," he says, bringing the beer to his lips and taking a sip. The white foam coats the top of his lip, and he reaches up and wipes it away with the back of his hand.

Okay, gross. Ick.

All-around no. Absolutely the hell not.

I steal a glance at the table where Cillian's sitting and see him watching us. He lifts a brow when he sees me staring, so I give him an eye roll and then turn my attention back to the hockey bro.

Who is becoming increasingly more unattractive by the second.

There is literally nothing, and I mean nothing, I hate more than a man who thinks that women don't have a place in sports. That our brains are just too small to comprehend what's happening when in actuality, they're the ones with small brains. And little dicks. So jokes on them.

"You know who I love? Matthew Everett. He's been such an advocate for women's sports, and I really admire how much he believes in women. You know, we rule the world." I laugh, batting my eyelashes at hockey bro. He blinks, the sarcasm going right over his head.

"That dude's the worst player in the NHL. Straight trash. You're telling me that's your favorite player?" God, this guy is a prick. And he has broccoli in his teeth, and you know what? I'm not saying shit.

I scoff. "False. He had one of the best assists of the entire season last year, or did you miss that?"

"Yeah, when he wasn't suspended. Sure, he had a good play. One. Of the entire season an—" He keeps rambling, but I've tuned him out because I can't do this.

Not even to prove a point. Gross.

I turn and walk away mid-conversation, making a beeline back to Cillian, who's staring at me with an unreadable expression on his face.

"It's a no," I say as I slide back into the booth, trying to erase the fact that I just spent the last fifteen minutes arguing with a guy who has the mental capacity of a toddler.

"Were you... arguing?"

My smile is dripping with sweetness as I say, "Of course not. We were just having a creative discussion. That guy is going to make some woman very happy one day but she's not me. He's not my type." When I'm done, he stays silent, his jaw working.

"Guess that means you've got to keep trying then," he finally says with a shrug, eyes flaring with something. Something that I wish I could read in the dim light of this bar. "The St. James I know isn't a quitter."

I resist the urge to roll my eyes and instead give him another bright, blinding smile. "Yeah, you're right. But *I* think this time I should be the one to pick the guy. Because you're one and oh tonight, Cairney. I think I'm starting to get a pretty good read on the kinda guy I'm interested in. One who can really... you know... handle me."

His gaze narrows, and I smirk, crossing my arms over my chest.

If Cillian wants to play the game, then I'm going for the try.

And if there's one thing I hate more than being wrong, it's *losing*.

CHAPTER 20

Cillian

"Go for it," I retort roughly. My teeth are grinding together so hard I'm surprised my jaw doesn't bloody pop. "Do your worst, St. James."

She smirks sassily from across the table before sliding out of the booth and making her way over to a tall, meaty bloke who's at the opposite side of the bar.

I watch her approach him, giving him a flirty smile that makes my fists clench and my gaze narrow into slits. When he leans in, whispering something near her ear, she tosses her head back and laughs, and a feeling much like jealousy pounds feverishly through my veins.

Fuck, I hate this shit. I hate that she's laughing with another guy.

The entire goddamn point of lessons was to teach her. To get her ready for this.

Then you kissed the fuck out of her and found out how sweet she tastes, the voice in my head says, repeating what I was very much already bloody aware of.

What a fucking mess.

I spent the week avoiding her because I needed to work out the shit in my head, and finally I came to the realization that this isn't happening. I'll never be the kind of guy who deserves someone like Rory.

The good guy who doesn't fuck up everything he touches.

She's too sweet, too kind, too pure for a guy like me. Not to mention that she's my coach's daughter. She's a complication I can't afford.

Regardless of how badly I want her, and fuck, it's so bloody bad.

My hands ache with how tightly my fists are clenched as I watch the arsehole place his hand along the small of Rory's back and lean in close to say something in her ear once more. Then her eyes widen slightly, and she rakes her teeth over her lip, nodding to whatever he's said.

It looks like they're actually getting on, and I fucking hate it. I knew from the second she walked over to the hockey dude that she wasn't interested, and my entire body sagged in relief.

But now...I realize she doesn't look over at me once, and that only frustrates me more, knowing that she doesn't need me. That she's actually enjoying talking to this tosser.

Maybe it's a bit fucked to think I actually don't want her to succeed. Not at all. I want her to find an excuse for why she isn't interested. But she's using all the same things I fucking taught her. The eye contact, the laughing, the leaning in, the touching his arm.

And I hate every fucking second of it.

When he reaches for her hand and leads her to the dance floor, I'm sliding out of the booth before I can stop myself. Purely on instinct I make my way across the bar toward them. I don't even think... I just act.

The dance floor is much more crowded than the bar portion, so I push through the crowd until I spot Rory and the dickhead. I walk up and tap him on the shoulder.

His head turns, and he looks confused as he says, "Yeah?"

"Time to go, mate."

"What?" He laughs like I've just told a fucking joke as he looks at Rory and then back at me. "We're dancing, *mate*, chill. Plenty of other people to dance with."

His hand that's curved around Rory's waist tightens, pulling her closer, and it takes every ounce of self-control that I've been working on for the past year to keep from hitting him.

"Take your hands off of her." My voice is deadly low. Venom dripping from every syllable.

Rory's mouth falls open, that spot between her brows crinkling and it's too goddamn cute for how I'm feeling right now. Her feet move backward, separating the two of them, and the bloke looks at us both before muttering something and leaving.

The second he's out of view, she looks at me, her eyes flaring with anger. "Are you serious right now, Cillian?"

Fuck, fuck, fuck. I should've probably thought this shit through before I walked over here, but that's the problem, I wasn't *thinking* at all.

Not when I saw him touching her.

My shoulder lifts as I cross my arms over my chest, trying to ignore the fact that she looks bloody angry. "Let's go."

Without another glance, she spins on her heel toward the exit. I follow behind, trying to work out how I'm going to unfuck this.

RED CARD

"What the hell was that, Cillian!?" she cries the moment she bursts through the exit of the bar into the parking lot. The heavy metal doors slam shut behind us, drowning out the sound of the upbeat music, leaving us alone in the frigid winter air. She whips to face me, her bright eyes burning. "Tell me what the hell just happened. What. Was. That?"

I clench my jaw as I tear my gaze away, leveling it on the rows of cars.

I don't even know how to answer that question because I have no fucking clue what came over me. All I know is that I couldn't stand to see him touch her. As if she were his to touch.

"No, you don't get to ignore me and go back to your broody bullshit, Cillian Cairney. Hell no," she seethes, stepping closer. Her chest heaves beneath her jacket, her fists balled at her sides. "You acted like a jealous prick back there."

Not going to lie, seeing her be the sassy spitfire she was that first day I saw her on the pitch is so bloody hot, but I keep that to myself because she's clearly pissed.

I don't blame her, but also, fuck, she's driving *me* crazy. I feel like I'm losing my mind, and I don't know what the fuck to do about it. I don't know how to stop feeling like this.

How to stop this shit before we both end up doing something that we can't come back from. Something that changes everything.

"I don't know, Rory," I finally mutter. I drag my fingers exasperatedly through my hair in frustration, tugging at the strands. "I don't know what you want me to say."

She shakes her head, peering up at me, her eyes searching mine. "The truth? That's a good start. Tell me why you almost got into a freaking fight with that guy. God, Cillian, you're the one who told me to go talk to a guy. Isn't that what you brought me here tonight to do? Isn't that what you wanted? I do exactly as you said to do and here you are acti—"

"I couldn't fucking stand him touching you, okay?" I cut her off, the admission rips out of me before I can stop it, my voice rising an octave and echoing around the empty parking lot. "Fuck, I just... I couldn't fucking do it."

Her mouth falls open as her expression flutters with surprise, her eyes widening. She inhales a shaky breath. "So someone else can't touch me, but you don't want me either, right?" I can hear the hurt in her voice, and I hate that I'm the cause of it.

My mouth opens, then closes. I'm struggling between fighting what I know is right and giving into what I want. "No, St. James. You're wrong. I want you so fucking bad that I'm losing my bloody mind," I say as I close the distance between us. "You think I haven't stopped thinking about kissing you?"

She swallows roughly, shaking her head. "I mean, you didn't even *acknowledge* it, Cillian. What was I supposed to think? I thought you weren't into it. I know I'm not very good at it, but st—"

"Stop. You're perfect," I say, cutting her off again. I hate that she thinks she's so undesirable, or because she's not experienced that it's a turnoff or would make me want her any less.

If anything it makes me want her more, knowing that I'm the one who would be teaching her these things.

That I would be the one creating these experiences for her.

That's an honor I don't fucking deserve.

My head shakes, and I reach for her, cupping her jaw in my

hand. I sweep my thumb along her bottom lip. "Stop doubting yourself. Everything about you is perfect, Rory, and I'm so bloody sorry that I didn't talk to you about the other night."

I feel her hands slide along the front of my shirt, fisting in the material, and I almost shiver.

"Kiss me," she whispers as she rises on the tips of her toes. "There's nothing stopping you right now. *Kiss me*, Cillian."

A low groan shudders out of me. "For once in my life, I'm trying to do the right thing, Rory. I'm trying not to fuck everything up."

"Stop trying to decide what I want or what I need," she murmurs against my lips. "I can make my own decisions. This doesn't have to be complicated. We can just...have fun. Hook up. Do what feels good for both of us. Clearly, we're into each other. I'm not asking you to date me. I'm asking you to kiss me."

But it's more than that. Whatever this is...it feels like more than that. It feels monumentally fucking dangerous.

I swallow. "And then what, St. James? I kiss you and then what?"

The pads of her fingers press into my stomach, and my dick stirs to life, pressing against the zipper of my trousers.

"Then we...do other things," she says breathlessly.

Motherfucker.

When I don't immediately respond, she continues, those pretty wide eyes flaring with heat. "It'll just be hooking up. Fun, low-key, easy. And I still have things to learn, remember. What happened to *I can teach you whatever you want, Rory*?"

She does a piss-poor job at an English accent, and I chuckle, shaking my head at how bloody bad she gets it every single time.

Her plump pink lips curve into a grin.

"You sure?"

There's not a moment of hesitation as she nods, leaning forward slightly and nipping at the pad of my finger playfully. She's never been shy or awkward when it comes to the two us, and it's the reason I've always wondered why she needed my help in the first place.

"I'm sure. I get orgasms. It's a win-win situation." Both her dark brows lift.

"It's almost like you only want me for my body, St. James. I'm feeling a bit objectified right now."

She laughs, tossing her head back and exposing the delicate column of her throat, and my mouth waters from my need to lean closer and drag my tongue along her skin and taste her.

This might be the worst idea in fucking history, but that doesn't make me want it any less.

"Can you blame me? It's the tattoos, I think. Apparently guys covered in tattoos are my new type."

I laugh, shaking my head. "Yeah, well mine is apparently mouthy little American girls who need their arse spanked."

I'm teasing, but I don't miss how her eyes flare and her lips part, as if the thought of me spanking her turns her on as much as it does me.

"Don't make promises you're not willing to keep, Cillian. Put *that* on our list of things to practice."

Bloody fucking hell.

* * *

Despite the fact that I got home at almost two this morning, I'm up at 6:00 a.m. on the dot. My internal clock refused to give me even a single morning of sleeping in, so I pull myself out of bed, and drink some pre-workout to fully wake up before heading to the weight room on campus to get a workout in.

If I'm going to be up this early, I might as well do something productive.

It's completely dead when I scan my pass and walk into the gym, the sound of my trainers echoing inside the massive space. Just as I expected it to be since most of the guys probably stayed out late partying and the last thing they want to do on an off day is train when they're not required to.

When Rory asked me to go back to her apartment last night, I was so bloody tempted to that I almost said yes. I *wanted* to say yes.

But I also want her to be sure she wants to cross this line with me, because there's no going back once we do. I respect her, and I don't want to fuck anything up by taking things too quickly, especially knowing that random hookups aren't something she usually does.

All I've done is fuck things up for the last two years of my life, and I refuse to let whatever this is with Rory be a part of that.

She's important to me.

I'm halfway through my workout when I hear the heavy double doors open, and a few seconds later Fitz strolls through with his gym bag hefted high on his shoulder, followed by Wren, Hollis, and Liam.

"Cairney, what up, dude? Did you watch that video I texted in the group chat?" Fitz asks as he comes to a stop in front of me. Unlike most of the blokes on the team, his dark inky black hair is buzzed close to his scalp, and his face is completely clean-shaven.

It makes him look like the youngest even though he's a junior like me.

I lift the bottom of my T-shirt and swipe away the beads of sweat lining my brow. "Yeah, that shit was hilarious, mate."

They added me to the "Scrum Lords" chat after the night at the cowboy bar, and truthfully, I still can hardly believe I'm *in* it, but I'm secretly... pretty okay with it.

Not that I'm making it a big deal, but it feels good to know that they are choosing me instead of Coach having to force us together.

It finally feels like things are looking up, like I'm becoming friends with these guys and forming a bond. It's something I didn't think I'd ever want to happen, but the longer I'm at Prescott, the more comfortable I'm beginning to feel here.

Wren and Hollis both fist-bump me and then move to grab weights and some plates for deadlifts.

"How long have you been here? It's barely seven on a Sunday," Hollis asks, lifting his leg in a stretch. "You go out and not sleep last night?"

I shrug. "Nah... I don't party much. Drink. None of that. You know after everything that went down in London, I stay away from shit that I can find myself in trouble with."

"Yeah, I get you."

Wren speaks up, his shoulder dipping as he lifts the weight in a curl. "I was thinking, we should have a guys' night that doesn't involve partying. I've been wanting to do one of those escape rooms."

"Dude, yeah, my boy that goes to LSU in Baton Rouge told me they have one there; it's supposed to be cool as shit. Super realistic," Fitz adds, coming to a stop beside me. "Perfect opportunity for team bonding. But no alcohol or partying involved. What do you say, Cairney? Guys' night?"

I don't need to think about my answer.

"Hell yeah, mate. Let's do it."

One step at a time is starting to feel like leaps toward where I want to be.

CHAPTER 21

♥

Rory

Since I was a kid, I've always spent most of my free time at the rugby pitch. Mostly because my dad was there, but also because it's one of my favorite places to be. Dad brought me along to practices, and as I got older, I tagged along so I could hang out with the guys and observe as they practiced.

Since becoming a student at Prescott, instead of using the library to study or do homework, I just pop my headphones in and sit in the stands. On the days I'm not participating with the coaching staff that is.

But today, the *real* reason I'm at the pitch pretending to focus on studying for anatomy is so I can watch Cillian practice.

I'm officially *that* girl.

The one who shows up to rugby practice just to see the hottest guy on the team and has read the same exact paragraph at least three times but can't remember a single word of what she read.

I'm irrationally, stupidly turned on watching him run down the pitch in his black sleeveless practice shirt, the one that's cut down to the waist on his sides and shows the toned, chiseled muscles of his obliques as he moves.

It's nothing I haven't seen a thousand times before, but it's different watching Cillian on the pitch. He's captivating, and I can't take my eyes off him, my heart pounding in my chest nearly in sync with the dull throb in my core.

His movements are instinctual and quick as he catches the ball and runs toward the sidelines, drawing out the defenders.

He has two options: he can offload to Fitz or he can break the line and go for the try.

My thighs clench together on their own accord as I watch him blow past Wren, successfully breaking through the line.

My brain can't even comprehend how someone who's so solidly muscled can have such speed and agility. His footwork is almost *graceful* as he moves down the pitch toward the try line.

God, it's hot.

He's hot.

So. Fucking. Hot.

Seeing him in action is inherently better than watching tape or hearing about how good he is.

"Rory?" a voice calls from beside me, and I practically jump out of my skin. The textbook in my lap falls to the ground at my feet and my pen goes flying.

Whipping my head to the side I see Dad standing there, his brow furrowed in worry. I was so lost in my Cillian daydream that I didn't even hear him walk up.

"S-sorry. Yes?" I say a little too loudly, pasting on a smile as searing heat floods my cheeks. "You scared me."

He laughs, shaking his head as he drops down onto the seat

next to me. He places his clipboard beside him and reaches for my fallen textbook, then hands it back to me. "You've been doing that a lot lately. Everything good?"

"Yeah, why wouldn't it be?" I swallow, willing myself not to glance back at Cillian on the pitch.

His brow lifts as his gaze bounces over my face, searching for something. "You seem...distracted the last few times I've seen you. I just wanted to check on you, sweetheart."

Of course he'd noticed that I've been...*preoccupied* lately; he knows me better than anyone.

But it isn't as if I could tell him that I've been with Cillian, so I just shrug, leaning into his shoulder with a grin.

"All good. I've just been busy with class and stuff."

"Okay, well, if you need anything you know I'm here. I was thinking we have a team dinner at the house in a couple weeks? It's been a while," he says as he drags his attention back toward the pitch, where the guys are currently breaking and talking with Coach Matthews. "Seems like we're finally moving in the right direction."

I nod, humming quietly. "Yeah. Practice has been so much... better."

The guys have started to incorporate Cillian more, making passes, talking to him as if he's their friend and not just the unwanted new guy, and it makes me happy to see them making progress.

"Wanna help me coordinate dinner? You know they're all going to ask for those damn cookies you spoil them with." Dad chuckles as he runs his hand over his salt-and-pepper beard and shakes his head.

He loves those cookies just as much as the boys do, but I stopped making them as frequently since his doctor said his cholesterol was higher than the safe range for his age. Someone's got to take care of him.

"Of course," I reply, a sudden pang of guilt rising inside me when I think of how much I've been absent recently. "How about we do a movie night this weekend and hang out? I'm sorry things have been crazy lately, but I miss you."

His eyes soften, crinkling slightly in the corners as he lovingly bumps his shoulder into mine. "I'd never turn down a movie night, sweetheart. I'm going to get back out there and wrap up practice, but I'll see you this weekend?"

His arm slides around my shoulder. He pulls me against him, and I feel his lips press against my hair softly.

"Sounds good, Dad. I love you."

"Love you too, sweetheart."

After he leaves, I reopen my anatomy textbook and attempt to resume studying, but I don't get very far—I still can't focus. When practice ends and the guys head toward the locker room, I slam the book shut and gather all my things, shoving them into my backpack.

I guess this means I'll be up late studying since I got absolutely nothing done and this test is worth way too much of my grade for me to fail.

But...so worth it.

I make my way off the training pitch and inside the athletic building. Inside I see Cillian walk out of the locker room.

His hair is wet and pushed back off his forehead from his shower, and he's wearing a fresh, sweat-free Prescott Rugby T-shirt with a pair of athletic shorts that hug his thick thighs. The ink on his arms seems even darker with his skin flushed from the hot shower he just took.

When he spots me, a lazy grin overtakes his face and his eyes move over me, making my skin hum from the attention.

I swear, I can almost *feel* the warmth of his gaze as it travels down my body, caressing each inch of me unabashedly.

I glance around, checking that we're still alone, and then I walk the length of the hallway in a few strides until I stop short in front of him.

He lifts a brow in surprise when I grab his hand, yanking him into the closest room I can find and slamming the door shut behind us.

Coincidentally, the equipment room.

A room I'm technically familiar with but couldn't tell him the first thing about.

Like where the *light* even is.

It's dark, but not entirely. There's a dim glow shining in from the sliver of space between the threshold and door that offers some light. It's a pretty small space, lined with shelves for equipment and little room for anything else, which means Cillian's almost pressed against my front.

I can feel the heat radiating off his massive body and smell the clean, masculine scent of his bodywash, and it makes me nearly dizzy.

Especially after I've spent the last hour practically panting as I spectated.

"Hi," I breathe, my gaze traveling up to his face.

He chuckles, amusement dancing in his hazel eyes as he

takes a single step closer. "St. James. Any reason we're hiding in the... closet?"

I step back slightly, dropping my backpack to the floor somewhere near my feet and my back hits the shelf behind me, noisily jostling the equipment on it.

"Equipment room. Not a closet."

Cillian laughs, the delicious sound washing over me. He reaches for a lock of my hair, casually twirling a strand around his finger. "Yeah? Why are we hiding in the *equipment* room then, baby?"

Baby?

That's a first.

I love that entirely too much. Like, an embarrassing amount. Now I'm convinced there's quite literally nothing sexier than hearing Cillian Cairney call you *baby* in that deep, raspy English accent of his.

"I—I—" I stutter, promptly shutting my mouth because I'm not entirely sure why I *did* drag us in here. Okay, yes I do. Because I wanted to have him alone and couldn't wait another second once I saw how ridiculously hot he looked fresh out of the locker room. "I don't... know."

I rake my teeth over my bottom lip, staring up at him.

His eyes seem to darken as he steps forward and lifts his other hand and places it on the shelf behind me, bracketing my head. The corner of his lip curves up in a sexy smirk. "I think you do know."

I gulp, trying to breathe steadily but failing, each inhale coming quicker than the last. He closes the little space left between us, molding to the front of me with every hard, sculpted muscle of his body and my pulse goes haywire.

I try to squeeze my thighs together, but his knee slides between them, stopping me.

"And you know what else I think?" he rasps, moving one hand to my chin and grasping it between his fingers. "I think that you watched me on the pitch today and it turned you on. Every time I looked into the stands, your eyes were on me, St. James. I think that's why you keep trying to press those pretty thighs together. Because it aches, doesn't it?" He trails his fingers from my chin, gently down my neck, where his massive, rough palm curves around my throat. The pads of his fingers create the most subtle hint of pressure, enough to have me squirming, and then he trails them lower, fingertips dancing over my collarbone.

Goose bumps erupt on my flesh, and my lips part as I suck in a stuttering pant. He's barely touched me, and my nipples are taut and pebbled almost painfully against my sports bra.

Leaning closer, his mouth dips to my ear. "If you wanted me to touch you, baby, all you had to do was ask." His warm breath on my neck has a violent shiver running down my spine. "I think that if I slipped my fingers into your panties right now, I'd see just how wet you are for me."

I'm almost embarrassed to admit how wet I am. How I'm *throbbing*, a deep, achy feeling spreading in my lower belly with each beat of my heart. My skin feels like it's on fire, a live wire of lust coursing through me and making my limbs heavy.

I swallow roughly. When I can finally form words, my voice comes out low and shaky. "What if I was?"

Cillian pushes off the shelf, his gaze lifting to mine. His smirk can only be described as devilish. His sensual, pillowy lips curve up slightly and reveal a flash of white, perfectly straight teeth.

Then his shoulder rises in a slight shrug and his fingers trail lower until they skim the space between my breasts, nearly beneath the fabric of my tank top.

My pulse is racing so hard I can hear it in my ears.

"Shall we find out then?" he hums against my neck, lips ghosting along my already heated skin.

God, we're in the equipment room, where anyone could walk by and hear what's happening on the other side of the door, and that should make me want to stop. It should make me come to my senses, pull me out of this lust-filled haze, but it doesn't.

And I'm not sure anything could right now, not with Cillian touching me. With his lips pressed to my neck. His molten gaze meets mine.

"Yes," I whisper breathlessly, nodding. I draw my bottom lip between my teeth as Cillian holds my eyes for another beat, then he drops his hand from my chest, fingers grazing over the expanse of my stomach through the fabric of my shirt, until he reaches the hem, where he toys with it.

Each palpable second that passes, my heart thrashes harder against my rib cage, anticipation snaking its way through my body in thick tendrils and taking root in my core.

Finally, I feel the rough pad of his calloused fingers slip beneath my shirt and dance along my stomach, causing me to suck in a shuddering breath.

Cillian's mouth twitches before he lowers his lips back to my neck and his tongue traces a path of fire that seems to burn me from the inside. Each spot that he touches creates a new inferno, and I'm almost dizzy from the sensation. My skin buzzes from the contact of his fingers, and once they dip below the waistband of my leggings and trail along the lace of my panties, I can feel myself trembling.

From anticipation, nerves, and raw, needy desire.

It's maddening how badly I want him. The air seems to crackle between us.

"Are you sure?" he asks. "Say the word and we can stop, Rory."

I nod, bringing my hand on top of his and guiding it lower, until his fingers skim over my sensitive core. "I'm *sure*."

I'm nervous because it's been a long time since anyone has touched me like this, but my arousal far outweighs my nerves, and truthfully...I *trust* Cillian. He doesn't make me feel like I need to be anything other than who I am. He makes me feel comfortable and safe when we're together.

Enough that I want him to feel how wet I am in the equipment room even when there's a chance we could be caught by someone.

I hear the low, hoarse groan rolling off his lips as his thick fingers brush over my clit through the damp lace. "Fuck, you're soaked, Rory," he murmurs before rubbing a firm circle on my clit that has my eyes rolling back and my toes curling in my shoes.

God, he's barely touched me, and I feel like I'm going to come, just from this.

Still with the barrier of my panties between us. Not even skin to skin.

My hips lift to meet his fingers, to plead for more pressure, and he chuckles darkly as he pulls back to look at me. "I can't wait to taste you. I want to bury my face in your cunt and lick all of this up." Pleasure pulses through me when he makes a slow, rough circle over my throbbing clit, his filthy words doing nothing but sending me further to the edge of whatever oblivion I'm ready to fall into. "I bet you taste as sweet as you smell."

He thrums steadily on my clit, and my arms slip around his neck, my own fingers curling through the hair at his nape as I hold on, hips rocking. The rough fabric of my panties only makes the feeling more intense, an added layer of friction, and I can't get enough.

I toss my head back against the shelf as a breathy moan tears through me. I tug at his hair, pulling him back to my neck, where he plants his lips, kissing and nibbling along the juncture.

"Are you going to come for me, baby?" he rasps, his voice gravelly and deep in my ear. I arch against his hand, my entire body humming with pleasure, and when he sucks roughly at the pulse point in my throat, I tip over the edge into an orgasm that has my legs trembling.

"Cillian," I gasp breathlessly, my voice breaking at the intensity of the pleasure sweeping through me in heavy waves, each a higher crescendo than the last.

I never knew it could be like... *this*. So all-consuming.

His strokes slow to a languid, lazy swipe of fingers on my clit, and he works me through my orgasm until the aftershocks finish coursing through me.

When I finally snap my eyes open, he's staring down at me with a cocky smirk and heavy-lidded eyes. His hair is messy from my fingers, standing in a hundred different directions.

I can feel his erection pressing against my lower stomach, hard and thick, and I swallow, trying to catch my breath.

"You did so good," he drawls.

Okay, I take back my earlier statement. There's absolutely nothing better than Cillian *praising* you post-orgasm in that stupidly hot accent. Nothing.

A laugh bubbles out of me, and his eyes gleam with amusement as I drop my hands from his hair and cover my mouth. "Sorry." My voice is barely recognizable, all raspy and hoarse from my orgasm. "That was..."

I rake my teeth over my lips as I watch him bring his fingers to his mouth and suck my arousal off, never breaking our gaze. "Bloody hot as fuck, St. James."

If the shelf behind me wasn't holding me up, I think my legs would give out. That was the hottest thing I've ever experienced, and I groan, dropping my face into my palms.

"Don't get shy now. I just tasted your pussy, it's too late for that," he says with a laugh.

"I'm not shy. I'm just trying to figure out how you're this... good. It's ridiculous," I respond as I lean back to look at him. "Actually, pretend I never said that. Your ego doesn't need any inflating."

"Come here." He laughs again, then reaches for me, pulling me into his warm, hard body and wrapping me up tight. I sigh against his chest. It's easy to be with him, effortless. It's the first time he's ever hugged me like this, and I love the way it feels, his strong arms surrounding me, and the comforting smell of him invading my senses.

"Consider it a thank-you."

I hum. "Thank you for what?"

His lips move against my hair as he says, "The guys in the weight room invited me out for a guys' night. Pretty sure that had something to do with you, St. James."

I pull back, my gaze whipping up to his. "What?!" I cry a bit too loudly. Wincing, I lower my voice but bounce on the balls of my feet. "Oh my God. Cillian! This is amazing. God, I'm so *so* happy to hear it. I knew that they'd come around. But that's all you. You've made the effort to bond with them, and it's paid off."

I'm so excited I could scream. This is exactly what Cillian needed. For the guys to accept him into the team by choice, not by force. Now it's just a matter of time before everyone else realizes that he's nothing like they thought he was. When they truly get to know him.

The way that I have.

He shrugs. "Either way. Thank you, Rory. I appreciate it."

My heart swells in my chest, and I hold back the majority of my excitement because I don't want him to feel weird about it.

"My pleasure. Actually, I know the perfect way you can repay me. And yes, it *definitely* has to do with orgasms." I pin him with a stare.

Cillian's lip tilts upward, and he shakes his head. "Shit, I think I've created a monster."

Oh, if he only had *any* idea.

CHAPTER 22

Cillian

"Okay, spill. Who is she?" Aisling asks, elbowing me roughly in the ribs and pulling my attention from my phone. "And why don't I know about her yet?"

I glance over at her, my brow furrowed. "Who is...who?"

She rolls her eyes. "Oh? Is that what we're doing? Pretending you haven't been glued to your phone for the past three days? I'm pretty sure I've never seen you text this much... *ever*. Like in your entire life, Cillian."

Yeah, well, I've never been much of a texter.

At least I wasn't until I met Rory.

We haven't seen each other for a few days because our schedules have been hectic with classes, training, and she had a group session for a project that she's working on, so we've been texting randomly throughout the day.

When I was leaving the weight room this morning, I almost ran into the fucking door because I opened my phone to a photo of her lying in bed wearing nothing but a tight tank top and those bloody nightie shorts that I dream about, curving high around her plump little arse. She's tiny, barely reaching my chest, but somehow those legs go on for days. I could make out the tight pebbles of her nipples straining against the thin fabric of the shirt, making perfect little mounds, and my mouth watered. I want to suck on them and drag my teeth over the sensitive peaks until she's writhing and begging for my cock.

I haven't stopped thinking about the way she came on my fingers, or how bloody sweet she tasted as I sucked her off them that afternoon in the equipment room.

It was stupid and reckless doing it on school property, and even so...I don't regret it.

Not in the slightest.

"Just been fucking off, watching videos" is all I respond, and it earns me a hard jab in the ribs from Ais. I groan, dropping my phone. "Fucking hell, Ais."

She lifts her chin, crossing her arms over her chest, and arches a brow.

I sigh and lean back against the couch cushion.

It's not that I want to keep anything from her; she's the closest person in my life. It's just...a little fucking complicated.

Even if Rory and I are just hooking up, it's still complicated because of who Rory is and who I am. What my past is like. And whatever my future looks like.

"It's...complicated."

Her eyes light up and she squeals, "I *knew* it! You better tell me everything right now, Cillian. I will not speak to you for an entire week if you don't. I can't believe you kept something this exciting from me."

Fuck.

My throat works as I pull my palm down my face, exhaling. I force my gaze back to her. "It's Rory St. James. Coach's daughter."

Aisling's jaw falls agape and her eyes widen. "*Cillian.*"

"I know. But it's...*casual*," I say roughly, slightly sharper than I intended. "It's not like I set out to get with the coach's daughter, Ais. It kind of just happened. But...I'm into her."

"You like her?" she asks.

I hesitate for a moment, not entirely sure how to answer that question. My jaw tenses when I move my hand over my mouth.

Of course I bloody like her. She's fucking gorgeous, smart, and witty. Funny and absolutely brilliant when it comes to rugby.

If things were different, and I was capable of giving her what she deserved, I would probably try to date her. Take her out, do anything to make her happy. Be the kind of guy that I know she wants.

That's not possible when the life I want is back in London.

Regardless of whether I *like* her. That doesn't make a difference.

Chewing on the corner of my lip, I nod. "She's great. But we're just...hooking up. Having fun."

Aisling shrugs, her dark curls bouncing with the motion. "Fun's good. As long as you're good...with fun?"

"Yeah, I'm good," I reply. My phone dings between us and we both glance down at the screen.

A picture message from Rory.

Fuck.

"So she must be the reason you've been so MIA lately?" Aisling teases, her dark brow lifted. "I've been here all alone."

Realization slams into me like the weight of a truck. "Shit, Ais, I'm sorry I—"

She holds her hand up, stopping me with a soft laugh. "Cillian, I'm just joking. I'm glad you're out having fun and not locked away in your room or working yourself to death in the training room. You need this."

"Yeah, but I shouldn't be leaving you here by yourself so much. What if your sugar drops and I'm not here?"

Guilt claws at my throat, along with a piercing shard of panic at the thought of something happening to Aisling when she's alone and I'm not here to help. It's my biggest fear.

Hell, I'm the entire reason she had to pick up her entire life and move to a new country, and I've been leaving her alone so I could fuck off with Rory.

"Cillian, stop," she says, placing her small hand on my forearm and squeezing gently. "Don't do this. Honestly, you're kind of suffocating, in the best way. You can't keep me in a bubble for my entire life, and you can't protect me from everything. I'm an adult now, and if you're not home and my sugar drops, then I know how to take care of it. I think moving to America is the best thing that's ever happened to me."

What?

My brow furrows, surprise flooding my face, but she continues before I can even speak.

"I can see you're shocked by that, but it's true, Kill. Being here has helped me find myself. Become more independent and not feel so much like a burden."

"Ais, you're never a fucking burden," I mutter quietly, shaking my head with a grimace.

Her expression softens, and she drops her hand, pulling her knees to her chest and resting her chin on top. She peers at me through eyes that look so much like Mum's it makes my chest physically ache. "It's just been hard since Mum died, and since coming here, it's the first time I've felt the sun in a long time. I'm happy and I want *you* to be happy too. And it seems like Rory makes you happy, whether it's temporary or not. You deserve happiness, Cillian."

The conversation's turned unexpectedly heavy, and emotion weighs thickly in my throat the way it usually does when we bring up Mum and everything that's happened in the past couple of years.

"I love you, Ais."

"Love you too, Kill." She gives me a cheeky smile when I reach out and ruffle her hair like she's a toddler, something she pretends to hate but that I've done all her life.

"I'm going to make an effort to be around more. I know what you said, but I don't like the idea of you being here by yourself so much."

Her eyes roll. "Grown woman now, remember? I'm fine. Plus, I've been hanging out with a few of the girls from the astrophysics club. We've been getting coffee sometimes."

Christ. That makes me so bloody happy to hear.

Aisling's been painfully shy and quiet since she was a kid, and making friends has always been a struggle for her. She's always been sensitive too. The nurturer while I'm the enforcer. Hearing she's making friends at Prescott takes a weight off my shoulders that I didn't even know had settled on them. It makes me worry less knowing she's got someone.

"That's great. No boys though." I grin, earning another eye roll and a scoff.

"Right. Because there's so many opportunities to meet guys when I'm drowning in classes and now tutoring on the side."

I shrug. "I love it. Maybe study more, yeah?"

Her giggle rings out through the living room, and I find myself smiling too.

"Remember the bubble you're not going to keep me in? Applies to guys too, Kill. Sorry, but the overprotective brute of a brother thing isn't going to stop my dating life, whenever there is one," she sasses, cocking a brow and giving me a pointed stare. "Not that it's even a possibility, but anyway, enough about my nonexistent dating life because this is awkward. How about you invite Rory over for dinner tomorrow? I want to meet her."

"I don't know if that's a good id—"

Aisling slaps her hand over my mouth, cutting me off. "I don't know why I even asked. What I meant to say is be sure to tell Rory that we're having a pizza-and-movie night tomorrow and to be here for seven."

I know better than to argue with her because it'll get me nowhere. Aisling knows she has me wrapped around her finger, and she's not afraid to use it to her advantage.

* * *

Once Aisling falls asleep, midway through the movie she forced me to watch—something about bloody dragons—I finally open Rory's message from earlier.

Another photo, but this time, it's just her face as she holds up her latest cross-stitch, a sweet smile on her face.

Christ, she's so bloody pretty.

Cheeks rosy pink, almost the same shade as her plump lips, and her eyes warm, rich chocolate as she gazes into the camera.

Followed by another text asking me to come over with a tongue out emoji.

And even though it's after midnight when I read the message, and I've got economics at eight a.m., I find myself at her apartment, standing on her doorstep.

I can't help myself. It's like I've had one single taste and now I'm addicted and desperate for another.

Or maybe it's because I like being around her. I like how everything seems quieter when I'm with her. I like laughing with her.

If I'm being honest I like everything about her.

It takes her only a moment to answer the door, almost as if she was waiting for me.

There's a lazy smile on her face as she peers up at me through her thick, dark lashes. "Hi."

Her hair is down and wet from a shower, and when she swings the door open wider, I get a whiff of her sweet floral scent and nearly groan.

I'm starting to realize how fucked I am. Lately, all I've been thinking of is Rory, and that's a problem.

I can't afford distractions. I can't lose focus on the reason I'm here.

"St. James."

Blinking up at me, she draws her plush pink lip between her teeth and reaches for me, fisting her hands in the front of my shirt and hauling me inside.

I slam the front door shut with my foot as she drags me through the apartment, only stopping when we make it down the hall.

I open my mouth to speak, and she crashes into me, her lips slamming into mine. I can taste the minty flavor of her toothpaste as her tongue sweeps along the seam of my lips, demanding access. Her fingers slide into my hair, tugging me closer to her, and my arms wind around her waist, hauling her tiny body nearer until she's pressed tightly to my front.

I never expected her to be as brazen as she is, but fuck, I love it.

Although she's hesitant and explorative in her touch, there's nothing shy or meek about it. Rory knows exactly what she wants, and even though it might not be something she's done a thousand times, she's assured.

Or at least she is with me, and that has a surge of possessiveness swirling in my chest.

My palms slide down the small of her back to the swell of her ass, and she moans into my mouth, pulling roughly at my hair. Something I'm starting to learn she's into.

Imagine when I've got my face buried in between her thighs, lapping at her pussy. How much she'll love pulling my hair *then*.

Fuck, I have to slow this down.

I tear my lips from hers, rearing back as I pant. "Did you ask me to come over just so I could make you come, St. James?" My mouth twitches, drinking in her blown pupils, flushed cheeks that have pink creeping down her neck, and swollen lips. Her tongue darts out, skimming the bottom one, and I almost say fuck it. Fuck going slow.

I'm so bloody tempted to haul her over my shoulder, carry her into the bedroom, and not let her out until the sun rises and she's come ten times.

On my tongue, my fingers, my cock.

"Why are you stopping?" she asks, peering up at me with her hands resting on my stomach. Her fingers slip beneath the fabric of my hoodie and trail down my abs, causing them to tighten and coil beneath her touch.

The little bit of restraint I have left is slowly fraying, but goddamn it I'm trying.

"Because... I want to talk."

Her brow knits together. "Talk about what?"

I grab her hands and pull them from beneath my shirt before capturing her wrists in my palms. "Because there's no rush."

I want her so bloody badly that my cock aches. I'm fucking *yearning* for her, but if I'm going to sink inside her, I want there to be absolutely no doubt that this is what she wants.

She's inexperienced, and I'm not a complete arsehole.

"Come here," I rasp, tugging her to me by her wrists. "Let's go sit."

We walk to the couch, and I sink down into the cushion, pulling her with me until she's seated in my lap.

"Okay, then let's *talk*," she says, emphasizing on the word. I hesitate briefly, and she huffs. "Out with it."

Chuckling, I say, "Aisling wants you to come over tomorrow for dinner."

Rory's eyes widen and her dark brow arches. "You interrupted a seriously hot make-out session to tell me your sister wants me to come over for... dinner?"

"And other things."

"And those things are?" Her gaze holds mine intently, and I sigh.

"I just want you to be sure. Before we go any further," I finally say. I have no idea why I'm hung up on this and holding out, but I think it's because I don't want to be the bloke who hurts her. The thought of hurting her makes my stomach twist into knots.

It's truthfully the only time in my life that I've cared enough about someone to put them first, outside of my mum and sister.

And I *do* care about Rory, casual hookup or not. She's my… friend.

She groans exasperatedly. "Cillian. I am a thousand precent sure that I want you to fuck me. Is that what you need to hear?" When I don't immediately respond, she says, "Yes, I've only had sex twice. And yes, they were admittedly horrible and not worth the memory, but that doesn't mean that I need to be handled with care. I'm not delicate. I'm not breakable. I want you to fuck me like you would any other girl. I want you to stop holding back and fucking *touch* me."

The words are barely out of her mouth before I'm crushing my lips to hers, my hands sliding into her hair as I tug her closer and groan against her mouth when her hips rock against my hardening cock. I pull back, staring at her for the first time tonight. I've been so caught up in doing the right bloody thing that I didn't even notice what she was wearing when she answered the door.

A faded blue, worn rugby T-shirt that has ridden high on her creamy thighs, revealing a pair of bright yellow panties that barely cover her pussy.

Bloody fucking hell.

Her tiny little clit peeks through the fabric, and I can make out the entire shape of her already wet pussy.

"You're driving me bloody crazy, woman."

"Then do something about it, or I guess I'll have to take it into my own hands," she retorts with a sassy bite that makes me want to put her over my knee and spank the fuck out of her, until her arse is blooming red from my hand.

"Keep taunting me, baby."

Rory's eyes darken as she rolls her lip between her teeth before letting it go with a flick. My gaze drops to her mouth, lingering there before I lean forward and kiss her. I nip at her lip, drawing it into my mouth and sucking.

When her head drops back on her shoulder, exposing her throat, I continue trailing hot, wet kisses along her neck, sucking on her pulse point down to the curve of her shoulder until she's a writhing, shaking mess in my arms. Her hips jerk against my cock, desperate for friction, and the moment she reaches between us, curving her palm over my erection through my sweatpants, my hand circles her wrist, stopping her.

She pulls back, staring at me with a stunned expression.

"Tonight's not about me. It's about you." My mouth twitches when her brow furrows deeper.

Instead of answering, I carefully lay her back on the couch beside me, hovering my massive body over her delicate frame. She's so bloody tiny, part of me is scared I'll fucking break her. My hands and body are meant to be used as a weapon, to take men three times her size to the ground.

"Let me make you feel good, Rory."

CHAPTER 23

Rory

I fear I might actually levitate off this couch.

Cillian hovers over me with his lips curved into a lazy, sexy grin that makes my toes curl along the cushions. He could have asked me just about anything and I would probably agree, if it meant "letting him make me feel good."

Warmth floods my lower stomach as his gaze drops to the hard, pointed peaks of my nipples, which are practically breaking through the fabric of my T-shirt. Hunger flares in his dark irises, and I swallow, feeling the heat of my flush creeping from my cheeks down to my neck and spreading throughout my body.

It can't possibly be this hot in here, can it?

"Can I?" he rasps, asking for permission, his hand splayed along my stomach, along the edge of the thin fabric.

I nod.

Not trusting myself to speak, I keep my mouth shut, drawing my lip between my teeth as I watch him.

The tips of his fingers slip beneath the T-shirt, ghosting along my skin as he trails them higher, past my belly button, the rough pads lightly sweeping along my rib cage.

A featherlight touch that leaves a trail of gooseflesh in its wake.

I'm thanking past me for forgoing the bra.

I'm nearly panting with every languid inch that he caresses. His movements are controlled and unhurried. I'm honestly impressed by how unaffected he seems, determined not to rush things, almost as if he's committing it all to memory.

The thought of a man like Cillian wanting to save this moment in his head makes my stomach flip.

It feels like an out-of-body experience, being beneath this man, his hungry gaze traveling over me.

Hence the levitate part.

I'm practically crawling out of my skin, needing him to go faster, to touch me where I've been *aching* for him since that afternoon on the pitch. I haven't been able to stop thinking about it. I could recall every moment in vivid detail, but it is nothing compared to the real thing.

Cillian inches the fabric higher until I feel cool air kiss the sensitive peaks of my nipples, and I hear his breath hitch. A low groan erupts from the back of his throat.

"How are you so fucking perfect?"

The whispered words wash over me, turning my insides molten. I've never felt as wanted or beautiful in my life as I do right now. I never knew it was possible to feel so revered.

"Touch me," I beg.

His throat works, and he nods, never taking his eyes off my chest.

I feel his rough, calloused palms cup my breasts in each hand, squeezing gently as a thumb sweeps across my nipple, causing my back to arch off the couch and a breathy moan to slip from my lips.

"So responsive. I've barely touched you, baby," he drawls, repeating the motion. His thumb and forefinger settle around my nipple and he rolls it, tugging gently, and I swear with each pull, my clit throbs in tandem.

Arousal tears down my spine, and my thighs close on their own accord, slamming shut around his hips.

Cillian continues to give attention to my nipples, tugging, rolling, flicking. I'm breathless, my chest heaving as I fight to keep my eyes open and not succumb to the pleasure.

"Christ, Rory, I think you could come, just like this," he says. But finally, fucking finally, he lowers his mouth to my chest, planting kisses around my nipple, until he closes his lips over it and sucks it roughly into his mouth. His teeth scrape over the peak, and my hips squirm, attempting to grind my clit against his erection.

I think I'm going to lose my mind. This is the best form of torture, but I'm desperate. Needy. Aching.

"Patience, baby," he says as my nipple slides out of his mouth with an erotic pop that fills the room.

When I try to slip my hand into the front of my panties for relief, he stops me, capturing my hand just before I make it there.

"That's not patient."

I groan, sagging back against the cushions. "Please, Cillian."

"I fucking love to hear you beg."

I open my mouth to sass him, but the words die on my tongue as he dips his head between my thighs and drags his nose up my slit, inhaling. "And I love how you smell as much as I love how you taste. So sweet."

God. If it was anyone else, if this was any other moment, I might feel too embarrassed to let a guy this close to my crotch, but with Cillian, there's none of the usual nerves or anxiousness. Seeing the raw hunger and desire in his eyes is all I need to be 100 percent in this. I'm not allowing my head to go anywhere but this moment.

In one swift movement, he gets off the couch. His hands fist on my hips and move me until I'm hanging off the edge, and then he's on his knees between my thighs. Apparently, he's had enough of driving me to the brink of insanity, because his long fingers slip beneath the lace of my panties, and he tugs them off, discarding them with a flick of his wrist.

Cool air hits my core, causing me to shiver.

Large palms run up my thighs, prying my thighs wider. Using his thumbs, he spreads my pussy open, eyes pinned on me.

"I'm going to eat this pretty little cunt every fucking day, and still never get enough," he murmurs as my face heats, my nipples hardening impossibly. I'm delusional enough to think I could come with just his eyes on me.

He leans forward and flattens his tongue on my slit, trailing up its length. His groan vibrates my sensitive core, my clit throbbing painfully at the desperate need for release.

I'm ready to detonate.

My hands fly to his hair, tangling in the strands, partially holding him in place and partially holding on like my life depends on it.

Cillian laps at my pussy, swiping his tongue through my arousal at a torturously languid pace that makes me squirm and tug harder on his hair.

At this rate, I may just pull it all out, which would truly be a tragedy because he has the best hair. Dark, thick, shiny.

God, why am I focusing on his *hair* right now when he's literally eating me like a man who's been deprived and I'm his last meal?

"So bloody good," he murmurs against my slick flesh before flicking the tip of his tongue over my clit in firm motions. Heat jolts through me as my back arches from the couch, a hoarse cry tumbling past my lips.

The pleasure is maddening as it pulses and throbs in my core, intensely unfurling low in my belly and blossoming.

All in a single breath, Cillian closes his lips around my clit, sucking it roughly into his mouth as he slides two fingers inside me, finding the spot that has my vision turning hazy. My eyes flutter shut.

It's hopeless, trying to fight the orgasm that rips through my body.

It's never been this...easy.

Never been so intense, so unrelenting.

My thighs tremble, shaking so violently that if it wasn't for his mouth latched on to my clit, his fingers stroking deep inside me, I might end up on the floor.

"That's it, baby. You're doing so good, taking my fingers like my good girl, soaking my tongue."

The filthy praise only sends me tipping further into oblivion, my toes curling along his back as my muscles tighten and clench with each wave of my orgasm.

Cillian hums in satisfaction against my pussy, drawing slow, soft circles on my clit as I come down.

I'm completely boneless and spent as I sag deeper into the cushions, desperately trying to catch my breath, form words. To say something, but my heart is beating so fast that my head feels light, my vision swimming slightly.

Oh God, that is something that would happen to me... blacking out from the most powerful orgasm of my life.

Cillian slips my legs off his shoulders and rises to full height, the evidence of my orgasm still glistening on his lips. He lifts the back of his tattooed hand to his mouth, swiping it away, and I think I might come again, just from watching him.

"You good?"

Fantastic actually.

I nod, giving him a sated, cheeky smile. My gaze trails down to his erection that's straining against his gray sweatpants, and I sit up, reaching for his waistband.

His head shakes. "Not tonight."

"But you're..."

"Yeah, because I just ate your pretty pussy, St. James." My cheeks flush, and he chuckles wickedly. "But I told you tonight was about *you*."

I don't even have the chance to pout or argue, which I absolutely was planning to, because he leans forward and slides his hands along my jaw, cradling my face gently in his big hands. And then his lips are on me, kissing me until I'm breathless, the faint taste of me still lingering on his tongue.

I'm slightly dazed when he pulls back to stare down at me. "I'll take *my* thank-you as you coming to dinner with Ais or I'll never hear the bloody end of it."

My head falls back as a giggle escapes me and I recall using the very same line earlier.

Cillian's smile is contagious, and I can't help but mirror it. He sits down beside me, gathering me in his arms. Realization hits me that I'm still completely naked, and he's completely clothed.

I reach for the blanket on the back of the couch and pull it over me.

"Isn't me meeting your sister kind of... not casual?" I ask, genuinely surprised that he would ask me this. He's so fiercely closed off and doesn't give very much of himself to anyone.

He shrugs. "My sister's persistent, and she knows we're friends. I think you'd like her. You remind me a lot of her."

This comes as a shock, especially now that I've gathered how close they are.

"Okay. I'll come," I say. "But I think that I'm going to need some thank-yous for this. Lots of them actually—*multiple* in one night. You know what, actually maybe you should go back down to my..."

Fingers press into my side, tickling me until I'm squirming and thrashing.

"Brat," he mumbles.

"All your fault."

* * *

I changed my outfit at least five times before settling on a pair of tight, dark-washed jeans that I know Cillian likes because he can't seem to stop staring at my ass in them, and a simple, silk camisole with my combat boots. And my leather jacket because it's one of my favorites now. Mostly because it makes me feel like a badass, and I need all the bad-bitch vibes I can get tonight.

I know that it's just dinner with Cillian's sister, and that we're just friends.

But it still has me feeling slightly anxious because I've never done *this* before, and therefore I have absolutely no idea what to expect.

I've never met the sister of someone I like...and have feelings for.

Exhaling, I run my palms down the front of my thighs once more.

I even wore my hair down. Well, half of it's pulled back by a small clip, but still.

I've started to realize that even though I'm probably always going to be a casual girl, I do like experimenting with new things. Even if they're not something I end up liking, a.k.a. the latex dominatrix dress that I will never speak of ever again, it's still good to try.

Before I can knock on Cillian's front door, it swings open and a girl around my age appears. I'm assuming this is Aisling, his sister.

Holy. Shit.

She looks so much like Cillian, it's startling. If I didn't know there was an age difference, I would think they were twins.

Dark, curly hair falls to her waist, wispy bangs brushing the tops of her eyebrows, and pale green irises partially veiled behind purple-framed glasses. When a wide smile overtakes her face, there's a slight dimple in each of her cheeks, and immediately, I feel my shoulders relaxing. Clearly, her brother got the broody gene because this girl seems like sunshine, and it immediately makes me less anxious.

My anxiety wasn't so much about Cillian but about meeting Aisling for the first time, and worrying if she'll like me. She's the most important person in his life, and I just want to make a good impression.

"Hi!" she says. "It's nice to finally meet you." She's about the same height as me, with a small dainty frame that's draped in a colorful baggy sweater and flared yoga pants, with a pair of fuzzy slippers. Her style is quirky, colorful, and fun, and I love it.

She comes in for a hug and my arms slide around her, returning it, and I realize that I'm smiling too. It's hard not to. She's got the same charismatic charm that I've seen her brother possess.

"Hi. You must be Aisling?"

She nods. "And you're Rory. I have a million questions, starting with how do you put up with my brother?"

"Aisling, Christ, can she come in the bloody apartment before you bombard her?" I hear Cillian's deep voice from behind her, and I giggle.

Aisling rolls her eyes. "See? Come in. We got pizza, and I thought we could watch a new horror movie? Cillian hates them, but he puts up with them because I love them so much." She gestures me inside the apartment and shuts the door behind us.

Cillian walks into view, looking exceptionally hot tonight in a T-shirt and sweatpants, his feet bare on the hardwood. He's rubbing the back of his neck, his expression apologetic. "Sorry, I've quite literally never heard her talk this much."

"Well someone has to carry on a conversation because we all

know it won't be you!" Aisling retorts beside me, giving him a pointed look.

He just grins.

I already know I'm going to love seeing the two of them together. He feels so different from the Cillian that I've come to know. He seems less reserved and more at ease.

Dragging his attention to me, his gaze travels over my body and back to meet my eyes. "St. James."

"Cairney."

We stand in the foyer, staring at each other stupidly for a few brief moments, that familiar magnetic tug appearing like usual, making me want to reach for him. Something that I've recently found myself wanting to do when we're together.

It's dangerous.

"Thanks for coming," he says.

I roll my lips together to bite back the smile, my face flushing at what he really means.

It is my way of thanking him after...

"Yeah, of course," I squeak, earning me a grin. It warms my insides, my stomach flipping in response.

He's entirely too attractive when he smiles. It's unnerving.

Aisling's brow furrows deep, and she looks between the two of us, shaking her head. "Why do I feel like there's something weird happening right now?"

We both remain quiet, until finally Cillian laughs. "Come on, we've got pizza, and this stupid bloody movie that Ais is bullying me into watching."

It's hilarious that Aisling is capable of bullying *him*.

He takes my jacket from me and hangs it on the coat hook in

the foyer, his dark eyes sliding appreciatively over the silk camisole. "New?"

I nod. "Another impulse purchase that worked out. I think it flatters my figure."

"You could wear a paper bag and still be beautiful, St. James," he responds with a shake of his head. "But I like it. It looks amazing on you."

My lip tilts upward. "Thank you."

I follow Cillian out of his foyer and into the apartment. It's small but cozy. Obviously his sister has taken to decorating some. There are plush throws and pillows on the couch and picture frames on the bookshelves in the corner. Hundreds of books are overflowing from it, and I turn to Aisling, who's seated at the table opening the pizza box.

"Have you read all of these?"

"Mostly." She laughs, scrunching her nose. "There are a few that are still on my TBR, but I'm always reading."

"*Always*," Cillian interjects. Aisling sticks her tongue out at her brother and rolls her eyes feigning annoyance, but I can see the hint of a smile playing on her lips. "She wouldn't leave London without them. Paid an arm and a leg to have them shipped over. I packed these bloody things for days."

God, he packed them all for her and had them shipped here? Cillian Cairney may actually be a big secret softie.

It's incredibly sweet and thoughtful of him to do that for his sister.

"Surprisingly, he barely complained. Though... there was a lot happening at once," she says in a strange tone, suddenly clearing her throat. "Anyway, yes. Thank you, big brother, for using your big strong muscles and packing all of my babies. Reading is kind of my escape."

"I totally get it. I actually do cross-stitch, and it's a way for me to just like...zone out? Like my brain can just focus on it without having to think very hard. Sometimes I just want to binge-watch shitty TV and do a cross-stitch," I admit. Mostly just *The Office* or *True Blood*.

Cillian pulls out a chair for me, and I drop down into it as Aisling hands me a paper plate.

"Yeah, that's the glory of finding something you love. It serves your purpose. Sometimes I just want to disappear into a fictional world and fall in love with a fictional man. They're always better than the real thing anyway. Oh, before you leave I have to give you a copy of this book that I read a few weeks back and loved. God, it was incredible."

Cillian blanches. "Please do not subject me to talk of your romance books, Ais. Please, I'm literally begging you."

The expression on his face is comical, and I can't help but giggle.

"It would be the most interesting thing to happen to you all week, Cillian," she retorts sassily.

And that's exactly the way dinner goes, the two of them teasing each other in between the questions Aisling asks me. It genuinely feels like she wants to know me, not just because Cillian and I are friends but because she's interested.

After we finish eating, we end up on the worn couch in the living room while Aisling grabs a snack. She told me tonight that she's got type 1 diabetes, something that Cillian had already mentioned to me in passing, and she has to monitor her blood sugar and be mindful about what she eats. Hence the cauliflower pizza she had for dinner. I make a mental note to try to find a type of dessert to bake for her that I could sub sugar for an alternative.

Cillian's sitting beside me, close enough that his leg is pressed against mine, but otherwise not touching me. It feels weird, being this close to him without touching him, and that realization makes a swirl of anxiousness appear in my stomach.

How easily I could become... attached to him even knowing that this is temporary, and that we're simply a casual hookup.

"You good, St. James?" Cillian whispers near my ear, his breath fanning along my earlobe and causing me to shiver.

I nod, forcing a small smile. I'm not ever going to mention the thoughts racing through my brain. They're fleeting anyway. As long as I remind myself that I knew exactly what I was getting into, what I practically begged him for, I'll be fine.

"I can take you home if you want. You don't have to stay for the movie if you don't want to."

I turn my head to face him, lifting a brow. "Are you trying to get out of this movie? Because you're scared?"

His head drops back against the couch as he laughs. "As if. I'm not scared of a fucking horror movie, Rory. I just get a bit queasy with blood."

"You're a *rugby player*..." I say, unable to keep the disbelief from my tone. "I don't think I've ever seen a rugby match that didn't have some type of bleeding injury."

"Nah, that type of blood doesn't bother me, it's the crazy shit on the screen that does. Guts and organs and shit."

I chew the inside of my lip for a moment before saying, "You know, this reminds me of Wren and the caterpillar debacle."

"Absolutely not," he deadpans, shooting me a glare.

I smile, shifting slightly to lean into his side. "It's okay to be afraid. Even if you are this big, broody, muscley guy, Cillian. Real men have fears too. Everyone does."

"Bloody hell," he mutters before throwing his arm over my shoulder and hauling me against his side, giving me the perfect spot to admire all of said muscles.

Aisling comes bounding back into the living room, a bowl of carrots with ranch drizzled over the top of them. "Ready? This one is gory, Kill. Your fav!"

The rumble of his groan fills the room around us, and I don't even try to hide my smile.

CHAPTER 24

Cillian

I'm bloody fucking exhausted.

I stayed late after today's practice to work on a few agility drills, and my entire body aches from overexertion. Even as conditioned as my body is, on days like today, I know I've pushed myself past my limits.

When it hurts to breathe... that's a good sign I should take a shower and go the fuck home.

Lifting the hem of my tee, I drag it down my sweat-drenched face as I make my way off the training pitch to the locker rooms, still attempting to catch my breath after so many ladder drills my head's still spinning.

"Yo, Cairney."

My head snaps to the unexpected voice coming from behind me. Fitz and Michaels are walking down the empty hallway toward me.

I'm surprised to see them here since everyone went home after practice.

"What's up, mate?" I respond, still a bit winded. I lift my shirt again and swipe at my brow.

They come to a stop in front of me and Fitz offers an outstretched hand to shake.

I haven't seen them much outside of the pitch because I've been spending most of my time with Rory and Ais, but we all talk in the group chat daily. We're supposed to have a guys' night soon and I'm actually looking forward to it.

Shaking his hand, I turn to Michaels and offer him my hand. He grins, slapping his palm in mine then bumps his fist against my knuckles.

"What the hell are you still doing here this late?" Fitz asks, glancing down at the watch on his wrist then back to me. "It's fucking eight o'clock. Practice ended like...hours ago."

I shrug. "Needed to work on some footwork. Felt a bit slow at practice."

Michael's eyes widen as he shakes his head. "Dude, *that* was slow?"

My lip curves into a cocky smirk at the underhanded compliment I'm not sure he even intended to give me. "For me it is. Anyway, what are *you* two doing here this late?"

"Forgot my damn phone earlier. We're getting ready to go to a party so we swung by so I could pick it up," Fitz says.

I knew practice had ended a bit ago, but I was too focused on the drills to realize how late it had actually gotten. Reaching into my gym back slung over my shoulder, I pull out my phone and open it. There's a handful of notifications.

A text from Aisling telling me she's studying late tonight with a group at the library and not to worry.

And then one from Rory, asking if I want to come over and watch a horror movie.

Fucking brat.

I'm still nauseous thinking about that damn movie they made me watch. Well, it's probably the workout I just put myself through but still.

I smirk, lifting my gaze back to the lads as I type a message, telling her I'm still at the pitch.

"Gotta head out, but I wanted to tell you about team dinner when I saw you walking up."

"There's a team dinner?" I ask.

Michaels nods. "Yeah, Coach hosts a dinner once in a while at his house for everyone on the team. Usually a barbecue, and Rory makes those famous fucking cookies." He clutches his stomach, a dreamy look flitting to his eyes. "Coach told me to make sure you knew about it and were going to be there."

It's crazy to me that just a couple of months ago we were barely able to walk on to a pitch together and now I'm going to an infamous team dinner.

"You gotta come, man. You're part of this team now and that means participating in team activities. Plus, I think it'll be good for Coach to see us all vibing, off the pitch that is," Fitz says, the two dimples in his cheek appearing with his grin.

"Yeah, and if you don't come, then you miss the cookies," Wren adds.

He has no clue that I could ask Rory at any time to make those damn cookies for me because no one knows what's happening between us, so I stay silent.

My mouth twitches when Fitz rolls his eyes, shaking his head. "You're obsessed. And ridiculous."

Michaels shrugs. "I'm a simple guy." His toothless grin turns into a shit-eating smile as he waggles his eyebrows.

"Okay. I'll be there. Text me the details? Time, place, all of that?" I say.

We exchange a quick goodbye, and when they leave out the double doors at the end of the hallway, I'm left feeling so much fucking relief.

I truthfully didn't know if being on this team was going to work, if I was going to somehow be able to gain the trust of these guys. To even push my own bullshit pride aside and allow them to extend an olive branch.

Pride's a funny thing. It can stop you from chasing your dreams and be the reason that you fail while sometimes being the only thing that keeps you in the game.

So I'm thankful that we've all come this far in such a short time. It's more than I could've hoped for.

Focusing my attention back on my phone, I pull up Rory's latest message, my brow knitting together as I read.

> **Rory:** Oh, that's actually perfect. I left my textbook there earlier in my dad's office. Could you wait for me? I'm going to run up and grab it. I have a key. It's kind of creepy being there alone at night.

Cillian: Yeah. I'm going to shower, I'm fucking disgusting.

Rory: Kay, sounds good.
See you soon.

She's not wrong. It is kind of eerie at night when it's empty. Usually the place is bustling with the coaching staff and team, so there's a strange quiet that settles over the building once the lights are out and everyone's gone.

It's so quiet you could hear a pin drop. I can hear myself breathing as I make my way to the locker room, the automatic lights flickering on above, illuminating the room. I set my bag on the bench and rifle through it, pulling out a change of clothes and my shower bag.

The locker room at Prescott is state of the art. Everything in their athletic department is thanks to the backers doling out thousands of dollars in donations to make sure the players have the best that money can offer.

It's nothing like the facility I used back in London.

Each shower is equipped with dual showerheads. Scalding hot water seems to massage every part of your body while you're beneath them. Exactly what the fuck I need after the grueling workout I just did.

Quickly shedding my sweat-soaked clothes, I turn the shower as hot as it will go, and step beneath the water. The hot water pelts my skin, and I nearly groan at the sensation, my muscles immediately beginning to relax.

I probably shouldn't have gone so hard today but I needed the distraction. A certain sassy, fun-sized brunette has been taking up all the available space in my head, making it next to impossible to focus, and the last thing I need is for my game to suffer because my head's not in it. I'm already busting my ass for my spot on this team without adding in a complication.

But Rory doesn't feel like a complication.

Exhaling, I drop my head back on my still tense shoulders, letting the hot water cascade over my face.

"Cillian?" My head whips to the doorway of the shower, wondering if I'm hearing things or if someone just whispered my name.

"Cillian?"

Fucking hell.

Rory?

Moving the thick curtain to the side, I poke my head out of the shower, the cold air hitting my face as I glance into the empty room. A second later, Rory appears, turning the corner, her gaze locking on me as a smile curves her lips.

Christ, she's fucking pretty.

But, hell, what is she doing in here?

"Baby, as happy as I am to see you...in the showers, do you realize how fucked we'll be if someone finds you in here?" My voice is a hushed whisper. Even though I was alone before coming in here, the way my luck goes, someone else has forgotten something and is going to catch us both in here *together.*

Not going to lie, my balls shrivel a little at the thought of that someone being Coach.

Truly, I can't think of a worse bloody scenario than *that.*

Rory stops short when she makes it to me. I watch as her throat bobs and her pink pillowy lips part. Steam billows around us, making the air thick and when her graze drops to the open spot in the curtain I'm leaning out of, she exhales shakily. "Well, I was going to grab my textbook myself, but then I started getting freaked out so I figured I would come find you. And I knew that no one else would be here this late, so I just…"

"Came to see me shower?"

Her cheeks flush even more, pink creeping down her neck and disappearing into the collar of her shirt.

"I…I…Yes," she finally admits with an eye roll. "I didn't want to be out there by myself. It's just a *bonus* that you're naked in there."

My lips twitch as I nod. "Right. A bonus."

She licks her lips, rolling them between her teeth.

We stare at each other for a moment until I finally say, throat thick with the need to reach for her, "Well, I'm going back in here because I'm freezing my balls off." I let the curtain drop back shut and add, "While you wait to decide whether or not you'd like to join me in here, St. James."

I hear her sharp intake of breath just as I step back beneath the hot spray and smirk.

A few seconds later she apparently makes her decision, because there's the faint sound of clothes rustling and cold air hits my back when she jerks the curtain open and slips inside.

I don't immediately turn, instead I remain facing away from her, my palm flattened on the tiled wall in front of me.

Although I've seen her completely naked, this is the first time I've been naked in front of her, and I want her to be comfortable. So I leave the ball in her court.

The shower stall isn't very big as it's meant for only one player at a time, so I can feel the heat of her body on my back as she steps closer.

"My God, Cillian. You have the best ass I've ever seen," Rory whispers.

I can't stop the laugh that bursts out of me that this is the first thing she says when we're naked and alone together in the fucking shower. "Christ, St. James."

She sputters, "I mean it's literally ridiculous. You could practically bounce a quarter off of it, and li—"

I turn to face her mid-sentence, and her words trail off, her mouth falling open, gaze falling down to my cock. Her rich, warm eyes widen, and she opens her mouth to speak, then closes it, swallowing roughly.

And I'm not going to lie, it's doing great fucking things to my ego having her look at me like that.

"I think...we might have a bit of an...anatomy problem, Cillian."

Her eyes are still pinned on my cock, which is hard and thick, bobbing against my abs from the attention and the fact that she's standing in front of me stark naked. The rosy pink buds of her nipples are pebbled and pointed, begging to be sucked, and her tits are the perfect handfuls that I want to weigh in my palms. Her waist is the shape of an hourglass, flaring at her hips down to thick thighs and a perfectly bare space between them that makes my fucking mouth water.

She's a goddamn dream, and she really has no bloody clue.

Rory St. James deserves to be worshipped, and I'm tempted to drop to my knees just to prove I'm worthy of her.

She draws her plump bottom lip between her teeth as she stares at my erection before lifting her gaze to meet mine. Her pupils are blown, flooded with heat I can practically feel as the air between us cackles.

"It's... *huge*."

I chuckle, my brow lifting as I reach for my cock, circling it with my fist and giving it a languid stroke that her eyes follow.

"C'mere," I rasp. I can't wait another damn second to touch her.

She takes a slow step forward and stops in front of me, her bare toes touching mine. The still-hot water cascades over both of us now, the heavy droplets clinging to her dark lashes as she peers up at me.

"Do you have any idea how badly I want you right now?" I murmur, watching the delicate column of her throat move as she swallows.

Her head shakes.

"Shall I show you then?"

This is reckless, being here with her when anyone could walk in at any time, but I push down the voice of reason and focus on the heady dose of need coursing through me that only has one specific goal in mind.

Rory.

An all-consuming need that drowns out anything else besides her.

She shakes her head once more, but before I can even ask what... she drops to her knees in front of me on the tile floor, peering up at me through her dark lashes. "I want to show *you* how bad I want *you*, Cillian."

"Rory, you don't have t—" I start, but her soft hand grips the base of my cock, and the words die on my tongue.

Holding my eyes, she leans forward and swipes her little pink tongue along the slit, capturing the bead of precum at the tip. "I know I don't have to, but I want to. So. Bad. Let me make *you* feel good."

Fire-hot arousal slithers down my spine, my stomach coiling tight when she closes her mouth around the head and hollows her cheeks, sucking me deep into her mouth.

Warm, wet heat envelops me and I groan, the feral sound bursting out of my chest.

Bloody fucking Christ.

I've never been a religious guy, especially not after everything I've been through, but this has me rethinking that decision.

I think if there is a heaven...it's without question Rory St. James's mouth.

"Fuck," I grunt, my jaw tightening and my fingers threading into her hair as she trails her tongue along the thick vein down the length of my cock.

I'll never last at this rate. I've imagined this moment so many times that now I'm fighting for control, the thread fraying until my restraint is left in tatters.

Or maybe it's just this fucking girl.

"Am...Am I doing it right?" she whispers.

I blink, water dripping from my face as I stare down at her, perched on her knees like the prettiest fucking girl. "Rory, I'm fighting for my bloody life here. I've been reciting stats in my head for the last five minutes trying not to come."

When she giggles, I shake my head and bend, grasping her chin between my fingers, tipping it up. "You're fucking perfect."

I can't stop myself from brushing my lips along hers and kissing her, my tongue sweeping into her mouth and tasting the salty, musky flavor of me lingering.

Possessiveness surges through me, catching me off guard.

Rory pumps her fist on my cock as I kiss her, forcing my attention away from the thought of her being mine and only mine. I make a noise in the back of my throat, pulling away and standing at full height, my gaze pinned to her as I watch her swirl her tongue on the head of my cock, lapping at it and then sliding my head back in her mouth.

My hips flex instinctively. I use my grip on her hair to guide her mouth up and down the length of my cock. Her nails dig into my thighs when I hit the back of her throat, a ragged groan rumbling from my chest.

"Fuck, Rory."

I lose the fight of keeping my eyes open to watch my cock sliding in and out of her mouth, my head falling back on my shoulders, my eyes dropping shut as the need to come tugs at my spine, making my entire body hum. One hand fisted in her hair, the other planted on the tile, are the only things keeping me upright.

My balls tighten, a warning sign that I'm close.

"Baby, I..." I trail off, briefly losing the ability to speak as the head of my cock hits the back of her throat again when she takes me deep, gagging around me.

For fuck's sake, my vision blurs, black spots dancing behind my eyes.

"I'm coming," I pant, pulling her off my cock. She stares up at me, a cheeky smile curving her lips, and I groan when she keeps pumping her fist, squeezing me tightly until I come, thick pearly ropes of cum coating her chest, spurt after spurt until I'm completely empty.

Seeing her covered in my cum stirs something awake inside me. Something slightly feral and unhinged.

I drag two fingers along her chest, gathering the cum that's dripping down the peak of her taut nipple and bring them to her mouth.

"Tongue out," I murmur.

Her lips part as her tongue darts out, her heavy-lidded gaze holding mine.

I spread it along her waiting tongue, my dick starting to harden again at the sight of her on her knees with my cum in her mouth and dripping down her tits.

"Now be a good girl, swallow me down. Every drop."

My cock twitches when heat flares in her eyes, and she closes her mouth and swallows, then licks her lips.

She's going to bloody kill me, and what a fucking way to go.

Lifting her off her knees, I wrap my arms around her waist and haul her against me, pulling us under the water as I kiss her, slanting my mouth over hers and showing her just how thankful I am for what she just did.

She whimpers against my lips as she lifts on her toes, threading her fingers in my hair.

I'm so fucking lost in her taste, in feeling her hard, pebbled nipples brushing along my chest that it barely registers when she pulls back, gasping.

"The water. Freezing!" Her voice is a squeak as she jumps back out of the spray that's gone ice cold.

I run hot on a good day, so add in the fact that she's naked and wet in my arms, I barely noticed. I laugh, reaching to turn the water off.

Rory's nearly shivering in the corner when I shake my hair, spraying her with water, and she shrieks.

"Stop it, you big idiot!"

I rush toward her, pulling her to me and wrapping my arms tightly around her. "Don't worry, baby, I'll warm you up."

She blinks, a slow, sultry smile spreading on her face. Her fingers ghost along my chest. "Then let's go home and finish what you started."

CHAPTER 25

Rory

My apartment always feels smaller with Cillian in it.

Not only because he's six foot four, two hundred something pounds of solid, unyielding muscle, but also because he's the type of man who commands the energy of whatever room he walks into.

But tonight, it feels like the walls are closing in. The air is thick and heady with palpable tension that makes my lungs constrict, anticipation humming through me like a live electrical current.

Cillian slams the front door of my apartment shut behind him with a quick flick of his foot and stalks toward me. My breath hitches audibly when his rough palms slide along my jaw, cradling me tenderly in his hands. "I don't think I've ever wanted anything as bad as I want you, Rory."

"Then take me."

Without hesitation, his mouth crashes into mine and he swallows down the needy whimper that escapes, sweeping his tongue past my lips and kissing me until my legs tremble.

Until my heart is in my throat, and my core is throbbing.

I kiss him back eagerly, my tongue stroking his greedily as his palms glide down my body to the flare of my hips, lower, until they're at the back of my thighs, and he's lifting me off my feet. My legs wrap around his narrow waist, and I moan when I feel his erection as it juts against my sensitive clit.

Cillian tears his lips away, panting heavily against my mouth. "Do you feel how hard you make me, baby? How fucking much I want you?"

God, I love when he says things like this.

It's so hot.

I nod, leaning forward and kissing him again, sucking on his bottom lip and nipping it with my teeth as he walks us down the hallway. He stops and presses me against the wall so his hands can roam.

They're everywhere.

Large hands cupping my breasts, sliding along my waist, palming my ass.

Everywhere but where I need him.

Where I'm so wet that I know I must be making a mess.

We're such a frantic jumble of limbs and teeth and touches, that I can't even keep up.

"Bedroom," I pant, breaking the kiss. "Please, Cillian."

I'm truly not above begging right now. If it made him move any faster, I'd do whatever he asked.

Thankfully, he carries me to my bedroom and gently lays me against the mattress. He stands between my legs, peering down at me with a heated glare.

"Tell me what you want. I need to hear you ask for it like my good girl. Ask for what you want." His voice is so gravelly, so heavy with desire that I swear I can *feel* the words as they wash over me.

"I want you to make me come."

His eyes darken as a wicked smirk tilts his lips. "How should I make you come?"

"With your—your mouth." I'm stammering not because I'm nervous, but because it feels like I'm going to combust at any given moment from how insanely turned on I am.

The locker room did nothing but make me want him more desperately. Watching him with his head thrown back in pleasure, his hands tangled in my hair, guiding my mouth along his dick was the most erotic thing I've ever experienced, and also the most *powerful* I've ever felt.

Knowing that *I'm* the one who gave him that pleasure.

His hands slide beneath my sweatshirt and in a single breath, he's tugging it over my head. Then his fingers dip into the waistband of my sweats and panties, and he pulls them down my hips until I can shake them off my foot and let them fall to the bedroom floor.

He's gotten me naked in twenty seconds, and he's *still* fully clothed.

His hungry gaze travels agonizingly slow over my naked body. "Christ, you're a fucking dream." Dropping to his knees between my thighs, he reaches beneath them and curves his hands around the tops, yanking me to the edge of the mattress.

"Watch me eat your pussy, baby. Keep those pretty eyes on me."

Deft fingers spread me open, and he lowers his mouth to my aching core and glides his tongue all the way up my slit.

God, nothing in the world feels the way it does when he touches me.

I whimper as he continues eating me, my arms trembling as I struggle to remain upright.

"Cillian," I moan. He latches his mouth on to my clit, sucking it into his mouth, rolling it between his lips in a slow, maddening pace that has my hips rocking against him.

Pleasure pulses and throbs inside me, my orgasm already beginning to unfurl in my lower stomach.

It's been the world's longest night of foreplay ever since I found him in the shower, and I already feel like I'm going to tip over the edge.

When he pulls back, his lips glistening with my arousal, and pushes two fingers deep inside me, my back arches off the bed. He finds my G-spot so quickly that it's actually a crime. He strokes it gently with the pad of his finger as he lowers his mouth back to my clit and swirls his tongue around the sensitive bud. Alternating between hard sucks and soft licks, he drives me out of my mind with lust.

I'm not sure I can handle another second.

"I need you," I cry out, my fingers disappearing into his dark mop of hair.

His chuckle vibrates through me. "When you come on my tongue, then you can have my cock. Give it to me, baby."

His teeth graze my clit lightly, and that's all it takes for me to come harder than I have in my life, my legs trembling as they slam shut around his head, my entire body quaking with pleasure.

I moan so loud, my neighbors can probably hear, but I can't even bring myself to care.

Cillian continues to flick his tongue along my clit until I'm too sensitive, and then with one last kiss to my pussy, he rises to his feet.

He reaches behind him and grasps the neck of his T-shirt, pulling it over his head and dropping it to the floor at his feet.

God, his body is fucking incredible.

He looks like he's carved out of the finest marble. Broad shoulders and hard, sculpted abs. Rows and rows of abs.

The delicious lines at his hips that disappear into the waistband of his pants are defined, and so sharp they could cut.

He's *gorgeous*.

It should be a sin for someone to be this effortlessly attractive.

I draw my lip between my teeth and watch him push his dark sweatpants and briefs down, freeing his thick, hard erection. It bobs almost angrily against the taut muscles of his stomach, a small pearl of precum beaded at the slit.

Cillian grips the base, giving it a rough tug as he glides his fist up to the swollen head, sweeping his thumb along the underside, and sucking in a sharp hiss. I never knew it could be so...hot to watch a guy touch himself like this, but it's undeniably one of the hottest things I've ever seen.

"Do you like watching?" he rasps darkly.

I nod, never taking my eyes off his fist as he strokes himself unhurriedly.

"Next time we can play, baby. Right now I need to be inside you."

I feel the mattress dip as he fits himself between my parted thighs and then lowers his mouth to mine and captures my lips, stealing the air from my lungs. My hands slide into the long hair at his nape and my hips rock, causing his erection to slide through my soaked core.

He pulls away with a sharp hiss, dropping his forehead to my shoulder.

"Fuck, Rory. That feels..."

"Amazing," I breathe, repeating the motion until my arousal is coating his cock. He flexes his hips, reaching down to fist his cock once more and rubbing the thick head against my clit.

My back arches, the sensation of our bare skin together...too much.

"Shit. A condom," he mutters.

"Drawer."

He lifts off me and reaches into the drawer next to my nightstand, pausing when he sees my vibrator inside. He flicks his gaze to me wearing a cocky smirk. "Next time too."

My cheeks immediately flood with fire when I picture Cillian using the toy on me and I swallow roughly.

"My dirty girl. You'd like that wouldn't you?"

"Yes," I reply breathlessly.

Cillian tears open the foil and quickly sheathes himself before he joins me back on the bed. My heart is racing, my pulse thrashing wildly because part of me can't believe this is even happening.

I'm about to have sex with Cillian Cairney.

His large body folds over mine, his hips settling perfectly between my thighs as he holds himself above me on his forearm. "Are you sure, Rory? Say the word and we can stop. At any time."

"I'm sure. Absolutely sure," I say without hesitation.

I know without a doubt that this is what I want. And one thing that I've come to learn about Cillian is that he wants to hear my consent. It's important to him that I feel comfortable, and that we take things at my pace. It's *achingly* sweet, and it makes my heart squeeze.

It only further confirms how positive I am that I want this. I want to share this with him.

It might not be my first time, but it's the only time I've ever felt safe and comfortable with someone. It's the only time I've felt actual pleasure given by a man.

And I don't think I could've chosen anyone better to experience it with.

Despite his bad boy reputation, I know that he's one of the good ones.

"We'll go as slow as you need," he promises as he drags his cock through my arousal, coating it, then lining up with my entrance. His hips slowly rock forward, the first inch of him slipping into me, and my breath hitches.

It's not exactly painful, no. It's more the anticipation of it happening that has me tensing, waiting for him to fully seat himself.

It's almost as if he reads my mind, or maybe he just reads my body the way no one else ever has, because his hand slips down my stomach to my clit, and he rubs soft, quick circles. He lowers his mouth to my neck and plants wet, hot kisses there, trailing his tongue along my heated skin, all while his talented fingers thrum my clit. He slowly sinks inside me inch by torturous inch.

Oh.

That's...

Good. Great.

"You're doing so good, baby, you're taking me so well," he murmurs into the curve of my neck, nipping gently.

I've always been a good girl.

Never missing class, never turning in assignments late, always doing what I'm told.

So it comes as no surprise that I love to be praised by Cillian.

With another slow, hard flex of his hips he buries himself to the hilt, hitting a spot that I think has never been reached before.

A deep, guttural groan slips past his lips, and I swear, a gush of wetness pulses from my core just hearing such an animalistic, feral sound rumble out of him.

"Are you okay? Did I hurt you?"

My head shakes, and I reach for his jaw, brushing my thumb along the stubble forming there. "I'm good."

For a beat, he remains still, allowing me to adjust to his size, but when he shifts, his pelvis brushes against my clit and my eyes roll back, pleasure surging through me unexpectedly.

It feels completely different from just having his mouth on my clit, or his fingers inside me. I feel impossibly...full. Overstimulated in the very best way.

When I suck in a shaky breath, his brow pinches. "Shit, I'm sorry I—"

"No. Please, move, Cillian," I pant, raw desperation snaking down my spine.

He reaches for my hand, threading his long fingers in mine as he withdraws, pressing his hips forward in a slow, impossibly deep thrust that has me panting.

"You're so fucking tight, baby. So fucking good."

I can tell he's holding back, trying to show restraint, but...I don't want that.

I want him to fuck me.

And he told me to ask for what I want.

"Fuck me. Stop holding back."

His dark eyes flare for the briefest moment of hesitation. And then he slides his rough hand along my side, down to my outer thigh, where he hitches my leg high on his hips, sinking even deeper.

And then he does exactly as I ask and *fucks* me.

Hard and fast and deep. His thrusts nearly moving me up on the bed from the force.

He rotates his hips in a circular motion that has my vision dancing, my eyes fluttering shut as my nails bite into the skin of his back.

God, whatever I thought having sex with Cillian would be like is not even in the same universe of what it actually is.

This is euphoria, and I can't get enough.

Cillian switches position, placing both my legs on his shoulders and slams back inside me. This new angle is even deeper than before, and with every thrust, he bottoms out.

The soft mat of hair on his pelvis drags against my clit, and suddenly, I'm tipping over the edge, free-falling as my orgasm hits me out of nowhere.

There was no building, a slow crescendo that eventually peaked.

This is all-consuming and unexpected, heat flooding my lower belly as I detonate like a bomb.

"Fuck yeah, come on my cock," he groans roughly, dipping to suck my pebbled nipple into his mouth as he fucks me through my orgasm. My walls tighten around his cock as my climax continues to ripple inside me. My legs shake violently as pleasure like

I've never known sweeps through me in a soul-shattering, torrential wave.

I'm still trembling when I peel my eyes open and stare up at Cillian.

"Wow." My voice is so hoarse, I barely recognize it. "Uh...did you come?"

He chuckles, pressing a sweet, lingering kiss to my lips before he shakes his head. "Oh, I'm not nearly done with you yet, St. James. We're just getting started, baby."

CHAPTER 26

♡

Rory

"Hey, Ror, can you do me a favor and grab my apron out of the kitchen?" Dad asks as he opens the top of the barbecue pit, then starts adjusting ten different knobs that I won't pretend I have any idea of what they actually do. This is why he handles the main course, and I handle everything else for team dinners.

Work smarter, not harder.

"Sure!" I call back, hopping down from the outside bar. I pull my phone out of the back pocket of my jeans, checking my notifications as I walk back inside, immediately opening Cillian's message.

> **Cillian:** I'm going to spend the entire night looking at your mouth and thinking about what you did with it last night. This is not good, St. James.

I can't stop the smile that flits to my lips.

Last night *was* incredible, and the night before... and the one before that. The past week has been an orgasm-filled haze that has left me deliciously sore and achy in all the right places.

And I fear that I'm becoming addicted. Not just to the orgasms, but to *Cillian*.

I quickly text him back, even though when I glance at the clock at the top of the screen, I see that everyone should be arriving in the next few minutes, including him.

> **Rory:** Be a good boy and maybe I'll do it again as *my* thank you. 😊

We seem to be doing a lot of thanking lately, and I still can't get enough. My stomach's bouncing with excitement and a tad bit of nerves that Cillian's going to be here tonight. His first team dinner. When I think back to just weeks ago, I honestly wasn't sure this moment would *ever* happen.

And granted, we're not completely out of the woods yet, but it's definitely a step in the right direction. A huge step. One that I will gladly take if it means that I get to keep him.

I mean, in the literal sense. On the team. Not like I'm going to keep him as *mine*.

Passing over the threshold into the house, I walk to the kitchen and grab Dad's barbecue apron off the hook he keeps it on in the pantry.

And that's when I hear voices in the foyer, signaling that the guys have arrived.

I shove my phone back in my pocket and take a deep breath.

It's showtime.

The moment I turn the corner from the kitchen to the hallway, I spot Wren and Fitz in the foyer.

"Rorryyyyyyyy! My favorite girl," Fitz says with a wide, cheeky smile. He tosses a heavy arm over my shoulder, dragging me against his side. And for a second, I stay there, letting the comfort of my best friend surround me. I guess I didn't realize how much I missed him until now.

Things have just been so... busy the last few weeks, I feel like I haven't seen much of anyone besides Cillian. He's been occupying nearly every minute of my free time.

And most of that free time includes mind-blowing orgasms, so no complaints from me.

"Oh, your *favorite*? Does this have anything to do with certain cookies, maybe?"

He has the audacity to look offended, like I can't see right through his facade. Best friends, remember?

"Can you blame me, Ror? Those things are literally the highlight of my month. Either way, you know you're my favorite girl. Always have been, always will be."

"Hey, she's *my* favorite too," Wren interjects, elbowing Fitz just as the doorbell rings.

"Well, good thing I love you both equally. Which means equal amount of cookies," I quip as I duck under Fitz's arm, tossing them a grin over my shoulder, before I walk to the front door.

Soon the house and backyard are filled with most of the team, except for... Cillian.

He hasn't shown up yet, and I'm starting to worry that he might not show up at all.

I check my phone again, sighing when I see that he hasn't sent me a text, and then shove it back into my pocket. I guess he could've changed his mind. It's not like tonight is mandatory attendance, more of something casual and fun we like to do together outside of the pitch.

"Ror?" Fitz calls from the barstool beside me, his thick brows pinched together beneath the brown beanie he's wearing.

I hum. "Hmm?"

"Everything good?"

I force a small smile and nod as the white lie spills from my lips. "Yeah, of course. Just thinking about the mountain of homework I have to work on later."

He laughs. "Worry about it later. Have fun with us tonight, Ror. Give it a rest, and think about it tomorrow."

Then Wren walks out of the house carrying a huge bowl full of salad and a few steps behind him is Cillian.

He came.

My heart gallops wildly in my chest, and for a moment, I almost forget that I can't just get up and go to him, throw my arms around his neck, and tell him how glad I am he's here.

That's the hard part about... falling for someone in secret.

His eyes find mine from across the yard, and his lips tilt slightly.

"Look who's here," Wren says, glancing at Cillian, who looks slightly uncomfortable at the sudden attention. He's wearing a pair of relaxed, dark-washed jeans, with a thick burgundy sweater and a thick black jacket.

Though I've spent the last week having hot, sweaty sex on every surface of my apartment with him, the sight of him still makes my pulse race.

He's the most attractive man I've ever seen, and even more so now that I've gotten to know him... beyond those concrete walls he puts up that I think have slowly begun to crumble.

Cillian lifts his hand in a small wave as he looks out around the backyard, pausing on Brooks and Ezra, who are sitting under the outdoor heaters.

I shift my attention to the two of them, watching as their expressions stay neutral. Brooks nods at him before going back to his conversation.

And Ezra just looks bored, barely acknowledging him.

While most of the guys on the team have made so much of an effort with Cillian, there's still a slight tension among the three of them. I think I can tell because I know all of them so well. They're not icing him out any longer, at least from what I can see, but things are definitely not rainbows and sunshine between them by any means. I don't think it ever will be, if I'm being honest.

The other night when we were lying in bed, I finally pulled out of Cillian what happened when he first got here... and where the black eye *actually* came from, since I know there's no way he fell into a locker.

And now I know it was Brooks. And that Brooks tried to goad him, and Cillian walked away.

He walked away without touching him.

Even after Brooks fucking *hit* him!

No one said anything. They all stood by and let it happen, and I'm honestly so disappointed and ashamed that these guys

I thought I knew and that I love so fiercely would take part in something like that.

Cillian made me promise not to say anything, especially to Dad, but I'm still upset about it. Even slightly at Fitz and Wren for not telling me.

But considerably more at Brooks and Ezra for being assholes. Ezra has always given me that vibe, but Brooks? I'm shocked, especially since he's supposed to be leading this team.

A small part of me wants to tell Dad what happened, but an even smaller part of me knows that I can't because it would mean betraying Cillian's trust. Which is something he doesn't give freely and I would never want to lose. Especially now that things have gotten progressively better. I would hate to undo all that progress.

Looking up, I see Wren and Cillian walking toward us after talking with Dad, and I pull my jacket tighter around me as a chill creeps up my spine. It's freezing even with the heaters, fire, and my thick jacket.

Wren flops his massive body into the chair across the bar and pulls out the one beside him for Cillian.

"What's up?" Fitz says, extending a hand over the table. Cillian clasps it as he gives him a rare smile. "'Bout time you finally showed up. I was getting worried that you wouldn't."

Cillian's shoulder lifts in a shrug. "Nah, I told you I'd be here. Just had some stuff at the flat to handle."

Is that why he didn't text me back?

"Well, I'm glad you're here, man. We're glad, right, Ror?" Fitz says as he bumps a shoulder against me gently.

I nod, and Cillian's eyes find mine, the two of us sharing a secret look that lasts for only a second. He reaches up, running a hand through his dark hair.

"Thanks for the invite. My first American cookout." His tone is light, a hint of playfulness shining through. "Can't say I've ever had barbeque in the cold though."

"Dad is...dedicated when it comes to team dinners," I say with a shake of my head. "He says they're imperative to team building, but I think it's just because he wants an excuse to cook for everyone."

Wren scoffs. "Yeah, and I swear he's secretly from Russia or something because the cold doesn't affect him ever. He could do this shit in the middle of a snowstorm and not bat an eye."

This is true.

His daughter on the other hand is still not accustomed to New England winters even though I've spent my entire life here. You'd think that after twenty years of blizzards and ice that I'd have grown used to it, but you'd be dead wrong. I think in a past life I was absolutely an island girl. From somewhere warm and tropical like Hawaii or Bora Bora.

"Oh shit," Fitz interjects. "Do you remember that time freshman year when he made us run when it was fucking freezing outside? Because we were still hungover that day at practice. Kill, I swear to God one of us puked and it froze on the fucking ground. I wish I was joking but I'm dead-ass serious."

Cillian laughs as he shakes his head. "No way?"

Fitz nods, lifting his hand to his heart. "Swear to God."

"It's been a while since any of us had to run like that," Wren says with an arched brow and a tight grimace.

I vaguely remember that happening. I felt terrible for the guys, but then again they shouldn't have gotten shit-faced drunk the night before an important practice, and they knew that.

"That's hilarious. Objectively. As someone who didn't have to participate that is," Cillian says.

The conversation continues to flow easily between everyone, and I sit back and observe, mostly remaining quiet. At one point a few of the other guys on the team come over and talk to Cillian, which makes my heart surge.

I'm slightly emotional about it, even though I'm not going to admit that to him. I'm just so happy to see them making such an effort with Cillian, and I can't wait to see how all their strides will affect their gameplay on the pitch.

Together? Playing as a team with trust and communication... these guys would be unstoppable. A true force.

And not only that, but I know it matters to Cillian that he's not seen as an outsider any longer, that he's fully a part of this team.

He might not think his feelings matter to anyone else, but they do. To *me*.

I care about him. Probably more than I should, but it's not like I ever truly had a choice in the matter.

"Shit, uh... where's the toilet at?" he asks us, and I speak up before anyone else can.

"I can show you."

I slide off the barstool, and Cillian rises from the chair, following behind as I lead him back inside.

We've barely made it into the kitchen when I turn to him, throwing my arms around him and burying my nose into the crook of his neck, breathing him in. His strong arms slide around my waist, and we stay like that for longer than is safe.

"I'm so proud of you for coming," I say quietly. "When you didn't show up I was worried that you weren't going to come at all...I was just worried."

"I was helping Ais with her new insulin pump. It was giving her issues, and I didn't want to leave until I knew it was working properly. I told you I'd be here, St. James." His palm on the small of my back pulls me tighter against him.

Suddenly, there's a flurry of voices right outside the back door, and I pull back, my heart nearly thrashing out of my chest in panic. I grab Cillian's hand and pull him into the guest bathroom, slamming the door shut just as the back door opens.

"Shit, that was close," I huff, letting go of the breath I was holding, studying his unaffected expression as he leans back against the bathroom vanity, fingers curving around the granite counter. "You know you are way too unbothered right now when my heart feels like it's about to beat out of my chest, Cillian!"

His mouth twitches in amusement and I sigh. "Is Aisling okay?"

"Yeah, baby, she's okay," he responds softly as he reaches for me. My feet propel me forward, as if there's an invisible magnet between us, controlling the pull until I land in his arms. His fingers grasp my chin, tipping it up. "Means a lot to me that you'd ask."

I swallow down the lump of emotion that's gathered at the base of my throat before responding. "Of course. I really like her. I'm glad that we got to meet."

"Me too."

"I heard Liam talk about your guys' night. I think they're officially accepting you." I wiggle my eyebrows. Being invited to go out with the guys? It's an official invitation if there ever was one, and it makes me *deliriously* happy.

I'm glad they're at least starting to pull their stupidly large heads out of their asses.

"Told him I might have plans though. Depends."

"On?"

"If I'm not between your pretty..." His words trail off as he dips his head near my ear, planting a hot, lingering kiss beneath it. "Perfect." Another wet kiss an inch lower, causing me to shiver. "Thighs."

My eyes flutter shut when he kisses the pulse point in my neck, the one that's racing wildly beneath his lips as he sucks on it. My knees actually go weak. A breathy moan tumbles from my lips.

"Don't quite want to go to any parties. I think I'd rather stay right there instead."

Why is this man so impossibly talented at saying things that make my brain short-circuit, and my clit throb?

"That sounds...good. Great. *Wonderful*," I say breathlessly, earning me a low chuckle against my skin.

"Later. Right now we should probably get back out there, yeah? Someone's bound to realize we've both been missing for a while."

Shit. He's right.

Fitz and Wren heard me say I'd show him the bathroom.

What if they realize?

"I can practically see your brain working, St. James. It's okay. I doubt anyone's even noticed," he murmurs, sweeping his thumb along the edge of my jaw.

Would it really be that bad if people...knew about us?

The question is on the tip of my tongue, and I open my mouth to ask, but at the last second, snap it shut.

I doubt Cillian wants to discuss our... relationship in the bathroom at his coach's house. I'm not sure if he even reciprocates the feelings that have been demanding to be known the past couple of weeks. It could just be me, lost in my head, romanticizing something that isn't even there.

"I'll sneak out, and then in a few minutes, you come out. That way we're not showing up back outside at the exact same time. 'Kay?" I force a smile, lifting on my tiptoes and brushing my lips against his in a quick kiss.

I give him one last look before stepping from his arms and slipping out the door.

The only thing I can think about as I make my way back outside is that even if he doesn't feel the way I do... it's too late to stop falling for Cillian Cairney.

That much I know for certain.

CHAPTER 27

Cillian

I should be used to change by now.

The last two years of my life had been nothing but temporary. In fact, the only thing that remained constant was that no matter how much I wished for things to be different everything would inevitably change.

It's how I view being here in America. *Temporary* until I could get both Aisling and myself back to Europe.

My spot on the team at Prescott... *Temporary.* A stop along the way till I could be back in London playing in Gallagher Premiership.

Except everything had changed between Rory and me in the past few weeks and it has knocked the fucking breath out of me because despite my familiarity with change, I didn't expect it.

It snuck up on me and once I realized what was happening, it was too late.

From the moment we started our arrangement, we said it was *temporary*. Only it doesn't *feel* that way anymore. It feels like something more, something that I can't just walk away from, and it terrifies the fuck out of me.

Maybe it had been changing since the moment that I met her, but I didn't realize it until recently.

Maybe it's always been something more and I was too stupid to realize it.

If there's anything that I've learned since Mum died, it's that running away from problems and things that scare me isn't the solution. It makes it worse.

Rory's the one thing I don't want to get wrong.

I might not feel like I deserve her, or can be the good guy that she deserves, but that doesn't mean I'm willing to give her up.

"Ugh, this is so good," she moans around a mouthful of lo mein as she sets the chopsticks back in the container. "I haven't eaten anything today."

I glare at her, ignoring the pouty lips she's giving me, as bloody cute as it is. "You have to eat, St. James. Yes, even when you've got class all day. Shall I start packing you a lunch?"

She scowls at me. "No. I'm going to get better about it. But for now I just want to enjoy my lo mein in peace."

We're sitting against the headboard in her bed, eating Chinese takeout and half arse watching a film on the TV. Thank fuck, not a horror because I've seen enough in the past month to last a lifetime.

Last night was the first night we've spent away from each other in...a while. After dinner at Coach's, she stayed over and had a movie night with him because she's been feeling guilty about how little she's seen of her dad lately.

Mostly my fault.

But it gave me time to try to sort through the shit in my head, or at least try to.

"I want to talk to you about something," I say, glancing over at her.

Her brows pinch together. "What's going on?"

I'm fucking nervous. I can't remember the last time my heart beat so fast. I think I've gone a bit soft for her, and I can't help it.

I set the takeout container on her nightstand and then turn to face her.

"Shit, I don't know how to do this, Rory," I admit, dragging my palm over my face.

"Do what exactly?"

I swallow. "I don't want to hook up anymore."

Panic moves over her face, and her eyes widen as she says, "W-what?"

Shit.

"No, no, baby. Fuck, I'm already making a mess of this. I'm bloody falling for you, Rory, and I'm fucking scared. I'm scared I'll fuck this up. And I'm scared that I don't deserve you and that no matter what I do to change that, I don't know if I ever will. I know this was supposed to be casually hooking up, but it's not for me anymore." The words rush out of me, and truthfully, they feel good to get off my chest. "I'm crazy about you. I can't stop thinking about you; I hate being away from you. It just…everything feels better when I'm with you. I feel like there's not a huge hole in my chest."

For a second, she's completely quiet, her expression unreadable.

Those seconds seem to stretch palpably, each one three times as long as the last.

Then she puts her takeout on the nightstand and launches herself into my lap, straddling my hips.

"I feel the same way. I wanted to talk to you about it yesterday at my dad's, but I was afraid that maybe it was just me feeling things, and not you. I'm glad that it's not because I'm really falling for you. And I've never actually been in a relationship so I'm not sure, but it kind of just seems like this is what it would be like if we were in one? No different?"

I nod.

We eat dinner together, study together, shower together, fuck, we do most things together now all under the guise of it being casual. Maybe it was at first. But it feels anything but casual now, and I can't pinpoint when exactly it was nothing but casual. All I know is that I haven't looked at another girl since we started our arrangement.

I have no desire to.

"It's not easy for me to…open up. But I'm trying," I admit. "Everything in my life feels temporary, and I don't want this—us—to be temporary."

"I'm not going anywhere, I promise you. I'm right here." She reaches up and cups my jaw, her warm eyes softening. "It's okay to be vulnerable, Cillian. Being vulnerable doesn't make you weak."

Her words wash over me, and my eyes drop shut as I swallow.

This feels like the hardest thing I've ever done. Everyone I've ever loved or cared about has left. My mum fucking died. The person I loved more than anything in the world.

And now I'm afraid I'm too broken to love. To let anyone else in.

"I'm going to try, Rory. That's all I can promise you, that I'll give it every fucking thing I have, okay?" I lean in, brushing my lips across hers. Needing the contact like I need air. "I don't know how this is going to work, or what happens next. I just know that I want you, and I'm too selfish to let you go."

She leans in, dropping her forehead against mine. "We don't have to have all the answers right now. We'll figure it out. I don't know, maybe once the season's over?"

My throat tightens.

"Your dad..."

Rory nods. "*I* will handle my dad. Later. I don't think he's going to have an issue with us being together, but things have just started to come together for you guys on the pitch. I don't want to hinder that in any way. With the guys, or with my dad. You've come too far. I think we just wait until the time is right, and then we'll figure it out. I'm happy with *us* knowing how we feel, and that we're together...everyone else can find out when they find out. It's about me and you, Cillian, not them."

"As long as you're mine, the rest doesn't matter." I lift a hand and tuck her hair behind her ear.

"Cillian..." Her voice cracks, emotion flickering in her eyes.

And then she leans forward, slamming her lips on mine, whimpering against my mouth as I sweep my tongue through her parted lips, desperate to show her that all that fucking matters to me is that she's *mine*.

Whatever that means, whatever the future holds or doesn't hold, I just want Rory.

I slip my hands beneath the T-shirt of mine she's wearing and gently pull it up and over her head, tossing it off the bed. As much as I love seeing her wear my clothes, I need it off.

I need to feel her right now. With nothing separating us.

She yanks at my T-shirt, a new sense of frantic desperation crackling in the air between us as we manage to get it off, only breaking the kiss to pull it over my head.

I lean forward and plant soft, lingering kisses along the swell of her tits, dragging my lips down the center of her chest before moving to capture her rosy nipple between my lips.

Fuck, she tastes so damn good. The sweetest forbidden fruit.

I want to slow this down, savor every second I have with her.

She's mine.

I take my time giving each nipple attention, sucking it into my mouth and rolling it, alternating pressure until she's writhing above me. I scrape my teeth gently along the peak, watching her shiver from the sensation, followed by rough tugs that have her hips rocking against my erection.

"Cillian, God…" she moans as her head falls back on her shoulders, and she pushes her tits toward my mouth. "You feel so good."

Her hand snakes between us, dipping past the waistband of my briefs and wrapping around my cock. I suck in a sharp hiss, dropping my forehead to the space between her tits.

She strokes me from base to tip, slowly, squeezing just the way that I like it.

Making me forget about going slow and taking my time.

My groan vibrates against her pink, flushed skin. "Fucking Christ, baby. I'm going to come before I ever get inside of you."

I raise my head to stare at her, seeing her brown eyes wide, pupils dilated, and heavy lidded. "Get inside of me then, please. I can't wait."

"You make me fucking crazy," I murmur against her lips.

She giggles softly as she lets go of my cock and tries to tug my briefs down. I lift my hips and help her pull them down enough to free it.

My fingers move to the front of the damp lace covering her pussy, and rub slow, firm circles on her clit.

I love watching her, the way she gives herself over to me so freely, letting me give her pleasure. Her plump pink lips part and her eyes flutter shut as her fingers curl around my shoulders, holding on tightly. There's a slight bite of pain where her nails carve half-moon shapes into my skin while she grips my shoulders, bucking her hips against my fingers.

I'm bloody obsessed with her.

Hooking my fingers on her panties, I drag them to the side, exposing the prettiest pink pussy I've ever seen. She's glistening in the dim light, already soaked and ready for my cock.

My mouth waters at the sight of her. I want to suck on her clit, and taste her, but I can't wait to be inside her.

Later, I'll have my fill, eating her until she comes on my tongue.

Rory rises on her knees as I line my cock up with her entrance. She's so wet that she's nearly dripping, and that's when I realize I didn't get a condom.

"Fuck."

She pauses, lifting her gaze to me. "What?"

"Forgot the condom."

"Oh," she whispers. "If you... If you want to go without one, that's okay. I'm on birth control and I've been... tested."

My throat tightens. "I've never been bare before."

"Me neither."

Fuck, I can't even imagine what it would feel like for her wet heat to clench around my naked cock.

"I'm clear. I'm tested for the team. Are you sure, baby?"

She nods wordlessly, holding my gaze as she sinks down slowly, inch by inch until I'm buried to the hilt inside her.

A strangled, stuttering breath wheezes out of me, and my hands fly to her hips, holding her in place. I squeeze my eyes shut as my fingers dig into the soft flesh at her hips. "Need a second."

It's never been this way before.

I've never felt so out of control, so lost in another person like this.

This is what Rory does to me. She's in my head, surrounding every goddamn thought.

After a moment, I lift her, guiding her slowly up on my cock, then I thrust up, causing us both to groan together.

My lips close around her nipple, tugging it roughly between my lips when she lifts onto her knees and begins to ride me. Those perky, full tits sway as she bounces on my cock.

"That's it, baby, fuck me," I say. "That's my girl."

I let her take her pleasure, carrying us both closer to climax. The closer she gets, her movements become choppier, her hips frantically rocking as she chases her orgasm. My gaze drops to where she's stretched around my cock, watching it slide in and out of her.

I fucking love it. Possessiveness swells inside me knowing that she's mine.

Mine.

"I'm... I'm about to... come," she pants.

My hands slide beneath her ass as I lift her, then thrust up roughly, fucking her so hard her entire body trembles.

My balls begin to tighten, and I know I'm seconds away from coming.

I bring my thumb to her clit, and it takes only one rough circle of my finger for her to fall apart. She tightens around me at the same time as I plant my cock deep and come, my climax ripping through me so violently that I swear I nearly black out.

I rock her slowly back and forth until I've emptied every drop of my cum inside her. And even then, it feels like I could go for more.

She collapses in a sated heap on my chest, both of us breathing heavily. I bring my hand to her hair, stroking the soft strands, and we stay like that for so long that I've already softened inside her.

And it's at this moment, when I have her in my arms, her ear pressed to my chest listening to the erratic beat of my heart, that I realize I'm never going to give her up.

I'm in too deep.

CHAPTER 28

♡

Rory

There's a delicious tenderness in my limbs as I stretch my arms above my head and sigh, drawing my lip between my teeth and sinking back into the mattress.

I trace my fingers over lips that feel slightly bruised from Cillian's kisses, recalling the hours and hours he spent exhausting me until I was nearly boneless.

Last night, it was like something changed between us, like we just couldn't get enough. An insatiable, frantic need that only seemed to grow with each kiss, each brush of our skin, each time he slid inside me and whispered that I was his.

And for the first time in a very long time, I shut off my alarm and skipped my morning classes because I was too tired to move, and also because playing hooky one time this semester felt worth it to spend the morning with him. Especially after last night.

When I run my hand along the sheets next to me and find them cold, I realize that Cillian must have been awake for a while.

I throw the covers off, find his discarded T-shirt on the floor, and pull it over my head. It hangs nearly to my knees and smells exactly like him. Clean and masculine. I inhale, breathing the scent in, and I can't help but smile.

I'm happy. So deliriously happy.

Part of me wishes I could keep us in this bubble, uninterrupted, just the two of us for longer. And another part of me can't wait for the day when we can eat at my favorite restaurant together or see a movie without having to worry if someone sees us or not.

I walk out of my bedroom and smell the scent of bacon cooking, and my stomach growls noisily. I'm starving, which makes sense after the hours and hours of strenuous physical activity last night.

My core throbs in response to that memory, and I cover my mouth, hiding my grin as I make my way into the kitchen.

I lean against the doorframe, watching as Cillian stands in front of the stove, skillets on every burner, humming while he flips a piece of bacon.

And I realize how *happy* he looks.

I wish he could always be this happy.

"Good morning," I murmur. His head whips toward me, a wide smile overtaking his handsome face. Arousal stirs inside me despite the fact that we spent the entire night fucking on every surface of my apartment... including the kitchen table he's set for breakfast.

"Morning, baby."

His voice is low and gravelly, the way it sounds when he's just woken up. The sleepy syllables rolling from his tongue in his delicious accent that makes heat pool in my lower stomach.

"I hope you plan on disinfecting that table."

He laughs. "Nah. I plan on having *you* for breakfast on top of it."

"As much as I would love that, I'm not sure that's possible. You've practically rearranged my organs with the monster that you keep in your pants." I wince slightly, and his brow immediately pinches in concern.

"Shit, are you sore?"

I nod wordlessly, pushing off the doorframe and walking toward him. He sets down the spatula next to the stove and moves to the cabinets, calling over his shoulder, "Where do you keep the painkillers?"

"I don't need painkillers, Cillian. I'll be fine."

Ignoring me, he begins to open each cabinet until he locates the one where I keep medicine and finds the Advil, pouring a few into his large palm.

"Here. Take these and drink some water. You need to hydrate, St. James," he says, his voice soft and coated with worry.

I can't help laughing. "You're cute when you're worried, but I don't think anyone's ever died from sex."

"Just take the bloody things," Cillian grunts, dropping them in my hand. "Let me take care of you, baby."

I take the pills from him, and grab water from the fridge. I toss them back and drink almost half the bottle. Damn, I guess I was thirsty. "Happy now?" I ask.

He nods, a devastating smile curling his lips. "Very. Now I'm going to feed you. Then I'll make your pretty little pussy feel better with my tongue. How does that sound?"

Glorious actually.

My stomach grumbles again, and he chuckles, turning back to

the stove as I sit down at the kitchen table and lean forward, placing my elbows on the top, watching him cook.

There's something incredibly sexy about a man who can cook. Especially a man who spent the entire night giving you orgasms and then offers to give you another as soon as he feeds you the food he's cooking.

I think I'd like to do this every morning.

The faint sound of ringing comes from down the hall, and Cillian grunts again. "Can you grab it for me? Probably Ais."

"Of course," I say, rising from the table and walking out of the kitchen. I go to my bedroom and find his phone on my nightstand just as it stops ringing. But then it rings again, and I see Aisling's name on the screen.

"It's Aisling," I call to Cillian. "Should I answer?"

"Yeah, please."

I swipe my fingers across the screen and hold it to my ear. "Ais, it's Rory. Cill—"

"Excuse me, I'm looking for Mr. Cairney? This is Logan Marks from Prescott University Medical."

My stomach plummets, and the phone shakes in my hand. Why is the hospital calling from Aisling's phone?

"O-okay, just one second please," I manage to say as I sprint back to the kitchen, almost running into the door as I carry the phone to Cillian.

He laughs when he sees me running, but then he sees my face and his own pales. "What's wrong?"

I thrust a shaking hand at him. "It's the hospital. Aisling."

I'll never forget the raw panic that flashes in his eyes. They go hazy for a moment as he lifts the phone to his ear. "Hello?"

His voice shakes, and it nearly kills me.

I can't hear what's happening, but I watch as his throat bobs, and he nods. The entire call lasts only a minute, if that, and then he pulls it from his ear.

"I have to go," he mumbles blankly.

"I'm coming with you."

It feels like he hardly registers my response as he brushes past me into my bedroom.

Less than thirty minutes later we burst through the doors of the emergency room, making a beeline for the front reception desk.

"Hi, my sister has been admitted. Her name's Aisling Cairney?"

The older man wearing dark scrubs nods. "Give me just a moment, please."

Cillian's frustration feels palpable with each second that passes as the nurse types away on the computer so slowly that even I start to get antsy.

"Sir, please, I'm very worried about my sister, can you please just tell me where I need to go?" Cillian says exasperatedly as he reaches up to run his fingers through his hair, his tone heavy with panic and worry.

Because I can't last another second without touching him, I grab his hand, lacing my fingers in his and squeezing reassuringly.

I don't care if someone sees.

I don't even care if my *dad* walked through that entrance right now.

Cillian needs me. And I need him to know that he's not alone.

"I'm trying, son, please give me just a moment," the surly nurse responds, and I squeeze Cillian's hand again, trying to offer any comfort I can.

Finally, the man looks up from his computer, takes Cillian's and my IDs, and tells him that she's on the second floor, room 293.

Thank God.

We take the elevator to the second floor, and Cillian bursts through the minute the doors open, dragging me behind him. The kind lady at the nurses' station points us in the right direction, and we easily find Aisling's room.

When we walk through the door, she's sitting upright in bed, wearing a pale blue hospital gown and a small frown. Compared to the size of the bed, she looks tiny sitting in the middle of it.

"Ais," Cillian says, his voice breaking on her name. "Are you okay? What happened?"

He strides over to her in two large steps, eyes running over every inch of her body looking for visible signs that she's hurt.

She nods. "Yes. I'm one hundred percent okay."

"You're in the hospital, Aisling. That's *not* okay," he deadpans.

"My insulin monitor must have glitched. My sugar dropped, and I fainted. I bumped my head against the table at the library, and the guy that witnessed it insisted that they call an ambulance. He actually um... rode with me here, so I didn't have to ride by myself. It was just a slight overreaction. I'm *fine*." Her sigh is heavy, her small frame shaking with the movement. It causes her glasses to slip down her nose. She pushes them back up before adding, "I mean it was the most embarrassing moment of my life having to be taken away in a freakin' ambulance, but other than being humiliated, I'm good."

Cillian curses as he reaches up and drags his hand down his face, shaking his head. "I was so fucking scared, Aisling. I—" I can tell how badly he's fighting for his composure, and I have to physically stop myself from reaching for him.

It's the worst feeling in the world when you care about someone and they're hurting, and there's nothing you can do about it. I feel helpless.

Aisling's expression softens as she gazes at her brother. She pats the bed next to her, beckoning him to sit beside her.

"Should I give you guys a min—"

"No, please stay, Rory," she says, giving me a smile. "I want you to be here."

I nod but hang back, taking a spot in the chairs beside the floor-to-ceiling window that gives a full view of campus and the rugby pitch. It would be gorgeous in any other circumstances, the sun shining bright and high as fresh snow blankets the ground and buildings.

"I promise you, I'm okay. You don't have to worry, Cillian, I can handle this," Aisling says when he sits beside her, fitting his massive frame next to her. "I have to take care of myself."

He huffs. "It's hard to do that when you're currently in a hospital bed, Ais. You could have been... You falling could have been very different." He reaches out, grasping her chin and turning her head to the side so he can inspect the spot that's bandaged.

"Yes, but it wasn't. It's not like I was careless and forgot. It was a malfunction."

"I knew we should've gotten another one after the issues the other day, but I didn't want to—"

"Cillian," she murmurs, cutting him off. "I'm *okay*. I'm not going anywhere."

In the panic to get here, I didn't even stop to think... Their mom. Oh God. Poor Cillian.

"I love you," he whispers gruffly, emotion flickering in his dark eyes. "I'm so glad you're okay, Ais."

"Me too. Thank you for coming. Both of you." When she turns her attention to me, I give her a small smile. "Did you read the book yet?"

Of course Aisling would bring up the smuttiest book imaginable when she's bedridden. My cheeks flood with heat, and I roll my lips together. "Uh... Yes, well I started it. It's..."

"Spicy." She giggles.

I nod.

A second later, a nurse walks through the door, pushing a small cart. "Hi, everyone. Can I ask you to step out for a few? I need to get Aisling's vitals, and the doctor will be coming by shortly to do a physical exam."

Cillian looks panicked. Aisling asks, "And that means then I can leave, right?"

The nurse's eyebrows raise, and she tuts. "Now, you know that will all depend on what the doctor says. I wish I could bust you out of here, sweetheart, but we need to make sure that you're okay. It's hard to tell with a head injury. There are a few tests I'm sure he'll want to run. And he's going to want to monitor your sugar for a bit with the new monitor."

Aisling groans.

I can tell it's the very last thing Cillian wants to do, but he slides off the bed and walks to stand beside me. "Ais, I'll be just out in the waiting room. Text me when you're done and I'll come right back, okay?"

"Stop worrying. Everything's okay. Okay?"

When he doesn't respond she pins a look on me. "Rory, you're up."

I thread my fingers through Cillian's tense ones, and squeeze. "You got it."

Once we're back out in the waiting room, surprisingly empty for the middle of the day, Cillian sinks down into the chair, propping his elbows on his knees and dropping his head into his hands.

"She's going to be okay," I say quietly.

Silence hangs heavily in the air between us until he finally lifts his head, and his expression nearly steals the breath from my lungs. His jaw tense and his eyes flickering with a hundred different emotions. Guilt, sadness... pain. He's hurting, and I don't know how to make it any better.

"Talk to me. Please, let me hold some of the weight, Cillian."

"When my..." His voice cracks, and I reach for him, placing my hand on his arm and sweeping my fingers soothingly across his skin. "When my mum died... no one would tell me anything until I got to the hospital. And today when I got the call about Ais, I just— I... I couldn't stop thinking about that night. About how I could lose her just like I lost Mum. It felt like it was happening all over again, Rory."

"Oh, Cillian," I whisper, my voice shaking with emotion as I slide my arm around his shoulders and pull him against me. He buries his head in my chest, and that's when I feel him trembling. Those big, broad shoulders that have carried so much weight, for so long, shaking as he begins to cry.

"She's all I have left. I..." The words break on a quiet sob.

I place my lips on the top of his head, stroking my fingers over his hair as I hold him.

It's the first time in my life that I've ever physically ached for someone. To want to take their pain away, even if it means making it my own.

Seeing Cillian break down, when he's so strong and steady, it... it's brutal.

"I miss my mum so fucking much that I feel like I can't breathe sometimes," he murmurs against my chest. "And just when I think that I'm going to be okay, that someday I'll stop just surviving and *live* again, it hits me with so much force that it nearly buries me alive. Sometimes I wish that it would. Then it wouldn't hurt so badly anymore."

I don't know what to say, what to even begin to say, so I stay quiet, moving my fingers along his hair as he keeps speaking, the words spilling out of him.

As if he's held this all in for so long now he can't stop.

I can't imagine that he's ever broken down like this to Aisling, not when he's always tried to be a pillar of strength for her.

"I've been so fucking lost for so long, Rory. So fucking lost." He laughs, but there's not an ounce of humor in the sound. It's devoid of all emotion. "She was a nurse. She took care of these tiny little babies. Premature babies who sometimes were born at barely a pound. I'd never seen a person in my life who was as empathetic and compassionate as Mum. She loved every baby she'd ever taken care of, and she'd even follow up with their parents after being with them for months and months. They became like family to her. Everyone would call her an angel on Earth and they were right."

My heart squeezes with each word. It's breaking for both him and Aisling. I can't. I just can't imagine the pain he's been living with.

I nod against his hair. "I'm so sorry, Cillian. God, I'm so sorry."

"It was pissing rain, like the sky had fucking opened up and dumped rain on London like we hadn't seen in ages. She was on her way home from the night shift." His shoulders tense in my arms, and I see his eyes squeeze shut, his breathing growing heavy as he recalls that night. "There was a truck that crossed the center lane... Head-on collision. She lived for three hours. And I didn't make it in time. I didn't fucking make it, Rory. You know the worst part? The part that fucking haunts me every goddamn day of my life? We'd gotten into some stupid fight that day. She was nagging me about something, and I had already had a shit day at the pitch, disappointed in how I had played, and I just lost it. We argued, and I said hateful shit that I will regret every day until I die. Shit that I didn't mean, that I could *never* really mean. I was just angry and lashing out, and she was the one standing in the way. And I never got the chance to say how sorry I was. I never got the chance to take it back."

Hot, wet tears slip down my cheeks, and I reach up, attempting to brush them away, but as soon as they're gone, more fall.

I hate that I never knew how badly he was struggling. In silence. All alone.

And I'm *heartbroken*.

"She forgave you, Cillian. You're her son, and that's what a mother's love is, it's... *unconditional*. She knew how much you loved her. She *knew*," I whisper through the thick emotion tightening my throat. "We all make mistakes, and we say or do things that we regret, but I know that she's looking down on both you and Aisling, and she's so proud of you."

For a moment he says nothing, completely still aside from the rhythmic rise and fall of his shoulders as he breathes. It feels like nothing I say could ever begin to touch the heartache that he's experienced, but I hope even the smallest part of it brings him some type of comfort.

There's no question that his mom would be proud of him. That she would've forgiven the things that were said in the heat of an argument. I believe it with everything inside me.

Cillian lifts off my chest, his eyes red rimmed and filled with unshed tears as he sits back in his chair, placing the heels of his palms over his eyes and exhaling shakily, attempting to regain his composure.

"You say she'd still love me, but you don't even know the worst of it. It didn't just stop there, Rory. I was a bloody fucking mess. An embarrassing mess. I barely made it through the funeral. I honestly don't even remember most of it. Just that I held on to Aisling like she was the only thing keeping me alive, and that's probably true." He sighs, dragging his palm over his face. "I was on a mission to fuck the rest of my life up from that night on. I was so fucking selfish, so goddamn stupid. I had Aisling to look after, and I was so fucked-up that I barely could open my eyes every day. How was I supposed to be what she needed when I was alive but barely breathing? I gave up. I went out every night, drank until I couldn't even think. Did drugs until I was numb. Physically. Mentally. Showed up late to practice, still fucked-up from the night before. Nearly failed every one of my classes. Got caught cheating on a midterm. Still, my coach put up with it because he knew I was a good player and that my mum had just died. I made excuses, promised to do better knowing I couldn't. I made promises that I never had any intention of honoring. I was a fucking disaster, Rory. When I think back to those days, I'm so ashamed of who I was. Who I let myself become. Someone my mum would've been disgusted with."

I reach for his hand, threading my fingers in his and squeezing. "You were hurting, Cillian. You were a kid yourself, and your mom died."

The tears in his eyes spill over as he sniffles. He reaches up to quickly brush them away, pulling his gaze from mine and out to the empty waiting room. "I pushed it all down. All of the pain, the guilt. How much I missed her and how I left things. I hated the world, but never as much as I hated myself. Not only did I fail her I failed Aisling when I was all she had left.

"It all came to a head one day at a game. There was a bloke from the other team, known for talking shit and goading and I knew that, but fuck...my mind was splintered. Broken into irreparable pieces. He brought my mum up, said she deserved what happened to her, and I just...snapped. We had just begun the game and I beat the shit out of him so bad that he had to be hospitalized. Fractured his skull. I blacked out; I barely even remember what happened. But that was it, I was off the team. I got a red card that day not just from the game but my coach had all that he could take, and I don't blame him. Not after all of the shit I put him through. I got arrested and my coach cut a deal to get me out, but that was it for him. He was done."

I lift a hand to my lips, and Cillian swallows roughly, shaking his head. "Aisling was the reason I woke the fuck up before I ended up in jail or worse...She cried, begging me to stop doing this to myself before it was too late. I'd never seen her so broken. It saved my life because I never wanted to see her like that again, let alone be the reason behind it. I could've died right then, when I was finally awake enough to see how much I was fucking up, how much of a mess I had made of my life. It made me realize how badly my shit was affecting her. Her health already wasn't good, and it got worse because she was constantly worried about me and not taking care of herself. She was fucking grieving *alone*, Rory. I wasn't there to help her because I was so fucked-up. She lost her mum too. Thankfully, my old coach...he called a favor in. I ended up here. That's all of it. The entire fucking nightmare that I've been living for the last two years, and most of it was my own doing."

There's so much of this I had no idea about. I knew he had been expelled, but I didn't know why.

"You lost yourself for a while, but that doesn't define you. Scars aren't always physical, Cillian. Sometimes the ones that are the deepest, the ones that hurt the most are the ones you can't see from the outside. They run like rivers inside of you, and sometimes they can make you someone that you're not. Because they have to heal, and when we put a temporary fix? We're just stitching them back together instead of really healing them. Now you're healing those parts of you and...you don't have to be strong all of the time, Cillian." My voice is barely above a whisper, but when I reach out and cup his jaw, he drops his hands and looks at me. "You don't have to carry it all alone. I'm here."

A dry laugh escapes him, the corner of his lip tugging up slightly. He slips an arm around my shoulder and pulls me against his side, dropping his lips to the top of my head. "You're too good for me, Rory."

He has no idea how much good *he* possesses. He's too busy

trying to fight the demons from his past to see the current version of himself and how far that person has come.

One who is strong, and courageous, and resilient.

"I think your mom would want you to be proud of who you are right now. She wouldn't want you to be drowning in guilt. She would want you to live your life, and to be happy. To be proud that you fought like hell and came out on the other side. No matter how hard you had to fight to get here. Because it takes so much strength and courage to pick yourself back up off the bottom, Cillian. And you don't have to feel guilty because she knew how much you loved her. No matter what. Give yourself the same love and compassion that you give Aisling. That you've given me. You have to stop punishing yourself for something that wasn't your fault. And I think now is the time to start."

CHAPTER 29

Rory

After everything I learned at the hospital yesterday, I understand why Cillian's so fiercely loyal and protective of his sister.

Aisling on the other hand does not want to be coddled nor have her older brother suffocating her.

Rolling my lips together, I sink back into the couch and watch the two of them having a... creative discussion, one that Aisling is absolutely winning, and Cillian has yet to realize that.

"Ais, for fuck's sake, you can't just pretend that you weren't in the bloody hospital *yesterday!*" he cries exasperatedly, tugging at the ends of his hair like a frustrated dad. My lips tilt into a grin, and I cover my mouth to stop the giggle that's threatening to spill. "You're supposed to be resting. You're being stubborn."

Aisling rolls her eyes, crossing her arms over her chest and lifting her chin in defiance. "And you're being overbearing. I got discharged, Cillian. That doesn't mean I need to stay in bed for the next week. I passed out. Barely hit my head. I'm *fine!*"

He groans as he stops his pacing and places his hands on his hips. "I'm sure when they discharged you they didn't mean go to a damn study hall. The test can wait. You can get an excuse."

"Nope," she retorts with a smirk. "Now, quit being so bossy and leave me be. My pump is working perfectly fine; you checked *three* times, remember? My blood sugar is fine. I have a huge test coming up that I'm going to sit in a chair and study for. End of discussion." Without another glance at him, she gathers her notebooks and laptop and puts them into her periwinkle-colored backpack, then stops and turns to me. "Oh! Rory. Thank you for the book. I'm so excited to read it."

"Of course. I was worried you already had this one, but the bookseller assured me that it was a new release, so I figured that lessened the chance of you having it despite your library," I say.

She reaches up to her curls and adjusts the bright yellow headband in her hair with a cheeky grin. Today she's got on a pair of light-washed overalls and a pink pastel long sleeve underneath with a frilly neck that I haven't the slightest idea of what the proper name for it is. What I do know though, is that Aisling has the most adorable style of anyone I've ever met. She's always wearing something girly and fun, and while it's quirkier than what most of the girls on campus wear, it's 100 percent her. It fits her personality to a tee, and I love that she's so comfortable with her self-expression.

Also slightly envious when I'm unsure of my own style, or lack of.

"When you're feeling up to it, would you possibly want to go... shopping with me?" A swirl of anxiety settles in my stomach.

I'm not sure if she would even consider us friends, but if so, she would be the first girlfriend I've ever had. Like, *ever*. All my friends are guys from the team.

Aisling's eyes light up as she bounces on the tips of her toes. "Hell yes! Literally nothing would make me happier. We could even get manicures? It's been so long since I've had one. Since I was still in London. There was this adorable little posh place near our flat that I loved. But you know you'll have to go through my *captor* if I'm ever to leave this tower." She cuts a pointed look at Cillian, who just shakes his head while muttering "bloody" something and my lips curve into a grin.

I think he's cute, like a worried dad, even though he *is* slightly overbearing.

But I get it. He feels responsible for Aisling even though she's technically an adult. And this is his way of showing that he cares and that he loves her.

"Perfect. We can make a day of it? Have lunch. I know this place right off campus that has the world's best lobster roll."

She nods as she slips her arms into the straps of her backpack. "Yes! I'll get your number from Cillian and shoot you a text. I've gotta run before I'm late." She walks over to her brother and throws her arms around his neck even though he's still grumbling. "Love you. I'll check in all day, okay?"

For a second he doesn't move. Then his arms wrap around her waist, and he holds her for a beat. "All right. If you don't, I'm coming there and making a scene."

She gasps sharply. "You wouldn't."

"Try me, Ais," he retorts.

"Fine. Whatever. See you lovebirds later!"

She lifts her hand in a wave as she bounds out the front door without another glance, slamming it shut behind her.

It's truly hilarious how different she and Cillian are, but I think at the end of the day, they balance each other out.

He looks over at me with a resigned expression before sinking down into the couch beside me and pulling me into his lap. I wind my arms around his neck, my fingers tangling in his nape, causing him to sigh.

"What do you think, St. James? Do *you* think I'm being overbearing?"

I draw my lip between my teeth and squinch my nose, giving him a subtle nod. "Maybe a little? I get it. I've got a different perspective though. I can see why she feels like she's being coddled, but also...you're worried. But you just have to remember, she's an adult now, and you have to let her make her own choices and mistakes."

Cillian's brow pinches, and I rub my finger over the tense space. "I guess you're right. It's just hard. Especially after yesterday. I'm scared something's going to happen, and I'm not going to be there."

"I know. But you can't *always* be there, and you'll drive yourself crazy trying to predict everything that could possibly go wrong." I press my lips to his when he sighs. "You have to trust her to make the right decisions and to take care of herself. Even though I know it's easier said than done." My lips ghost along his, to the corner of his mouth where I press a kiss, then one to the edge of his jaw, then pull back to look at him. "Maybe you just need a little distraction. You know, to get your mind off of worrying for five seconds?"

"Yeah? What kind of distraction?" His lip twitches and his dark brow curves.

Instead of responding, I rock my hips in his lap, feeling that he's already half hard brushing against my core.

Leaning forward, I hover my mouth just a few centimeters above his. His warm breath stutters as it fans across my lips.

I love that he's so affected by me, and that I'm not the only one who feels like this when we're together. Like there's this invisible string tethering us together, and with each breath it pulls us closer.

His large hands curve around my hips, his fingers digging into the soft flesh as he drags me over his erection, causing us both to groan in unison.

I think it might actually be a crime for him to be this good at making my body light up and come alive with such little effort.

I feel his hands slip beneath my sweatshirt and slowly trail up my back as he pulls me closer until I'm molded against his hard body and still... it doesn't feel close enough. I want more.

No, I *need* more.

Cillian moves to pull my shirt over my head when his phone begins to ring on the coffee table. He groans, dropping his forehead against my chest. "Bloody fucking hell."

I laugh. "Get it, it could be your sister. You told her to check in, remember?"

He reaches past me and grabs it from the table, his brow knitting together.

"What?" I ask, glancing down at the phone.

His eyes lift to mine. "It's Coach."

Surprise sears through me. Why would my dad be calling

him in the middle of the day? Maybe he wants to go over tape or something.

I shrug. "Answer it!"

He swipes his finger across the screen and brings it to his ear. "Coach. What's up?"

I can't hear what's being said, but I can hear my dad's voice low through the phone. Cillian nods to whatever he's saying a few times before he says, "Yeah, sure. I can be there in a few."

A few moments later, he hangs up and looks at me with a confused expression. "He just asked me to meet him down at his office. Said it's important, and it can't wait. You know what it's about?"

My head shakes. "I have no idea. I actually haven't talked to him in a few days, so I really have no clue."

Cillian's dark eyes move over my face as he lifts his hand to cup my cheek. The slow, steady sweep of his thumb along my jaw makes my heart falter. "Do you wanna wait here till I get back? Probably won't take too long."

God, I want to, but... clearly the universe is at work and knows that I've been neglecting my homework for the past few days and is sending me a sign to get my shit together. I don't think I've ever been this distracted in my life from school, but without a doubt, it has been worth it.

Sighing, I poke my lip out slightly. "I'm going to head back to my apartment. I'm so behind on homework, and I don't want to fall behind. But call me after? Tell me what happens?"

"Of course. Maybe I can help you... study later. You know how good of a teacher I am, baby." His grin is wolfish, causing his eyes to crinkle.

"I need to be a good girl for one night." I laugh, stealing a quick kiss before sliding off his lap and fixing my sweatshirt. "I think you can survive a single night without me. How else would you have made it this long?" I walk over to his kitchen table and grab my bag, checking that my phone and house keys are inside.

Cillian strides over to where I'm standing and wraps his arms around my waist, hauling me against him. "Can't bloody help that I'm addicted to you, St. James. It's your fault that I can't get enough."

I smirk as I roll my eyes. "Go, before you're late. He hates when people are late. I'll see you tomorrow, though?"

With one last lingering, toe-curling kiss, he walks me to the door and then I turn in the direction of my apartment and start walking home.

Ignoring the swell in my chest at how out-of-my-mind crazy I am about the guy I was never supposed to fall for.

And how I don't even care anymore.

CHAPTER 30

Cillian

There's a heavy feeling in my gut as I walk through the double doors of the athletic building toward Coach St. James's office. I can't tell if it's because the last forty-eight hours of my life have been an absolute shit show or if it's a sense of foreboding.

Not sure why else Coach would call me to his office unless something was wrong. It's not like we've got much to talk about outside of the obvious issues we've already discussed, but things have felt better in the past few weeks. Yeah, I mean, we're not all going to sit around and braid each other's hair and make friendship bracelets, but things have definitely improved since the first day I got here.

At least that's what I keep telling myself as I walk to his office.

I find his door open when I finally get to the end of the hallway, and Coach lifts his gaze from the paper on the desk in front of him, waving me in without a word.

When I walk inside, I see Coach Matthews seated in one of the leather chairs to the side of the room, and fuck, that only makes me more suspicious.

He hasn't been in any meeting I've had yet with Coach St. James.

"Please shut the door and have a seat, Cillian," Coach says, and I nod, closing the heavy wooden door behind me, then lowering myself into the chair across from his desk.

I can't read his expression, but I notice Matthews shifting uncomfortably from one side of his chair to the other, and the vibe I'm getting says that something's definitely fucking wrong.

The first thing that comes to my head is Rory. How could it not? I've spent the last month with her. Knowing the risks and that if we were caught there would be consequences.

Maybe we weren't careful enough or someone saw us and that's what this is about.

And maybe I'm going to have to face those consequences today.

But I highly doubt he'd have Matthews in here for an audience over a conversation that has something to do with his daughter.

"Thank you for coming in on such short notice." Coach sighs, his gaze darting to Matthews. Something unreadable passes between them before he forces his eyes back to me. "Cillian, there's been a very serious allegation made against you. And while I know that there has been some tension since the beginning, and it very well could be a baseless allegation, but as a coach, I cannot ignore it without verifying the validity."

What the fuck?

My throat tightens. An allegation? "I'm sorry, I'm confused. What type of allegation?" I say, my voice low.

Coach St. James hesitates for a moment before sitting back in his office chair and crossing his arms over his broad chest, his jaw steeling. I never really noticed how much he and Rory look alike until now, and it makes my stomach sink with the weight of lead. "There was an anonymous tip submitted through the student hotline that stated you've been witnessed doing drugs, and that you may be dealing those to other students. And due to the... your past history at your university in London and the fact that your position here on the team is currently probational, I have no choice but to take these claims seriously."

A low chuckle slips past my lips as I shake my head.

"Drug test me then, yeah?" I retort sharply. My fists are balled so tightly by my sides that I can practically hear my knuckles cracking as I try to keep my shit together. "Solves the problem quick. I'm not on drugs, and I'm not bloody dealing shit to anyone. I'll take the test right now."

"I'm sorry, Cillian. I hope that there's nothing to this allegation, and I wish that I could simply take your word for it," he says, and I'll give it to him, he does truthfully look like he's sorry.

But I'm fucking pissed and unwilling to see an ounce of reason right now.

Not only because he's accusing me of doing drugs when I've been busting my arse to earn my spot on the team, but also because why would anyone submit an allegation that's a blatant lie?

Fuck.

"If what you're saying is the truth, then we can administer the drug test and immediately lay the allegations to rest. And trust me, Cillian, there is nothing that I or Coach Matthews want more. We've seen the strides you and the rest of the team have made in the last few weeks, and we're both immensely proud that you've come together to make that happen. I truly hope this isn't the case."

I nod, tightening my grip on the chair.

I'm not worried about failing a piss test. I know I haven't done shit, and the test will prove it, but fuck, it just feels like a slap in the face that as far as I've come, this is where I'm back at.

In this very fucking chair that I sat in when I got to America, determined to turn it all around.

"I haven't done anything wrong. I'll gladly take the test. No questions."

Coach St. James reaches for the piece of paper on this desk, turning it to face me. "Okay. Coach Matthews will administer the test with me as a witness, and we should have the results immediately. I'll need you to sign a release form stating that you understand Prescott's drug policy and the substances that are prohibited. Also, giving your consent to perform the test and share the results with us."

I take the paper from him, my eyes barely scanning what's on it as I pick the pen up that he's slid across the desk and messily scrawl my signature at the bottom of the page.

I've got nothing to hide. I hope like fuck when I do this, then he'll realize that I'm not the problem on this team. As much as I hated being here in the beginning, since meeting Rory, I've given this shit everything I've got.

It's not just Ais I have to worry about disappointing now. It's Rory too.

And I'm not going to let either one of them down.

He nods when I set it back down on the desk. "Let's get this over with so we can get back to doing what we're all here to do. Play some rugby."

Both he and Matthews follow me into the bathroom at the end of the hallway, where they watch me piss in a cup, then administer the test.

I lean back against the stall, arms crossed over my chest while we wait. No one bothers with small talk to fill the painfully tense silence that seems to drag on slower than I ever thought possible.

There's nothing to say. He's sorry he's having to do this, and I'm...feeling a lot of shit.

Most of that I don't need to say out loud to him.

When the timer on Matthews's phone goes off, he picks the test up and peers down at it, comparing it to the legend.

Wordlessly, he passes it to Coach St. James, who just fucking stares for so long that I'm beginning to worry.

Finally, he lifts his gaze to mine.

"It's positive for amphetamines, Cillian."

CHAPTER 31

Rory

My eyes are burning after staring at my anatomy notes and textbook for the last... however long I've been studying.

It feels like hours, but truthfully, I've lost track of time.

Glancing out of the large arched window above my desk, I see the sun has started to go down over the horizon. I set my pen on my textbook and lift my arms above me in an attempt to stretch my stiff, aching muscles after being stationary for so long.

I probably should've taken a break before now, but I tend to lose myself in my homework easily and after severely neglecting it the last few days, I had a mountain to work on.

I make my way to the kitchen to search for something to eat, but I'm pretty sure the last time I went grocery shopping was... weeks ago?

I've been a tad preoccupied, so it's not at all surprising when the only thing I come up with after rifling through my cabinets is a protein bar and a pack of ramen noodles.

The quintessential college student's survival diet. As cliché as it sounds.

I'm putting a pot of water on the stove when I hear a soft knock at my front door.

It's probably Cillian. I haven't heard from him since the meeting, and even though I told him I was going to be studying this evening, I'm hoping he decided to come anyway. It hasn't even been a whole day, and I already miss him.

I walk through the entryway and open the front door with a grin. "I kne—"

Only it's *not* Cillian.

"*Dad?*" I say, my tone full of surprise.

He smiles, but it doesn't quite reach his eyes. He looks tired tonight. His normally bright eyes seem dull and heavy with bags beneath them. His salt-and-pepper hair is slightly disheveled, as if he's been running his fingers through it. "Hi, sweetheart. Can I come in?"

I swing the door open wide and step to the side. "Of course. What's... what's going on?"

Usually, he doesn't show up unannounced so I'm starting to get worried. When he walks into the living room and sits on the couch, dropping his head into his hands and not meeting my eyes, that worry morphs into something bigger.

Something's not right.

"Dad, what's happening?" I ask, sinking down beside him. I bring my thumb to my mouth to chew on the end. I need something to do with my hands with the anxiousness coursing through me.

He lifts his head, his expression fitted with apprehension that does nothing for the knot tightening in the base of my throat. "I...I wanted you to hear this from me, and not anyone else. I'm sure the entire campus will find out by morning. Cillian's been kicked off the team, permanently."

The floor seems to sway beneath my feet, and if it wasn't for the fact that I'm already sitting, I might actually fall.

What?

How is that possible? I don't understand.

I swallow, trying to keep my tears at bay. Out of everything... this is the last thing I expected to hear. And I can't show the emotion that I'm currently fighting to hold back. My dad has no clue that Cillian and I are together and...

"W-what happened?" My voice cracks slightly, the tremble evident.

He exhales, shaking his head as he shifts beside me. "This needs to stay between us, Rory. I'm only telling you this because I know you've had your hopes set on making this work, and you've developed a friendship with him. Like you have with the other guys."

The knot in my stomach tightens until an ache begins to form.

What I feel about Cillian is nothing like I feel for any of the other guys. He's become my best friend but...he's so much more than that.

And I can't even be honest with my dad about it, and that just seems to make the feeling worse.

"I know that you worked hard to get the team working together, to get them through the transition, and I want you to know this is not your fault, and you are not responsible for someone else's actions." He pauses as he reaches for me, squeezing my hand gently. "I received an anonymous tip that Cillian was using drugs and may be dealing them around campus. I didn't want to believe it. Shit, I *didn't* want to. But as a coach, I have responsibilities. I had to investigate it. When I brought Cillian into my office this afternoon, he agreed to a drug test."

My brow furrows in confusion. "Are you saying..." When I trail off, he nods, rolling his lips together.

"He failed, Rory."

No. No. *No.*

Cillian's not on drugs. There's no way.

I'm shaking my head, over and over, but I can't even find the words because this is just...insane. He's not on drugs. I know that he's not on drugs.

"I didn't want to believe it either, sweetheart. I really believed that he had turned things around. I'm so disappointed."

I spring from the couch, shaking my head. "No, Dad. He wouldn't. He wouldn't do drugs. He was working his ass off to keep his spot on the team. He wouldn't do all of that and be taking drugs. Not when it would get him off the team."

The hot sting of tears behind my eyes threatens to spill, but I suck in a shaky breath, willing myself to calm down. Obviously, this is just a big misunderstanding. One that we can easily fix.

"Retest him. It could be a false positive. You can't kick him off the team for a test that could be a false positive, or even a faulty test. That happens."

Dad shakes his head again. "We did, Rory. We immediately retested him with the same results. I saw it myself. He failed for amphetamines. Both times."

I feel like I'm going to puke. I can't believe Cillian would be on drugs, but my dad...he would never lie to me.

He reaches into the pocket of his jeans and pulls out his phone, turning the screen to face me.

I don't want to believe what I'm seeing, but... I can't. Because there's two positive drug tests.

Cillian failed. *Twice.*

My head begins to swim so I slowly walk to the couch, dropping my head into my hands as I breathe.

"Rory, it's not that difficult for me to believe that he went back to what he was doing in London. The boy has been through a lot, more than I can imagine honestly, and I'm not saying I condone it... I'm just saying that history has a way of repeating itself. As badly as I wanted this to not be true, it is, and now we have to deal with it. I have a responsibility to my team, and my guys."

I just don't understand. Why would Cillian *ask* for a drug test if he was going to fail it? None of it makes sense. Why would he do this knowing that it would result in an immediate dismissal from the team? Why put that work in?

"I'm sorry, sweetheart. I know how hard you tried. That's one of the things I love most about you... your heart. You always see the good in people." His arm slides around my shoulder and he tucks me against his side, rubbing a hand soothingly down my arm. I squeeze my eyes shut to stop the tears from falling.

I just... I can't believe Cillian would do this not only to the team but to *me*. Surely, there's some kind of explanation for this.

There has to be.

I know that his time at Prescott hasn't always been the easiest, but the Cillian that I know wouldn't do this. I can't truly begin to understand the heartache he's experienced in the past couple of years, and I know how hard it's been on him after he finally opened up to me.

I thought that I had gotten past those concrete walls around his heart, and that I knew who he really is beyond all that.

And after everything, he's been lying to me?

The thought of him hiding this from me feels unbearable. A type of pain I've never experienced before, and it *hurts*.

"Dad..." My voice cracks, and I tell myself to hold it together for just a few more minutes until I can let it go. It feels like an impossible feat right now. I clear my throat. "Um, I think I just need a little time to process this. I'll call you tomorrow, okay?"

I untangle myself from his arms and stand from the couch, facing away from him. I don't even know if I can look at him right now without breaking down.

"Yeah, sweetheart, of course."

I hear him stand from the couch, and on the way out, he presses his lips to my head in a lingering kiss. "I love you, Rory. It's going to be okay. We're a strong team, and we'll make it through this."

If only he had any idea.

I nod. "Love you too."

The second I hear the front door shut, I lock the deadbolt and fall back against the wood as a strangled sob rips free.

My hand shakes as I pull my phone out of my pocket and press Cillian's name in my contact log.

I have to talk to him; I *need* to talk to him.

Straight to voicemail.

Shit. Immediately, I call back. Over and over.

Every single time his phone goes straight to voicemail.

Rory: Cillian I need you to call me asap.
Please.

Everything was going great, Cillian was finally making strides with the team, they were building trust, bonding in a way that I couldn't have even imagined they would, and now... this.

It has to be a mistake. I want to believe I know Cillian better than this, that somehow this is an error or a misunderstanding but another part of me knows that my dad would never kick him off the team unless there was irrefutable evidence.

I saw it myself, and still... the way I feel about him clouds that.

I feel like I can't even trust myself right now. Not to take Cillian's side, to not believe him despite what proof is being shoved in my face.

Sliding to the floor, I let the hot tears stream down my face, my breath shaking with my sobs.

I'm hurt, and disappointed, and confused.

Because if he was struggling this badly, if he felt he had no other choice but to turn to drugs... he didn't trust me enough to come to me. To be honest and tell me that he needed help.

I had to find out like *this*.

Not even from him.

I don't know how long I sit on the floor, crying until there's nothing left, until I think I can somehow lessen the hurt and confusion I feel. My apartment is dark and my face is stiff and puffy from dried tears. And if anything, I just feel worse.

He never answered my text messages, and his phone is still going straight to voicemail. Radio silence.

I pull myself off the floor, wincing because my limbs are asleep after sitting on the hardwood for hours. I walk to my bedroom and strip out of my clothes before slipping beneath the covers and burying my face into the blankets that still smell like Cillian.

There's a fresh new wave of tears, and the last thing I remember before sleep pulls me under is all I want is Cillian to prove to me that this was all a mistake.

* * *

A loud noise rips me from sleep, and I shoot up in bed, my heart pounding as I glance around my darkened room. A flash of lightning lights up the room followed by a ferocious clap of thunder that nearly shakes the walls. A thunderstorm apparently moved in, and now I can hear the heavy sound of hail clinking against my window.

God, what time is it? I look over at the glowing alarm clock.

1:28 a.m.

Then I hear the noise again and realize it's not the storm. Someone's pounding on my front door frantically. I toss the covers off and walk to the entryway, then peer through the peephole on the front door.

My heart thuds heavily in my chest.

Cillian.

I wrench the door open and find him standing on the doorstep, completely drenched. Jesus, it's fucking freezing; he's going to catch hypothermia.

"Cillian, my God," I whisper thickly, opening the door wider so he can step inside. I can feel the chill radiating off him as he passes by, shrugging out of his soaked jacket, rain covering his shoulders. He hangs it on the hook with a shaky hand and turns to face me.

When he reaches for me, I take a step back and hurt flashes in the depths of his eyes.

"So I'm assuming you've heard?" His voice is low and hoarse. Heavy with emotion.

I nod, running my hands up and down my bare arms for warmth. Even with the heat on, the chill from outside has seeped its way in and sends shivers down my spine.

"I..." I start, trailing off. My throat feels so tight that I don't know if I can even speak. "My dad came by earlier. He wanted me to find out from him first. I texted you all night. I called you probably a hundred times and you never called me back."

His eyes are solemn, dark and stormy like the one he just walked in from. "Do you believe it?"

My brow pinches. "I don't know *what* to believe, Cillian. I saw the test. Both of them. They were positive for amphetamines."

For a second he's quiet, and then he shakes his head, rubbing his palm roughly over the back of his neck. "It's bullshit, Rory. You bloody know that I'm not on fucking drugs."

I wince when his voice raises an octave, and he sighs as his eyes drop shut briefly like he's trying to hold on to his composure. When he opens them, the raw pain and betrayal I see shining back almost breaks me.

"I asked for the test because I knew that I would pass, Rory. I haven't taken any drugs, and you of all people should know that. I would never fucking do that; not after everything in London.

I would never hurt Aisling or *you* like that. I would never leave the team in a spot like this. Baby, please believe me. I need you to believe me. Believe *in* me."

"I do believe *in* you, Cillian. I have believed in you since the moment you got to Prescott. Hell, I've believed in you before I even really knew *why* I did. I just blindly put faith into someone I didn't even know. I trusted my gut. I knew deep down that there was more to you than the rumors that swirled around me like wildfire. You shut everyone out because you didn't want to feel any more hurt, and I still wanted to be here, trying to break past your walls," I cry, waving my hands in the air with each word, exasperation taking root and blossoming into something that feels bigger. "I have never doubted you. Not until now. What am I supposed to believe when my father, the man who has never let me down in my life, who has never lied to me, who has never given me reason to doubt him, shows up at my doorstep with proof that you failed a drug test? Not once but twice. I'm so confused, Cillian, and I'm just...I'm *hurting*. I don't know what to believe anymore. When I tried to reach you and I couldn't, I was so worried. God, Cillian, I've been worrying for hours about you. Where you were. If you were okay. If you were hurt."

"I'm sorry that I disappeared, Rory. I turned my phone off and sat by the river walk. I just needed a little space to get my shit right in my head. In the past, I've always shut down, pulled away from those who care about me when shit gets to be too much. I'm proud of the guy I am now, and pushing everyone away is not who I am anymore." His jaw clenches, his nostrils flaring as a darkened look passes through his stormy eyes. "But you're right. There is one piece of the truth I've kept from you."

My heart drops into my stomach. It feels as if the floor has fallen from beneath my feet as his admission floods through my veins like pure ice.

In two strides he closes the distance between us, lifting his freezing palm and curving it around the edge of my jaw, the rough pad of his thumb forging a path along my skin. I feel the slight tremor in his touch, whether from the cold or the intensity of this moment, I can't tell.

"It's the only thing I've never been a hundred percent honest about. The *only* thing I'm guilty of. That night in your bed, I told you that I was falling for you, but the truth is I'm *already* in love with you, Rory St. James. So fucking in love with you that sometimes it feels like I can't breathe. And I would rather take a hundred beatings on the pitch until every inch of me is black and blue before I ever purposely hurt you. Rather rip my heart out of my chest than be the reason behind your tears."

Those tears are falling freely now, hot against my cheeks. He swipes them away carefully, so tenderly that my heart aches to the point of pain.

"I'm sorry that I didn't tell you right then, drop to my fucking knees and tell you that every single piece of me belongs to you. I was scared and that's not an excuse. But, baby, you *know* me. Better than anyone else in my life besides Ais. You know that I'm not on drugs. I don't drink. *I don't do drugs.*"

He pauses, his eyes searching and holding mine intently while I try to process everything that's happening. My pulse is pounding so loudly that I can hardly hear anything over the steady woosh in my ears. Tears well in my eyes, and I shake my head, a strangled laugh bursting free that's partly a sob. "You idiot, how dare you tell me you love me *right now*? I'm supposed to be angry at you. I was so worried, Cillian."

"Be angry then, baby, but don't fucking cry. It makes me want to die. Throw shit at me, hit me with a fucking shoe. Push me. Do whatever you need to do that helps. But it's not going to make me love you any less. It's not going to change the fact that I'm laying my heart at your feet and begging you to trust me. To help me figure out how the fuck this happened. Because I left that shit in London, along with the broken version of myself and, Rory, I never want to go back to him. I *can't* go back."

His tortured gaze hits me full force, and the ache in my heart feels unbearable. I hate this. I hate it so much.

I hate that I doubt him.

"I truly don't know how or why I failed that piss test, Rory. It has to be a mistake. I don't understand, and I swear to you on everything that I love, I'm *clean*. I didn't do this. All I can think is that the test is faulty, or it's a false positive. I know that sounds crazy and I can't explain it, but the tests have to be wrong. They *have* to be."

It's not as if I didn't think the same thing when my dad told me that he failed the test. I thought there had to be some explanation, some reason that the test could be wrong.

And now that Cillian is standing here in front of me, and I can look into his eyes, seeing the unshed tears shining back at me and the fierce determination to prove his innocence, I can't help but... *believe* him. Not just *in* him. In his potential. I believe he's telling me the truth, and that he would never hurt me.

Believe in what my heart is trying so desperately to tell me. To ignore my head and the what-if.

To trust my gut, the same way that I did when he first arrived at Prescott. Cillian isn't the same guy he was the day that he walked onto the pitch. And he's not the same guy that he was when he was drowning in grief back in London. Numbing himself the only way he thought would help.

He's the guy who trusted me when almost everyone he's ever trusted gave up on him. He put that trust in me, and right now I have to put the same trust in him.

"I believe you, Cillian." My voice is barely above a whisper as I reach for him, cradling his jaw in my hand.

I feel his entire body sag in relief, and those tears that were welling in his eyes fall. "Fucking hell, thank God. Baby, I swear on my mum's life that I didn't do anything to fail that test."

His words sink into the depths of my soul. I swear I can feel the weight of them piercing my skin. He would never swear on his mom unless this was the truth. "I know. We'll figure it out. Whatever it takes, we'll figure it out. Together? Okay?"

Leaning forward, he drops his forehead gently against mine. "I love you, Rory. You breathed life into me again, and now I just... I can't live without you."

My hands slide around his jaw, curling around his nape, and pulling him into me. I feel his breath fan against the slope of my neck as he buries his face there.

Steadily, inhale, exhale.

"I love you, Cillian. I'm not going anywhere."

Even if that means going to war for him.

CHAPTER 32

Cillian

Three months ago, I was packing my life up to leave London and feeling like there'd never be another place in the world that would ever feel like home.

How could it when everything I've loved was there? My mum. Aisling. Rugby. My teammates. Friends. The flat I'd spent my childhood in.

I remember the overpowering sense of dread in the days leading up to our flight. Each minute that brought me closer to coming to America was a constant reminder of the sentence I'd been dealt. A new prison to hold me for my sins outside of the grief that I'd been suffering with for so long.

It wasn't bad enough that I lost Mum, but I had to leave my entire life behind too.

And now I'm facing the same reality once again. I'm no longer on the team, and everything is going to subsequently fall apart.

Which means I'm not going to be able to remain at Prescott.

And I'm fucking devastated because somewhere along the way

it became *home*. Something that I never imagined I'd feel again. Not when my life has been temporary.

Only I found a home in Rory St. James.

I've realized that houses with walls, roofs, and memories, they're not home. They're simply somewhere you live. Where you go to bed each night and wake up every morning.

But your real home? It's the beating, breathing heart of the person you love.

The one you'd do anything in the world for.

That's who she is for me. She nestled her way into my heart, into the seams of my soul. Into my bones, my breath. Everything belongs to her.

I didn't even realize I still had a fucking heart until it started to beat again for *her*.

I'm lying beside her in her bed, my arm tucked beneath my head, my fingers gently moving through her long, silky hair as she sleeps, brushing along the soft skin of her cheeks, trailing along the bare skin of her arm that peeks out from beneath the sleeve of my T-shirt.

I love seeing her in my clothes almost as much as I love seeing her out of them.

Last night, after everything that happened, I was going to leave, give her space to process the revelation I dropped on her. Telling her I'm in love with her in the midst of everything falling apart is not at all what I had planned, but I couldn't go another second without admitting my feelings. Because if it all went to hell, and I couldn't convince her that I was being truthful and she did leave, I needed her to know that I loved her.

Even if it was the only time I got to say it to her.

But she didn't ask for space. She didn't push me away or keep me at arm's length. If anything she pulled me closer. It's like she knew I needed that more than anything tonight, to feel her with me.

There was nothing sexual about us crawling into bed together, her in my T-shirt, me in a fresh pair of dry athletic shorts that she had tucked away in a drawer. We just lay on our sides, staring at each other, talking about everything until she started to doze off, her eyes fluttering shut from exhaustion.

Despite the exhaustion that I felt—emotionally, mentally, physically—sleep evaded me. I couldn't get my brain to shut off. To stop replaying the last twenty-four hours in my head like a broken record.

Trying to figure out how the fuck it was possible that I failed the tests, and how thankful I am that Rory stayed. That she believed me even though she had every right not to.

How I'm going to try to fix this shit and try to keep my spot on the team. My home at Prescott.

Rory stirs in her sleep, her rosy lips falling open as whispers a string of indecipherable mumbles that I can't make out.

Except three distinct syllables.

My name.

Fuck, my girl is whispering my name in her sleep.

My chest swells, my heart galloping wildly beneath my rib cage. Sometimes I think Rory is the only thing I've ever truly gotten right. She saved me in ways that I know she couldn't possibly understand.

I've been lying here for hours, watching her sleep, trying to savor every single bloody second that I have with her because in truth... I don't know how long it'll last.

I don't know what's going to happen. My entire future is up in the air. When I first arrived in America, I thought the stakes were high, but now it's no longer just about playing for a professional team. It's about Rory.

The thought of leaving her makes me physically ill. An entire fucking ocean separating me and the girl I'm in love with sounds like torture unlike anything I've ever known.

"Are you creepily watching me sleep, Cillian Cairney?" she murmurs, eyes still closed but her pillowy lips curving up into a sleepy grin.

"Of course not."

Her grin widens into a smile that makes my heart race. As if her smile commands her pull on my heart, increasing the tempo with each time she looks at me. She's so fucking beautiful.

"Mmmm. Not true. I can feel your eyes on me."

My hand shoots out and slowly curves around her waist, tugging her across the mattress until she's plastered against my chest. She heaves a sleepy sigh, burrowing into the crook of my neck, hitching one leg around my hip.

It's perfect like this, wrapped up in her.

"That's because I can't take my eyes off you, St. James. Can you blame me?" I mumble into the silky hair on top of her head, pressing my lips there, lingering.

The tips of my fingers glide along her thigh lazily, spelling letters that I wonder if she'll be able to decipher.

"I've been thinking. About everything from yesterday..." she starts, then pauses, lifting back slightly to stare up at me. Her pretty brown eyes are my favorite shade, darker in the morning when she's first waking up and still sleepy. "I was so worried about finding a guy who could see me for who I am, who I really am. It felt impossible, but I think that's what I found. I think that you've seen me, for all that I am, for exactly who I am since I met you. The same way that I have you. I never saw you as a guy who could never escape his past, and you never saw me as the hopeless girl who would never make it out of the friend zone. Kinda feels like fate to me."

I've never really given it much thought. Fate.

But I think she may be right. Whatever I've experienced in my life, the immeasurable hurt and heartache, the good and the bad, the pain and the healing.

Every piece of it must have led me right here, right to this moment.

"It does." My throat feels tight with emotion, the same way it has countless times in the last day. "Loving you is effortless, Rory. I have no doubt that I was made solely to love you."

Her eyes glisten, fresh new tears welling in the depths like pools. "I'm scared, Cillian. That you'll leave, that we'll lose this."

"Hey." I clasp her chin between my fingers. "We're going to figure it out, baby. I'm not giving up. I'm going to fight, not just for myself but for you. For Ais."

"What are we going to do?"

I swallow hard. "I don't know yet, but I'll figure it out."

Rory's lips find mine, the softest, sweetest brush of a kiss that sucks all the air out of my lungs.

I want to deepen it, swipe my tongue through her parted lips and lose myself in her, but the sound of someone knocking on the door stops me from doing so.

She pulls back alarmed, eyes wide. "Shit. It might be my dad. I wasn't exactly... put together when he left yesterday." In a breath, she's off the bed, grabbing a pair of sweatpants from her dresser and dragging them on.

I follow her through her apartment, prepared to hide in the damn closet if I need to. A second later, I watch her sag with relief when she looks through the peephole. "It's just Fitz."

When she opens the front door, he steps past her into the apartment.

And then I remember Fitz has no fucking clue that we're together. Fuck.

His shocked expression meets mine, and his brow shoots up to his hairline. "Cairney? What the hell are *you* doing here? I've been freaking the fuck out, man. Trying to figure out how the hell we're going to fix this shit an—"

Rory steps between us, lifting a hand to stop him. "Fitz, wait. You know about Cillian?"

"Yeah, duh. The whole team knows. Your dad sent an email earlier today, before breakfast." His ass hits the chair as he flops down into it, crossing his arms over his chest. "Fuck that. There's no goddamn way that shit is for real. I don't believe it for a second. That's why I'm here; because we gotta figure this shit out and *pronto*."

A weird, fuzzy feeling blooms in my chest that he's even here, believing that I wouldn't do this, ready to fight.

I hoped that the guys on the team would believe me when I said that there has to be a mistake, but shit, I wasn't sure. The same with Rory. There're two positive tests so I get the doubt.

We've been through a lot in the short time that I've been here, but it feels like we're forming a brotherhood. The way it should be between a team, especially in rugby. Rugby's about family. Maybe not blood, but the family that you find. That's part of the reason this is such bullshit because the timing is something.

Right when we've bridged the gap between us.

"I know. We know. We just haven't exactly figured out how we're going to do it," Rory says, sinking down beside him on the couch.

"So.... let's just get the elephant out of the room, yeah?" he says, looking between Rory and me.

Then Rory's head whips to look at me, and I look back at Fitz. And we're all bloody looking at each other.

I stay glued to my spot, unsure of how to go forward. Is this the right time to tell him what's been going on between us?

"Someone's set you up. I mean, that's the only logical conclusion to be drawn," he finally says, and Rory deflates beside him, eyes still wide.

What he says should be a relief, not having to drop this bomb between us in the midst of everything that's going on, but if anything it makes my chest feel heavier. I don't want to keep things between us a secret, and if there's anyone I trust outside of Rory or Ais, it's Fitz.

"Rory and I are together."

The space between his brow furrows. "Yeah, I know. We're all together."

"No, mate, I mean together, *together*. She's my girlfriend," I say quickly, clearing up the confusion written on his face.

"I am?" Rory blurts out.

"You are?" Fitz says at the same time, their words overlapping.

"I mean, I thought that's what was going on here. I mean, we love each other, that means we're dating, yeah?" I respond, reaching up and rubbing the back of my neck.

Rory rolls her lips together. "Yeah, but like you hadn't officially asked me, so I wasn't sure if we were going to, like, put a label on this."

There's a loud whistle, and we both look over at Fitz. "Can we focus for a second? We'll come back to...this in a minute. First of all, we have to figure out how the hell we're going to prove Cillian's innocent. Kind of hard to have a relationship from two thousand miles away, Ror."

He's right.

But also, now I'm fucking grinning at Rory, and she's smiling at me so sweet that I wanna scoop her off the couch and carry her to her bedroom and pretend the whole world isn't burning down.

"I have an idea. But...we're going to need some help," Fitz says slowly.

My brow lifts. "What do you have in mind?"

CHAPTER 33

Rory

"Everyone, be strong. Remember, his bark is way worse than his bite. Right, Michaels?" Hollis mumbles in a hushed whisper from beside Wren, and I have to cover my mouth in order to stop my giggle from bursting free.

Wren nods, feigning a way too nonchalant shrug, "Yeah, for sure. Totally." I watch his throat bob in a swallow as he looks around nervously. He glances down at me with wide eyes. "Fuck that. Rory, I'm scared. *Hold* me."

"Jesus, Wren, where the fuck are your balls. We do not have time for this right now. *Get. It. Together*," Fitz whisper yells as he shoulders his way between the both of them. "Look, this is going to work, and if it doesn't then you know what...we pivot. Always fucking pivot. We do whatever we have to do to make sure that Cillian stays, right?"

Great, now I'm going to cry.

My heart flutters as my eyes burn with unshed tears taking in the scene in front of me. When Fitz said he had an idea, I truly had no clue what it would be. I'd already spent the entire night racking my brain over and over trying to figure out what we could do to prove Cillian's innocence. And came up completely blank. I felt totally useless and helpless at the same time.

Turns out the idea Fitz has was the least complicated of all the things I thought of, and yet somehow the most important. The most impactful.

He texted everyone on the team and told them to rally for Cillian. To show up at my dad's office and all vouch for the newest member of the team. Demand a retest. Do whatever it takes to keep him on the team.

And even if that failed, which there was a huge possibility that it would, Cillian would still see how many people love and care about him. How his teammates *want* him here. That they will go to bat for him even after the rocky start.

Most of all, he gets to see these guys show up as his family. And know that no matter what, they'll be here.

Everyone from the team showed up. Aside from Ezra and Brooks. It makes me sad and disappointed, but I don't have the time or energy to focus on the people who didn't show up. Instead, I'm going to focus on the ones who did.

Cillian's hand slips into mine, giving me a tight, reassuring squeeze. So much comfort in a single touch, when really I should be the one comforting him. He's steadfast and strong not only for me but also Aisling. The team.

I want to be the same for him.

The door of the athletic building bursts open and my dad steps out, his hands shoved in his pants pockets, eyes roving over the crowd of his waiting players. "What's going on?" When he sees me standing with the guys, his expression shifts slightly, confusion marring his face.

Fitz steps forward with his chin raised and a flare of determination in his eyes. I've never been prouder of my best friend than I am at this moment.

"Coach, we're here today because we want to stand with Cillian. He says he's not on drugs, and we all believe him. I know what the test said. We all do. And we all think it's wrong. That there has to be an explanation. It's a false positive, or a faulty test, something. You've always told us to have each other's backs and stand together, no matter what. That our team is more than just rugby, that we're a family. That means more now than it ever has. He's part of our family, and we have to fight for him."

Even if I wanted to stop the tears from falling, I couldn't. I am so incredibly proud to be a part of this family. For these guys to be my best friends.

"We're not leaving. Not till you agree to retest Cillian. To investigate whatever is going on. Even if we have to run. Even if you have to bench us. Right, guys?" Fitz says loudly, looking around at his teammates. I watch as they all nod, a sea of agreement passing between them. "Cillian is one of us."

I can hardly breathe while waiting for Dad to speak. To say anything at all.

Silence permeates the air, heavy and tense, and for a full torturous minute, he says nothing. Not a single word. He just drags his gaze over his players, jaw working, hands still stuffed into the pockets of his slacks.

"Shit," I hear Wren whisper, furthering my panic.

"Guys," Dad starts, finally, freaking finally speaking. "I'm touched by this show of support for Cillian. Truly, I am. All I have wanted from the moment that he got here was for him to be a part of this team. A part of our family. So seeing this today has touched me in a way that I've never experienced in all the years that I've coached rugby. It speaks volumes for your loyalty and respect for him. I appreciate it, and I wish that it would change the outcome. My hands are tied. I'm sorry. I truly am."

My heart sinks. All the way to the floor.

I knew this was a possibility; I knew there was a chance our presence would make no difference.

But I was wholly unprepared for how badly it would actually hurt.

"I'm sorry," Dad repeats, his voice low and full of remorse.

Part of me is also hurting for my dad because I know this is not easy for him, and that his position is impossible, but it doesn't help make this any better.

"Am I too late?" An out of breath voice sounds to the right, and we all turn to see Brooks standing there, cheeks red from exertion, panting as if he's been running.

"I mean sort of, y—" Hollis starts, but Brooks cuts him off, turning to Dad. "Coach. I need to talk to you. It's important and it can't wait. Um...Cillian too."

What in the hell is going on?

"My office. Now."

* * *

I'm not entirely sure that I should be here, but Cillian insisted I join them. I know it's so he doesn't have to face this alone.

Of course I said yes because right now, I just want to be here for him.

We all file into Dad's office, and the door creaks loudly as he shuts it behind us.

While Cillian takes a seat in the leather chair in front of his desk, I hang back, leaning against the bookcase and cross my ankles, fingers curled around the edge of a shelf.

"What's going on, Brooks? Talk to me," Dad says quietly.

Brooks paces along the small space in front of the door, running his hand over the back of the dark blond hair along his neck before he finally comes to a stop, a frantic edge to his words as he begins to speak. "Ezra came to me last night. He was boasting about something he'd done, and he thought I'd be on board with it I guess because of the circumstances, but... I'm not. I'm a lot of things, but I'm not a piece of shit," he says, his Adam's apple bobbing as he swallows.

"Brooks, I'm sorry I'm not following. What's going on? What did he do?"

He hesitates, opening his mouth, then snapping it shut before he flops down into another leather chair in front of the desk and drops his head into his hands, running his fingers through his hair roughly.

Unease shoots down my spine, a tight knot twisting in the pit of my stomach. I don't think I've ever seen him so on edge in all the years I've known him and that makes my anxiety spike.

Hesitation flickers in his gaze. "Ezra has been putting Adderall in Cillian's water bottle before practice this week. That's why he failed the piss test."

I sway on my feet, only remaining upright because of my white-knuckled grip on the bookshelf.

Oh my God.

I bring my hand to my mouth to cover the shocked gasp that threatens to fly out of me.

As painful as it is to hear, a staggering sense of relief flows through me.

The truth.

It'll set Cillian free.

Brooks groans, his shoulders falling. "Ezra's my best friend, but fuck... sorry, Coach. I just... I can't be responsible for someone's whole life being taken away." Lifting his head, his shoulders still hunched in defeat, his eyes flick to Cillian. "I might not be your biggest fan, but this is just too far. I haven't been able to sleep. I can't fucking eat. My stomach's in knots since he told me."

He looks back at Dad. "I should've said something as soon as I found out, and I'm sorry. I really am. I know that telling you is the right thing, but I'm going to lose my best friend for doing this. It'll ruin his entire rugby career. He'll be expelled too, and I'll be responsible for that."

God, how the hell could Ezra do this?

I'm just so angry, so in absolute disbelief that this is happening, I can't even properly process the emotions running through me right now.

Ezra nearly ruined Cillian's life by drugging him. And now Brooks has to ruin Ezra's by turning him in.

Dad shakes his head, that vein in his neck bulging. "Son, if this is the truth, then you're not responsible for anything. No one is responsible for someone else's decisions, and that is a decision that he made. A stupid, reckless decision. The only person you are responsible for is *yourself*. You can't bear the weight of Ezra's bad judgment."

I can't stop looking at Cillian, my hands aching from the need to reach for him. To make sure he's okay. He's completely still, his hands curved around the arm of the chair, his knuckles white. The expression on his face surprisingly blank despite what I know is probably happening inside him right now. I know there's probably a small part of him that's relieved we have answers for what happened, but there's probably an even larger part of him that is so angry he's seeing red.

Despite that, he keeps cool, his jaw grinding together as he keeps his gaze pinned on Brooks before moving it back to Dad.

Brooks finally nods, running another hand through his hair and tugging on the strands. "We've been best friends since *third grade*, Coach."

I understand where Brooks is coming from, I really do. I can't imagine having to be put in a position where you have to betray someone you love, someone so important to you. But this is not something you can just pretend you didn't hear and move on from.

Keeping quiet would have meant ruining Cillian's life, after he's fought so hard to be here, and it makes me physically sick to know that Ezra's responsible for it.

His teammate.

Someone I trusted.

"Why did he do it, Brooks?" I say quietly, speaking for the first time from behind them.

He doesn't even turn to look at me, instead hanging his head in his hands once more. "Because he hates him. He hates that Cillian is a better player than he is and that he feels like competition to him. He was proud as fuck that he did it too. That he finally got him off the team. But drugging him and destroying his whole life? That's fucking crazy, Rory."

It's not crazy, it's absolute psychopath behavior and he needs to be arrested for it.

I exhale shakily.

"What's going to happen now, Coach?" Brooks asks, his voice barely above a whisper. "I know I'm the captain, and I need to own up to all of this, but my head is just a mess."

All of this is such a horrific mess.

Dad sits back in his chair, rubbing a hand over his tense jaw, his eyes hard as he sighs. "Well, I've got to contact the NCAA and the authorities. What Ezra's done can't be swept under the rug, Brooks. He committed a crime, and he's got to answer for that."

Brooks doesn't immediately respond, the creased space between his brow furrowing deeper, like the thought of Ezra facing consequences outside of Prescott hadn't yet crossed his mind.

There's no doubt in my mind that my dad is going to do whatever he can to make this right. I truly can't imagine being in his shoes right now.

Part of me can't even believe that Ezra would do this. I'm shocked. That he would stoop so low and be so desperate to get rid of Cillian that he would do something *criminal*. I would've never seen this coming. Not in a million years.

I knew they had some tension between them, but I didn't realize that Ezra *hated* him.

It makes me wonder what other low, fucked-up things he has done that we're none the wiser to.

"I know," Brooks finally says with a slight tremble to his voice. "It fucking sucks, but what he did wasn't right and I can't stand behind it."

"You did the right thing, Brooks. Even if it might not feel like it right now. No one deserves to have their future stolen from them. I know Ezra is like your brother, but that's what a true captain does. They do the right thing, even if it's hard. *You're* doing the right thing, even when it's hard," Dad says quietly.

He nods silently.

"I'm sure the NCAA is going to ask for a statement, as well as the police. And the president of Prescott. I need to make some phone calls and start to get this under control before it's leaked to the press," Dad says, eyes running over all of us. "Brooks, I'll be in touch with you soon. I need some time to get this handled. Get some sleep and keep your phone by you. Please don't talk about this with anyone."

"I won't," he says, rising from his seat. I think he's going to make a beeline for the door, but he pauses in front of Cillian, staring down at him. "I'm sorry I didn't call last night. I know you probably don't give a shit, and I don't blame you, but for what it's worth... I am sorry."

Cillian's jaw clenches, but he nods, saying nothing in return.

When the door shuts behind Brooks, my dad looks at Cillian. "I'm sorry as well, Cillian. It might not mean much right now, but I will make this right. I promise you."

CHAPTER 34

Cillian

When I walk into the athletic building the following morning, every eye is trained on me. I barely make it through the door before my teammates are rushing over, pulling me in for hugs, offering their support, clapping me on the back.

It's overwhelming in a way that makes my chest constrict. These guys didn't have to go out on a limb for me. They had nothing to go on to prove that I wasn't guilty of what I was being accused of. But they did anyway. They stood beside me and showed up in ways I never imagined.

Aisling came over to Rory's last night, and we stayed up half the night talking. Long after my girl had fallen asleep with her head in my lap, my fingers tangled in her hair. She loves when I play with her hair, and after the last few days, exhaustion took over. She was asleep in minutes after lying down.

Then of course, Ais had to spend the next thirty minutes talking about how cute we were, and how she's happy that I've found love.

We talked about everything that happened with Ezra, and she was enraged. And wondering why *I* don't feel the same.

Of course I'm mad. But I'm not letting it control me. Not the way it used to. I've worked too hard to be a better man than I used to be, and hanging on to something I can't change isn't going to make that any easier.

Instead of being pissed off and holding on to resentment, I'm going to try to move forward. In part because I'm not letting that arsehole win. This is exactly what he wanted, and the biggest fuck you I can give to a piece of shit like him is to rise above it. To make sure he knows that he hasn't broken me, and he doesn't get the satisfaction of knowing he succeeded in his fucked-up plan. He's the one who's going to sit in jail until his mum bails him out.

When Coach called this morning and asked me to meet him at his office, I could hear the remorse in his tone. I could tell he was being authentic, and I know all this is a fucked-up spot for him to be in. He did what he had to do as a coach.

Didn't make it fucking suck any less though.

I woke Rory up and told her I was headed to the pitch. She insisted on coming and would hang out with the guys until the meeting was over.

Now here I am. Ready to walk into the meeting that's going to decide what happens with my future at Prescott.

My knuckles tap lightly against Coach's door. His gaze raises to meet mine as he lifts his hand and gestures me in with a wave.

"Cillian."

I nod. "Coach."

"Thank you for coming in. I met with the dean and the president of Prescott this morning," he says, reaching for the folder in front of him and opening it. A few sheets of paper sit inside with the Prescott University letterhead printed boldly at the top. He flips the top piece around, sliding it across the desk toward me. "This is your official reinstatement to the team and Prescott. Ezra has obviously been suspended from the team until a full investigation happens. The disciplinary committee will decide next steps, but I do know that he has been arrested and is going to be formally charged. I'm sure the police department will be reaching out to you soon with questions, and to take your statement. That's what I know as of now and Cillian, again...I'm sorry."

Sincerity shines in his eyes and he frowns, shaking his head. "It's not enough, but I am sorry. It's your decision if you'd like to come back to the team, and I can't say I blame you if you decided not to. But I want you to know that you earned the spot on my team, and I want you here, son. And clearly your teammates want you here too."

A strange sense of relief floods my chest as his words wash over me. Logically, I knew I'd be reinstated to the team because I hadn't done anything wrong, but hearing it brings more relief than I thought it would.

This team was supposed to be a temporary stop toward my future, but everything changed along the way. In huge part because of Coach's daughter. I can't imagine walking away from her. I can't imagine leaving her behind.

And now? I don't have to leave my team behind. My friends. Prescott as a whole.

"I'm sorry that I didn't recognize what was happening between the two of you. If I would've, I would've taken care of it from the start. I would've never allowed it to get this far. I'm sorry for that.

I'm disappointed in what's happened, but nothing like the disappointment I'll be facing if you don't come back, Cillian. What do you say? Will you rejoin the team?"

For a second, I say nothing, letting the silence hang between us.

"I will. I just need you to know that I understand why you drug-tested me, and that it was hard for you to believe that I wasn't lying when the test showed positive. But I also need you to know that I'm not that guy anymore, Coach. And I've worked my arse off to be someone that I'm proud of. I don't want that to hang over my head anymore. All I want to do is leave my mistakes in the past and move forward."

Coach nods, understanding flitting through his gaze.

At first, all I wanted was to get in and get out, so the irony isn't lost on me that somewhere along the way, my plans changed. *I* changed.

The future I want for myself changed.

I don't want to live in guilt and pain any longer. Shutting out the world as a defense because I'm too afraid to be hurt or lose someone I love again. That's no fucking way to live, and Aisling was right.

Mum would hate to see me like that. A shell of the man she raised me to be.

I want to be more. If not for me or for Aisling, for Rory.

"I understand. I failed you as a coach, and I'm sorry for that. I've been coaching for almost as many years as you've been alive and still...I learn every day. I'm not immune to making mistakes, and this time, I made a big one. I should've supported you more, should've made sure you felt like you were a part of this team from the start instead of focusing so much on making sure the rest of the team could handle it. Cillian... you're a part of this team whether you're here, or in London."

After a beat, I say, "I appreciate that. I'd like my spot on the team back."

"It's yours. I want to add that I'm really impressed," he says, rising from his chair. "You've shown maturity and grace in a situation that most people your age wouldn't have the ability to do, and I admire that. It's clear to me that you're not the same guy that you were back in London. Thank you for being willing to move forward and stay a part of my team, son. I'm hoping we can put this past us and move forward from here."

Extending his hand over the desk, he holds it out for me to shake.

I rise from the chair and slide my hand in his. "I'd really like that."

He nods but doesn't drop my hand. "Probably should discuss you and my daughter, though."

Bloody hell.

I should've known he wasn't going to let me walk out of here without addressing shit about Rory. She told me they talked last night and said they had a heart-to-heart, where she came clean and told him everything. It made me feel so much better about him finding out. The fact that it came directly from Rory.

Coach might not kick me off the team for what just went down, but I had no doubt in my mind he'd not think twice when it came to his daughter.

"Coa—" I start, but his grip on my hand tightens, the corner of his mouth lifting slightly.

"Don't need the details. Nor do I want them, honestly. I trust

Rory and the decisions that she makes. Always have, and I'm not going to stop now. All I'm going to say is that if you hurt my daughter, we're going to have much bigger problems than this. Got it?"

I nod, pushing down a swallow. "Got it."

With that, he drops my hand and chuckles, entirely too relaxed about this whole thing, and it's a little unnerving if I'm being honest.

Because I apparently lack any and all self-preservation, the words come stumbling out of my mouth before I can stop them. "That's it?"

His gaze narrows and his brow lifts. "What do you mean?"

"I mean..." I trail off before I sputter out, "You're not upset that we're...dating? I don't know, I just kind of expected you to lose it on me. Scream a bit, throw some shit?"

Coach laughs. "If you want me to throw some stuff, I can. Not much my style though."

"No, no, I just—"

"Look, yeah, sure, I wish Rory would have told me before last night. I don't want her to ever feel like she has to keep anything from me, but at the end of the day, I'm her dad and all I want is what's best for her. I want whatever makes her happy. And apparently, that's you. I could be mad that she got involved with one of my players, but I'm not sure what good that would do. I trust her decisions, and I trust that she'll always choose something that is good for her because that's the way I raised her to be. And if she doesn't, then it's a lesson that she'll learn from."

Yeah, I don't want to be a lesson that Rory has to learn from. I want to be the guy that protects her heart and shows her the same love that she's shown me.

"I'm not going to do anything to hurt her, I promise. I...I love her, Coach," I say thickly, my voice tight with emotion. "All I can do is prove to you that I'm going to treat her the way she deserves to be treated. With actions, not words. This isn't temporary for me."

He nods. "That's all I ask. Give her the respect she deserves."

"I will."

"Then I'll see you on the pitch."

Just like that, the conversation is done and I'm not sure what's more shocking: the fact that Ezra fucking drugged me to get me off the team, or the fact that Coach actually *doesn't* care that I'm dating his daughter.

As I'm walking back down the hallway toward the locker room, still replaying the conversation with Coach in my head, I see Rory burst through the double doors.

Her dark hair is pulled back low on her nape, her cheeks flushed red as those pretty eyes land on me and a smile tugs at her lips.

Christ, she's gorgeous. She's breathtaking, something that never ceases to take me by surprise when my eyes land on her. More than anything...she's *mine*.

Yeah, I didn't need her father's approval, but I *wanted* it. I wanted him to accept that I'm in love with his daughter, and if he didn't approve of us being together, then it was just something that we would have to work through.

Together.

It just makes this a hell of a lot easier knowing that he's not going to be an issue for us.

In the end, all I know is that Rory is mine. She's a part of me, buried deep in my chest where my heart resides. I think the entire beating thing might be hers if I'm being honest.

"How'd it go?" she breathes when she comes to a stop in front of me. "Tell me everything."

"I'm back on the team."

She squeals, tossing her arms around my neck tightly and burying her face in my neck. "Oh, thank God." When she pulls back, I see the relief shining in her eyes. "I mean, I knew that they would because you didn't do anything wrong. I'm just...I'm so, so happy. You belong on the team, Cillian. You deserve that spot. I'm so thankful all of this is going to be over."

"Me too," I murmur as I wrap my arms around her waist, pulling her soft curves against me.

Then realization rushes through me.

This is the first time we've ever had a moment like this in public. Hell, aside from holding her hand outside yesterday, this is the only time we've openly touched around the team.

And neither of us hesitated for a second. We didn't even think about it as we came together. It was instinctual. Two magnets drawn to each other by force.

The hallway is busy with the athletic staff and my teammates, and now that I'm aware, I can feel the stares.

"Rory..." I start, my gaze flicking to the people passing by. "I think we have an audience."

Her eyes widen briefly, and she goes to drop her arms, but I pull her tighter, not letting her step out of my arms.

"Let them stare," I say. "We're done hiding. Your dad knows, the coaching staff knows. Everyone else can know that you're mine, Rory. I don't want to have to keep our relationship in the dark. I want to be with you, out in the open, without giving a shit about what everyone thinks."

Her eyes soften, and I feel the tips of her fingers running along my nape. "Really? That's what you want?"

"Are you surprised by that?" I chuckle, reaching to cradle her jaw in my hands. My thumb sweeps along the edge, her skin soft beneath the rough pad. "Baby, I'm crazy about you. Let the whole world know that *the* Rory. St. James is my girlfriend. That if they even bloody look at you, I can fight."

Her laugh wraps around me, filling every empty space inside me.

The last thing I ever expected to do when I came to Prescott was fall in love. I didn't think it was possible to love someone the way that I do Rory because my heart was too bruised and broken. I was still piecing myself back together, picking up those fragmented shards and attempting to make myself whole again.

I failed time after time, sabotaging myself and everything I love. Because I thought it was what I deserved. But the moment I met Rory, everything changed.

She broke down the walls that I built high around my heart and forced her way inside a fortress that was forged of heartache, guilt, and pain.

For the first time in a long time, I see the other side. I see the old me. The one who wasn't broken. I'm working on healing, on a permanent fix instead of a temporary one.

I owe that to her.

To the girl who showed me it's okay to lean on the people who care about you. To give them some of the weight from your shoulders so you don't have to carry it all alone.

Who taught me that I can't be great *just* on my own.

Because of her I found a *family* who loves me despite all my faults and the past that haunts me.

I used to think that leaving London was leaving my life behind, but the truth is, it's just beginning.

Rugby may be my future, but Rory St. James is my *end game*.

EPILOGUE

Cillian

"Remind me again why the hell we agreed to this?" Fitz mutters from the seat beside me, a wrinkle forming between his brows as he glances down at the kitchen table.

Wren scoffs, answering for me, "Because our boy Cillian here has this problem where he can't tell his girlfriend *no*."

"Bullshit," I retort in defense, even though fuck...okay, maybe it's a bit true. Shit, this *is* my fault. After that realization, I blow out a breath and wince. "Sorry, mates."

A chorus of groans rings out around me from my teammates, and I roll my lips together, shrugging. "What do you want from me? You know what, you're one to bloody talk, both of you." My gaze bounces back and forth between Wren and Fitz. "She's not even your girlfriend and she's still got you by the balls."

"What was that?" Rory asks as she walks back into the living room with a plate of cookies.

Wren's eyes widen, almost comically, and he licks his lips, stuttering, "N-nothing Rory."

I bite back a grin.

They can say whatever shit they want about me being wrapped around Rory's finger, but they've been wrapped far longer than I have. My teammates would do anything for Rory St. James, and it's been like that long before I ever arrived at Prescott.

They're not wrong though. There's nothing I wouldn't do for my girl, and if that means I'll be teased relentlessly for it non-bloody-stop by my teammates, then so be it.

I'll take it any day if I get to be with Rory.

"We were just talking about how lucky we are that you make us cookies." Fitz smirks as he swipes a still warm cookie off the plate and shoves it into his mouth, talking around a mouthful, "*And* put up with Kill's shit. He's the lucky one now that I think about it."

My foot shoots out under the table, nailing him in the front of the shin, causing a low pained groan to tear out of him.

Arsehole.

His eyes find mine, and I just smirk and lift my middle finger, flipping him off while Wren snickers and eats his fourth cookie in a five-minute time span.

Three months have passed since the day I sat in Coach's office and thought my future at Prescott was over. That my rugby career was over, for good this time.

Three months since Ezra was arrested and expelled for illegally drugging me.

When I think about that day, I should probably feel angry, or betrayed, but the truth is, I'm not anymore. Part of me is glad that it happened, however fucked up it was, because I'm not sure where I would be right now if it hadn't.

If anything, the shit Ezra pulled brought me and my teammates, the guys I now call my *brothers*, closer than I ever imagined we would be.

In the last three months we've formed an unshakable bond that has made us unstoppable on the pitch. I've never seen a rugby team play together the way we have. Seamlessly. A complete force to be reckoned with.

It might sound like we're cocky arseholes, but it's the truth.

We're more than teammates. We're family. I've got their back just the way they have had mine. Because of that…we brought home the championship, and it was truly one of the best moments of my life. I'm so bloody proud of what we've been able to accomplish. *Together.*

And none of that would have happened without Rory, because she's the glue that holds everyone together.

I love her so fucking much that my chest aches. And not in the way that I've experienced over the past two years since my mum died. This is something entirely different. It's an all-consuming feeling, and every bloody heartbeat belongs to her.

"Mm-hmm. You weren't complaining about the game I chose for tonight, were you?" Rory mutters as she slides into my lap, looping her arm around my neck. "Because we could always play Twister. I know how much you guys love Twister. Maybe we should play for old times' sak—"

"No!" Wren screams in horror at the same time Fitz blanches, face tight with alarm, "Absolutely not. No fucking way, Rory."

Her plump lip curls up into a shit-eating grin, a glint of amusement shining in her pretty chocolate eyes as her fingers slide through my hair at the nape of my neck. I've been letting it grow out slightly for the summer, and she loves it. She especially loves tugging on the strands when I'm between her thighs devouring her. My *favorite* meal of the day.

"You sure, because I've got it right there in the closet," she says. Her shoulder lifts in a shrug, and my mates shake their heads, pleading.

I bring my lips to her ears, brushing them against the shell, grinning when she shivers from the contact. "The only way you're getting me on that damn mat is if you're on it, naked."

Rory pulls back, her eyes flaring with heat, tugging her lip between her teeth.

I smirk.

"Can the two of you stop whatever weird thing you're doing right now? We're literally sitting right here," Fitz says. When I glance over at him, he's wearing a horrified look, but I see his lip curving into a grin.

"Are you jealous, mate?" I ask.

Wren snickers. "Of course he is; you know the only thing he's committed to is his hand."

"Fuck off," Fitz mutters, shoving Wren. "I told you: I'm not looking for anything serious. Now, can we play Hungry Hungry Hippos or not?"

I bark out a laugh, the sound vibrating through me as I shake my head.

Of course, Rory would pick bloody Hungry Hungry Hippos for our game night. It could never be something like poker. No, it has to be something for primary school kids, and I swear she does it just to fuck with Wren and Fitz.

"Yes, yes, we can, Fitz. See, I knew you'd love this one," Rory says with a blinding smile, which makes my chest do that funny thing where it races and pounds at the same time.

Like it always does.

She excitedly leans forward while the guys start goading each other, bickering back and forth about who's going to win. I'm not even paying attention to the game, my eyes staying trained on the love of my life.

I don't give a shit who wins because I've already won.

The girl who brought me back to life, piece by piece.

She's fucking beautiful, and so fucking *mine*.

ACKNOWLEDGMENTS

I can't believe I'm writing this right now. That *Red Card* is finally, at last, done and ready to be put out on shelves and in the hands of readers everywhere.

This book started as a fleeting moment; the smallest crumb of an idea that blossomed into something bigger than I ever could have dreamed.

This story, and these characters, changed my life forever, and I can't begin to put into words how grateful I am to be the one to tell it.

Although my love for this world runs soul deep, woven somewhere deep inside me, Cillian and Rory's story was the hardest I've ever written. It was a brand-new world, a new sport that I'd never written about, new characters with new voices and their own personalities, flaws, problems. I fought so hard for them, and in the end, it's a story I'm immensely proud of.

And there are so many people to thank for helping me take this book and shape it into something utterly magical, so without further ado...

To the entire team at Forever for not only believing in me but believing in Cillian and Rory. My editor Madeleine for taking the roughest first draft to ever exist and helping me make it something beautiful. To Dana, who first read one of my indie books and championed so hard to have me as part of the Forever family. I still think about that first email so often, and I am so grateful you took the chance on me.

To my incredible, wonderful, truly brilliant agent Jess, whom I would be lost without. You changed my life the day you became my agent, and saying thank you will never be enough. You have been endlessly supportive and patient through this entire process and never hesitated to answer my billion and five questions, or to made me feel silly for asking them. I feel so lucky to have the privilege to work with you, and I am so eternally grateful for you. Thank you for everything you have done for me.

To my sister, Reanne, the person who has always believed in me, even when I didn't have the strength to believe in myself. My soulmate and my best friend. Forever and always. I love you.

To my mama, who has always been my biggest fan. It's because of you that I'm brave enough to chase my dreams. You are the kind of woman I will always strive to be. I love you so much.

To MJ: We sat on the couch of that Airbnb nestled in the mountains and this idea took shape, becoming what it is today; I owe that to you. You are the best friend I've ever had, and I will never take that for granted, till the stars call us home, no matter where the world takes us. I love you.

To Katie, I owe you more than I can ever say. God, what would I have done without you, not only while writing this but for the past five years? We've been through so much together, I cannot imagine what it would be like to do this without you. Thank you

ACKNOWLEDGMENTS

for wearing many different hats, but more importantly, thank you for your friendship. For never leaving my side, and for helping me always see reason. I love you.

To Sandy, who was one of the first people I ever told the idea of Cillian, Rory, and Prescott to. From that very first day, while I was holed up in a cabin in Georgia with MJ, you believed in them. In me. You encouraged me to stop being afraid, and to follow my heart and my dreams, and I'm so glad I trusted you enough to jump. Without that push, I would still have the idea in the back of my head, begging to be written. You were the first person to ever read this, and I know if I didn't have your feedback from the very beginning that this book would not be what it is today.

To my lovely sister across the pond, Lulu: Thank you for holding my hand even though you are thousands of miles away. Somehow, it feels like this friendship was always meant to be. Thank you for double-checking all my English in this book and being so steadfast and supportive. You have the best heart, and I love you so much.

To my darling angel, alphas, and betas: Logan, Mia, Sahara, Chas, Haylie, LB, Caro, and Tabitha. Truly the dream team. I am so beyond thankful to have you in my life. Thank you for reading this when it was a mess of sentences and incorrect grammar, believing in it, and seeing it through to the end. I couldn't have published this book without your feedback. Love you, girls.

To all my friends who held my hand, dried my tears, and cheered me on when the finish line felt so far away. Thank you for writing with me and being there every step of the way. I love you endlessly.

ACKNOWLEDGMENTS

To B. K. Borison, Hannah Grace, Peyton Corrine, Helena Hunting, Elle Kennedy, Becka Mack, Chip Pons, and Hannah Bonam-Young for the voice chats, invaluable advice, and friendship through this journey. You have my endless gratitude, *forever*. I am so lucky to have people like you in this industry.

To Elizabeth Stokes for this stunning cover, and Alina for the forever beautiful art you always seem to create for my books.

To my husband and boys: I love you more than words can ever say. Everything I do is for you. *You are my reason.*

And to my lovely readers, thank you. Without you, there is no dream. Thank you for picking up my books and screaming about them, making the most creative, amazing content, for sharing, recommending to friends, for being the best readers I could have ever asked for. This has been the most transformative journey of my life, and I owe it all to you. Love you always and forever.

ABOUT THE AUTHOR

Maren Moore is a bestselling sports romance author. She writes love stories that are equal parts heart and heat and *always* end in a happily ever after. She resides in southern Louisiana with her husband, two little boys, and their three mini dachshunds. When she isn't on a deadline, she's probably reading yet another romance book, rewatching her favorite cult classic horror movies, or daydreaming about the nineties.